SECOND CHANCE
ON
Sunrise Ranch

L.E. WAGENSVELD

Contents

Words of Caution

This book contains sensitive topics, but listing them here could cause spoilers. Most heavy themes take place in the past and are off-page, though they are discussed on-page. If you are concerned about your mental health, please take precautions and check the list at the back of this book before reading. You will find a complete list (to the best of my abilities) after the bonus epilogue. Happy reading!

L.E. Wagensveld

To all of us who needed a second chance to find our way.

Prologue

2009

ONE THOUGHT FLOATED THROUGH Jasmine Reynold's sleep-drenched mind, iridescent as a bubble in sunlight.

She got to see Theo today.

He'd been gone since Friday, and sure, it was only Monday, but each day was precious on a timeline such as theirs, with the summer slipping through their fingers as quickly as hourglass sand. Memories of the evening they'd spent together before he left for a quick trip with his uncle cascaded through her.

Jasmine pressed a fist against her belly. Whenever she thought about him, pictured his storm cloud eyes, or the way he watched her as if she were the answer to all the world's mysteries, she got a sick, swoony ache in her stomach. She wasn't sure if she loved or hated that feeling, but it had been there since she first saw him all those months ago. Ever since the day she looked up from giving that shithead Tommy Bacus a talking-to about theft and her gaze first snagged with Theo's. Time had gone sticky and still something unnameable stretching between them. The feeling hadn't eased, even after being away from him for two seasons, and doubled in potency when Theo returned to Jamieson Creek after the school year, four inches taller, shaggy, and lean—a Great Dane puppy growing into his legs.

It was the second summer she and Theo Bridger had spent grasping every moment together that they could. They swam, explored, and galloped horses through the fields until they were breathless. They fell into discovering the joy of each other's laughter, the sweet, salty tang of stolen kisses consumed along with melting ice cream cones, and what it was to shatter and be put back together in someone's arms.

They graduated and turned nineteen this year, Jazz six months after Theo. That was *different* somehow—a promising future that hung inches away from the skimming grasp of their fingertips. Maybe, and that was a word she tended to shy away from, he would stay. After all, she'd given him everything, opening herself body and soul in a way she had never done. Hell, her body was still a bit sore from all the ways she'd given herself to him. She wished she could talk to her best friend. Valley would tell her what she should do next. At this point, Jasmine would consider talking to Blair, though she could only imagine the type of crap he would say. He would likely start singing, "Theo and Jasmine sitting in a tree k-i-s-s-i-n-g." Both were gone with their families, though. Valley at her grandparents in the Okanagan Valley, and Blair in the East at his dad's in Prince Edward Island. She'd have to navigate what to do about her feelings for Theo alone.

Should she ask Theo if she could go home to Vancouver with him when the summer ended? The thought brought a staggering tug-of-war of emotions to life in her chest. Leave her father—excitement and an irresistible curiosity over how it would feel to be *free*. But... the other side of that coin was leaving the ranch. That thought brought a stab of pain; saying goodbye to the land that nurtured her since her birth would tear a chunk away from her soul, scarring her forever. She'd have to ask Theo to stay; it was the only way. He could live with his uncle; they could save money until they could get their own place. Then they would both be free, and they would be together.

Pressing her fingertips against her lips, Jasmine tested the smile, stretching them. She wasn't one to walk around with a goofy grin, but damn that Theo, he did it to her. She had to get a handle on the happiness before she went downstairs. Her father would sense any iota of joy and do his best to steal it from her. Maybe—shit, there was that word again; she knew better than to hope—he would be out in the barn.

Throwing back her quilt, Jasmine slipped out of bed. She showered quickly, taking much more care in shaving her legs than usual, and then rubbed on a sweet floral lotion Valley gave her. Tip-toeing down the stairs, she stepped over the one that creaked, then paused in the hallway, listening. The tinny old radio her father refused to replace crackled out an old Alan Jackson song, but Jasmine didn't hear any other sounds from the kitchen. Maybe it was her lucky day?

Cramming bread she didn't bother to toast into her mouth, Jasmine bounded down the back steps and grabbed her bike. Halfway down the long driveway, she heard her father shout her name from the barnyard.

"Jasmine! Jasmine! Where the hell you goin'?"

She was far enough away to pretend she hadn't heard. She may have earned herself a smack when she returned, but it was worth it. She flew over the gravel and out onto the narrow road leading to town, wearing a grin so vast, she was lucky she didn't catch bugs in her teeth.

Theo was jogging down his uncle's driveway when she saw him. The brakes on her rusty old bike squealed as she hit them. She leapt off before it stopped entirely, letting it plummet to the gravel. His arms were around her, holding her to him, quenching the ache of missing him. Jasmine breathed in his summery scent, male sweat, and fresh air. His headphones were hanging around his neck, and she could hear the faint sound of Chris Cornell's voice growling through the tiny speakers.

"I missed you," Theo breathed into her hair as he let her slide down his body. She could tell that was the truth and giggled.

"Shut up," he grumbled, cheeks pinking as he fought a smile. "I can't stop thinking about the other night."

"I know," she admitted, biting down hard on her lip to trap that ridiculous fucking smile. What was wrong with her? How did he have this power? "Want to go back to the river?"

"Um, of course I do. I want to go wherever you go."

Lifting her chin with two fingers, Theo brushed a kiss over her lips, once, then twice. Then he sighed, adjusted his shorts, and bent to pick up her bike. After propping it up against the gate at the end of the drive, he slipped his hand through hers.

"Tell me what you did while I was gone," he commanded as they walked. "Don't leave anything out." They would arrive at the river sunburnt and drenched, but neither cared. It was private enough to swim all they wanted, wearing as little or nothing. He always asked her for an account of her day, even though one rarely differed from the next. She got up and did her best to avoid her father. She fed animals, cleaned stalls, and then escaped into town to work at the store or... not be at home. At dinner, she would return and sit with Betty, hoping her father would stay at the bar and leave them in peace. She'd told Theo all that a time or two, but it didn't bear repeating.

"It was fine, but it is much better now," she said, tipping a smile up at him and allowing her shoulder to bump against his. Days were better with him beside her.

They lay on the grass, letting the warm air play over their skin and lick away the droplets of river water still clinging to them despite the heat.

"We only have fourteen days left," Theo whispered. Jasmine, nearly asleep, lulled by the caress of his fingers twisting dandelions into the strands of her hair, sighed. His words made her gut plummet like she'd missed an anticipated step at the bottom of the stairs.

"Do we have to think about it? It will go even faster if we dwell on it." Nerves ricocheted through her limbs. Though she'd thought of asking him to stay that morning, now the question was momentous, clogging her throat like a boulder in a creek bed.

"I wish we could pause right here." Theo raised one arm in the air, clicking as if holding a remote. "I'd freeze us so I could lie beside you forever."

"Well," Jazz said, rolling to her side to face him, forcing a smile she didn't quite have the happiness to power. "That was a huge load of sentimental bullshit." She grinned as she said it because the butterflies rioting in her gastrointestinal tract were back in action.

Theo didn't mirror her smile, though Jasmine could tell she hadn't upset him with her joking. There was something else bothering him.

Reaching out, she pressed her fingers to the horizontal crease between his dark brows. "What is it?"

"I... there's something I've been meaning to say."

"Okay. Shoot."

Theo swallowed hard, his throat bobbing with the pressure. "I love you, Jasmine."

Her world narrowed to a pinpoint, a drawing in until he was her only focus. Her friends told her they loved her. Valley and Blair said it often, coming from homes where the words were freely granted, unlike hers. But hearing them had never felt like *this*. A cocktail of hope and joy mixed up with laughter. She found herself nodding stupidly; she wanted to say it back, but she hadn't grown up with those three words crossing her lips. Had she ever told her father she loved him? Why would she?

"I... I love it when you call me Jasmine," she whispered. "I used to hate my name. My father chose it, and he has this way of saying it that makes my skin crawl, but when you say it–" she battled down a lump in her throat. "When you say it, it feels clean and pure, like the flower itself. I never thought

it suited me, but then I hear you say it and think, may̧
could."

Maybe... maybe.

Theo stared at her, his storm-grey eyes a mass of emotions. And then, all at once, without her full permission,
the words were there, at her lips and flowing free. "I love
you too, Theo Bridger."

$$\text{♪ ♪ ♪ ❋ ♪ ♪ ♪}$$

"Do you really have to go home?" Theo punctuated the
words with nibbling kisses along the curve of her neck.
Jasmine shivered.

*Say it. Ask him to stay. Ask for a future. See if he wants
to make your maybes come true.*

"Yes," she sighed. "He's already going to be pissed. I
skipped out this morning without doing chores."

Theo's lips stilled, body tightening against her, but not
from desire. "Is he... is he going to hurt you?"

Probably.

...be okay. I'll do some grovelling and

...xtra chores this week. If I'm lucky, he'll be

...nd not even hear me come back."

...e this." Theo's voice was molten with rage. "I hate

you have to go back there. Can't you leave?"

Jasmine snorted. "And go where?" Maybe now he would ask *her*, suggest they make a life together, and save her from trying to pry the words from her stubborn throat.

Theo was silent for so long that she thought he wouldn't answer. The rush of river water and faint sounds of Pearl Jam from his headphones swirled around them.

"I don't know," he whispered, and Jazz's heart wrenched away from her ribs and fell right to the depths of her, breaking on impact.

They were both quiet on the walk back to town. The day was cooling as the sun slipped behind the jagged peaks of the mountains that cradled them. And as despondent as she felt, Jazz, as always, couldn't help but admire their beauty. There was nowhere on earth she'd rather be.

"Goodnight, Jasmine." Theo's voice was hesitant, nearly shy. She knew he sensed her despair but wasn't sure if he knew what had cast her into it. "I'll see you tomorrow, right?"

"Yes, of course." Jasmine pressed onto her tiptoes and let her mouth meld against the familiar shape of his lips.

"I love you," Theo told her, his voice low and rough. It tangled in her hair's wild, river-tossed strands as he hugged her close for a long moment. "I think I'll always love you."

It was five a.m. when Jasmine finally rolled from the bed where she'd spent the night not sleeping. Fuck it. She was asking him. She was asking Theo Bridger to stay. She was asking him to take a chance on an emotionally bruised girl from a small town ranch. The thought of standing in front of someone, offering up her heart like the squishy inside of a cactus without its protective spikes, sent anxiety spiralling through her. More uncomfortable, though, was the memory of Theo leaving last year and how it felt to only hear his voice over a phone line for so long. It would be more complicated now. They'd become so much more this summer.

Jasmine dressed quickly and once more slipped from the house as quietly as she could. It didn't take her long to get to Ted Bridger's farm, but she arrived breathless and sweaty.

Without considering what time it was, she raised her fist and pounded on the door—kept pounding until a dishevelled Ted flung it open.

"Jasmine?" The older man blinked at her, sleepily confused. "Are you alright?" He looked exhausted, deep crescents pillowing his large dark eyes and lines marking the sides of his usually smiling mouth.

"I'm so sorry that I woke you," Jasmine said, her voice catching as she panted. "I just... I have to talk to Theo. Right away."

Ted drew in a shaky breath, jostling his head back and forth so the loose skin of his cheeks jiggled a bit. "What do you mean? Can't you call him?"

"I needed to see him. It's not a phone conversation." She could feel the blood pooling in her cheeks.

"But, sweetie, he's gone. Didn't he call or text you?"

Jasmine's heart fell again, shoved right back from the height that hope had allowed it to climb to. "What do you mean he's gone?" she whispered.

"Greg picked him up late last night." A muscle in Ted's jaw bulged. "I'm sorry, honey. I know you two are fond of each other, but I don't think he will be coming back. Now, I have a horrible headache; I must lie down." His voice had a suspicious break, and before Jasmine could answer, Ted swung the door shut in her face.

She wasn't sure how long she stood, staring at the peeling blue paint.

Theo was gone.

How could that be when he'd kissed her, told her he loved her, and asked to see her tomorrow, *today*? Jasmine's father always said guys would use her for whatever she'd given and then try to take more. Was that it? She'd given Theo what he wanted, and now he—holy shit, had he known she was going to ask him to stay with her, and he had called his father to help him escape.

Jasmine pressed her shaking hands over her mouth, ugly, strangling tears rising in a gush, threatening to drown her.

No. No. No.

Not her, Theo.

Not the sweet boy who loved music and animals and kissing her along the riverbank. Surely, she couldn't have gotten it that wrong. Was she really as stupid as her father said?

Jasmine wrapped her arms around her middle, a gag grasping at her throat. She thought she might be sick. Staggering down the steps, she made it to the side of the drive before she doubled over, heaving up bile, the only thing in her stomach. Tears coursed down her face as she threw her leg over her bike. She had to get away. She couldn't be here, looking at the end of the road where he had met her so many times.

Stupid. Stupid girl.

She could barely peddle with the ache clenching in her stomach. It was no longer the sensation of butterflies. Acid poured through her digestive tract, eating away at the fragile walls. Betrayal, not love. She was no longer sure she knew what love was. If this all-consuming need to curl herself into a ball and wail was love, she didn't want to feel it again.

Chapter One

JASMINE

F EW THINGS CAN SNAP a girl out of a daydream faster than the gritty slurp of a bovine tongue prodding at her ear. With a shriek that may have been the most feminine noise she'd emitted in months, Jazz Joyce launched herself away from the fence she was leaning on.

"Was that necessary?" she growled. Scrubbing away green-tinted slime with the sleeve of her worn denim shirt, Jazz threw Henry, the black Angus who'd accosted her, a dark look. All she wanted was to stand in the morning stillness and watch the sun stretch its coral rays over the surrounding mountains while drinking her coffee. Was that so much to ask?

Henry returned Jazz's gaze with a baleful brown-eyed one of his own before plunging his tongue deep into his left nostril.

Well, that wasn't disgusting at all.

Jazz gave her face one more wipe for good measure. Cattle left a lot to be desired as far as creatures went. Nevertheless, she loved the fuckers. Her fondness for the meatheads spurred her to shift the ranch from beef to breeding, to...whatever it was now. These days, it was more of a home for wayward souls. She needed to devise a plan for the ranch that spawned some monetary influx.

"Come on, Loki," Jazz called, slapping her thigh and bringing the border collie to her side. Of the three dogs on the ranch, Loki was the most inclined to be nearby and in the mood to listen to a command.

With one last disparaging glance at Henry, Jazz yawned and set down her mug. She could never sleep the night before a new guest arrived on the ranch. There were so many unknowns about the situation, and though she trusted her contacts at social services and the employment centre, she could never quell the gut-churning anxiety. As much as Jazz knew she helped people, that didn't excuse her from the occasional nerve-induced case of diarrhea. More than one neighbour told her she was crazy for living alone and allowing people she knew nothing about to stay with her.

They didn't understand it was *because* she was alone that she did what she did. Jazz could use her good fortune to help others while simultaneously helping herself. She needed workers on the ranch, and the people who came to stay provided most of the labour she needed. In exchange, Jazz gave them food, shelter, hard work, and breathing room while they learned to banish their demons.

Besides, when was she ever truly *alone*? Even discounting the number of animals surrounding her, her ex-husband popped in unannounced at least once a day.

Jazz threw back the dregs of her coffee, then pressed a hand to her brow, squinting against the sun. "Right on time," she muttered. At her side, Loki looked up from where he'd been turning circles on a pile of loose straw, ready to settle in for a nap. As Blair's truck drew closer, the dog's ears went up, and he released a belated bark. Thirty meters away from his customary spot on the porch, Odin's deep answering *woof* sounded. Somewhere in the south field, Titus's excited ruckus joined the chorus.

"Really, guys," Jazz grumbled, pushing away from the house and toward the driveway. "I should revoke your guard dog's licenses."

The rusty old Dodge groaned to a halt, shuddering as Blair killed the ignition. "Hey, gorgeous." Jazz's ex-husband unfolded his long body from the cab, shoved his unruly blond curls off his brow, and bent to rub the bellies of the dogs who flung themself at his feet.

That figured, now that she finished the morning's chores, the rest of them appeared. Loki was her only friend. Jazz crossed her arms and scowled. "I drank all the coffee," she said in greeting. "Maybe next time you could show up sooner, lift a finger to help in return for treating my house as your personal cafe."

Blair looked up, blue eyes sharp and twinkling despite the early hour. A pillow crease bisected his handsome face, and his hair looked like a family of rats had fought over the right to nest in it. He flashed her the grin that stole her heart when she was five, leading to a well-attended playground wedding complete with a dandelion stem ring.

"Who says I came for coffee?" His voice croaked as if those were the first words of the morning, and he winced.

"Your track record," Jazz snapped with no real venom in her tone. Blair was one of those obnoxious people who charmed everyone they met—in a genuine way—not even a sleazy used car salesman sort of way. Jazz was no exception despite being married to and then divorced from him. It didn't hurt that she knew all too well the quality of the heart beating within his muscular chest, which was one of the finest. Blair would do anything for anyone, despite his outward attitude of douchery.

"You're in a mood," Blair remarked, dusting off the knees of his jeans as he stood. Leaning in, he brushed a kiss on her cheek. "Better make more coffee. That will get you sorted out."

Jazz punched his arm, but Blair only laughed and followed her toward the house.

The porch steps creaked as they walked up, reminding Jazz to add replacing the old boards to her to-do list. Her father had ignored or failed to accomplish a meter-long list of repairs in the year leading up to his death.

She and Blair toed off their boots in unison and walked into the kitchen. Blair's nose lifted, scenting the air like a bloodhound before he cast her a narrow-eyed glare. "I thought you said you drank all the coffee?"

Jazz shrugged, brushing past him to refill her cup. "I guess I lied."

"Wait a minute. You're being pricklier than normal. Is there a new one coming today?" Blair asked. Bracing himself, he hopped his Wrangler-clad butt onto her kitchen counter and leaned over to pull his cup from the drying rack by the sink. Jazz hated that he could read her with such ease; it made her twitchy.

"Yup." She gave him a tight-lipped jerk of a nod. Of course, he knew her well enough to understand why blue bruises pillowed her eyes and a general vibration of anxiety shimmered in the air like heat waves.

"What's their deal?" Blair jerked his chin to the half-full coffee pot and waggled his cup at her.

"I don't know their *deal*, Blair. I never know their deal." Jazz did not try to hide her annoyance. It wouldn't faze him, anyway. With a hefty exhale, she grabbed the mug, filled it, and passed it back.

When Jazz took on a new ranch guest, she requested no details of the person coming be given to her to avoid prejudice. She hoped she wouldn't judge anyone based on their past, but she took precautions. She partnered with several therapists, and once they shared their client's interest, Jazz sent the paperwork. It was up to them to ensure all the pieces were in order from then on. The parameters of the agreements were arranged to safeguard the program participants. If the new person didn't want to, they didn't even have to share their real name with Jazz.

She didn't take violent offenders and knew the therapists carefully considered candidates before referring them. Since starting the program, Jazz applied for and received several grants from the government, which helped supplement the ranch's income. But it wasn't enough—nothing ever was. Her dad had left her so deep in the pit of debt that she wasn't sure she would ever see the sun.

After a minute, Jazz asked, "Do you think it's weird that we have coffee together almost every morning?" It occurred to her that she couldn't remember a morning she hadn't shared with him, ex or not.

Blair set his mug down, blinking at her sudden change of subject. "Not really. We've done it for years."

Jazz closed her eyes with a sigh of equal parts annoyance and fondness. "We were married for most of those."

Blair lifted his mug, his eyes dropping before flicking back to hers. "We got divorced, Jazzy," he said, his voice uncharacteristically serious. "We didn't stop being best friends."

Chapter Two

THEO

THE WELL-WORN RIBBON OF asphalt snaked into the foothills, bringing Theo Bridger closer with each kilometre to the only place he'd ever felt at home. He wondered, not for the first time, if it was ridiculous to return to Jamieson Creek. The two summers he spent in the small town as a teenager had shaped him during his formative years, but they were only a fraction of his 'real life.' How did he know everything that made Jamieson Creek special hadn't died with his uncle?

When Theo's therapist suggested the rescue ranch and told him its location, he said yes to the opportunity before he had time to consider its potential meaning. He knew he would run into people from his past in Jamieson Creek. If he stayed, those memories would filter into his present and possibly change what he hoped to achieve by coming here. The knowledge left the sour sting of uncertainty in his mouth. The months he'd spent here flew by, exhausted by hard physical labour, nights drinking with friends, and *her*.

Even the flash of memory made his thoughts skitter away. She was gone; she moved away with a husband and probably some kids. He'd come back here for himself and only himself—to heal and discover his path in life—not because a splinter of hope still festered in his heart. He was confident in those facts, yet he couldn't shake the worry he was chasing ghosts by returning.

Theo's pulse pounded in his throat when the first buildings appeared on the horizon. The road led him along the short main street, and he slowed the truck, drinking in the sight of the places he hadn't seen in fifteen years. So many remained unchanged. Their paint jobs faded to the same dusty grey as their neighbours, porches sagging in the middle, but there was recent growth, signalling the town wasn't done for yet. Theo passed a bowling alley that would have been a godsend when he was here as a teen. There was another pub at the end of the street and a pharmacy that didn't exist then.

Blinking hard, ashamed of the sudden mist in his eyes, Theo exited the other end of the town and sped up, following the GPS directions into the mountains. It was only a few more kilometres to Sunrise Ranch.

Turning onto a winding gravel drive, Theo slowed. Fields, coated in the first growth of spring, unfurled on either side of him, shining emerald in the morning sun. A handful of animals lifted their heads as his truck rumbled past; a glossy black bull and a barrel-round grey horse stood side by side, probably wondering who the stranger was.

Theo drew the truck to a crunching stop before the small blue farmhouse and killed the ignition. He sat for a moment in the cab's silence, listening to the tick of the cooling engine as he surveyed his surroundings. It was a habit he hadn't been able to shake, even after being back in Canada for almost two years.

Chickens shuffled around the yard, and two goats were free-ranging on weeds near the porch. One looked up, a clump of greens hanging from its mouth, and let out a bleat at the sight of his arrival. With a deep breath, Theo pushed open the door and stepped out of his truck. A sea of animal faces turned to look at him when the crash of his door closing echoed through the barnyard. They all studied him for a moment and then returned to the more pressing task of eating.

A screen door slammed, and Theo looked up as a lean, blond man stepped from the house onto the porch. With his hand against his brow, he gave Theo a long look.

Theo stepped forward, intending to introduce himself, but the guy turned and yelled over his shoulder into the house. "Jazz, your new one is here."

Then, tipping his head at Theo, he trotted down the steps two at a time and ambled toward his truck. "Good luck, man," he muttered as he passed.

Theo stared after him, taken aback. Maybe the guy meant it as a well wish: 'You're new here, good luck,' but something in his tone unsettled Theo. The words sounded an awful lot like a warning.

Attempting to push down the nerves souring his gut, Theo headed up the stairs. The ranch house was smaller than he'd expected, built in the classic two-story, gabled style with double dormer windows. It was nearly a twin to his uncle Ted's, and that fact alone cooled some of his anxiety.

Theo extended a hand to knock, and the screen door flew open outwards at the exact moment, missing his face by a mere inch. He jumped back with a yelp and nearly fell backwards off the porch steps.

That was precisely the first impression he wanted to make.

"Shit!" The voice was throaty and slightly deep for a woman. It struck a cord of recognition thrumming in Theo's chest. "You're *right* there."

"I am."

No apology from the woman. She stepped outside into the light, and Theo instantly forgot that she had nearly destroyed his face seconds ago. He was too busy falling back through time.

"Jasmine?" The word scraped out of his throat: a question, a curse. A plea.

Chapter Three

JASMINE

"**H**OLY SHIT," JAZZ STUMBLED back a step, shock wrapping its icy fingers around her trachea. "Theo?"

Theo stared back at her mouth, slightly agape. The landscape of his face, a terrain she'd once known by heart, was altered by time and hardship yet still familiar. His thick, black hair hadn't met a pair of scissors in some time. Strands swept over his brow and curled against the sweat-damped collar of his faded blue work shirt. Deep lines bracketed the full mouth in a face too sharp to be handsome but too intriguing not to be. The touch of boyhood softness that still rounded his cheeks at nineteen when she'd last seen him was gone, lost somewhere in the life that had marked him with scars and lines. But those eyes, the tumultuous grey-blue of water mirroring a storm-drenched sky, drowned and left her gasping for more, as they always had.

She was eighteen the last time she saw Theo Bridger. They'd spent two months together as each other's confidants. Then passed seasons devouring long-awaited letters and emails hastily typed on molasses-slow computers until the sticky days of summer rolled back around.

Best friends.

First loves.

First lovers.

Those combined four months painted Jazz's memories, bright and permanent as tattoos. What came after branded her heart, searing the meat with one smoking scar.

"I ..." Theo stammered, shoving a hand through his hair and taking a half-stumble step back. He squeezed his eyes and then opened them, shaking his head as if they may be playing a trick on his mind. "Jasmine?" He repeated.

"Yeah," Jazz said. "But nobody calls me that anymore."

"What are you doing here?" he stammered.

Jazz crossed her arms over her chest, hoping they would help contain her thundering heart. "Well, since I have lived in

Jamieson Creek my entire life and was born in this house, I think the better question is, what are you doing here?"

"But—" Theo squeezed his eyes shut, then opened them again, shaking his head slightly as if he expected her image to change before him. "I thought you moved?"

She frowned. "Why would I move?"

"Facebook... I thought–"

"You stalked me online?"

"I...well, no. Yes. Sort of. A long time ago." The words were sticky burrs in his throat, and he stammered them out, colour rising in his cheeks. "Is this your place?" he asked in an evident bid to change the subject.

Well, fuck her running. Was Theo Bridger honestly the guy who was supposed to live with her on her ranch for half a year? How could this be happening? If there was a God, he sure had one fucked up sense of humour.

"Dad left it to me. Three years ago."

Theo nodded. "He's dead?"

"Yup."

"Good."

Jazz's mouth twitched, but she killed the wry smile attempting to escape. Anyone listening would have been appalled by that single word, but Theo knew her. He knew what she went through with her dad.

He knew so much about her.

Memories clamoured through her brain, making her stomach twist. They created so many memories in their short time together. The first time she'd seen Theo's face, his eyes had been wide in a mix of appreciation and fear as she reamed out a kid she caught stealing. The little shit was pocketing candy bars at the little corner store where she'd worked each summer of her youth. When the kid had looked ready to piss himself, Jazz had chased him out and looked up to find Theo watching her. Their eyes met that first time, and her gut swooped, the sensation of missing a stair. Over the next two summers, Theo learned whatever he could about her, gobbling up any tidbit she would feed him. Jazz had allowed him into her heart in a way she'd never done before or since. The man standing before her now knew what made her laugh, her favourite flavour of ice cream—how to make her come. Jazz's face heated, and she swallowed.

Fuck her running; how the hell was he standing on her porch?

Theo stared at her, his lean cheeks bleached pale as if he had seen a ghost. For the first time, Jazz noticed the scar bisecting his left eyebrow. It ran thin and jagged down to the middle of his cheek. Whatever caused the injury could easily have blinded him. A twinge of something uncomfortable plucked at her heart when she thought of him in pain. She realized she didn't want him marred; didn't like the idea of him being hurt and bleeding. And she didn't like that she didn't like it. Theo wasn't hers to be concerned about.

"What do we do?" Theo asked, his voice hesitant.

Jazz realized he thought she would tell him to leave. That was what the girl who still lived inside Jazz, whose heart Theo broke, longed to say to him. She wanted to order him to get his ass in his truck and get off her property. She ached to yell after him that she managed fine when he broke his promise to love her forever. She never allowed herself to remember how she cried herself to sleep for weeks after he left.

But it wasn't so simple. Jazz operated her ranch the way she did for a reason. She believed in helping people, and the fact Theo stood before her now meant he needed to be here. So, she would do what she did best. She'd lock her feelings down, put the past behind her, and try to help him the same way she had with the others. Hard work, good food, and clean air were the most authentic ways to heal a person, in Jazz's opinion.

"Get your gear." Jazz jerked her chin at his truck. "I'll show you your room. You can have the rest of today to settle in. Work starts tomorrow at daybreak. As far as I'm concerned, this is our first time meeting."

Theo stared at her for a long moment, shadows of emotion shifting across his face. Then his chin jerked up, and he saluted sharply. "Yes, ma'am."

Jazz spun away without acknowledging his words, but she was acutely aware of his presence following her as they entered the house. How was it possible he was here after all these years? They passed through the boot room, and Theo paused to toe off his well-worn Ropers.

"Breakfast is at 7 a.m., after morning chores are done, lunch is at noon, and dinner is at 6 p.m., after evening chores," Jazz said. "We don't eat until the animals have." She gave this speech often, but her skin had never crackled under the scrutiny of her new ranch hand.

"I don't care what you do after dinner, as long as it doesn't break your contract. Don't come in late and wake me, or I'll be pissed the fuck off. No drinking, no drugs. And—" Jazz paused, and Theo nearly crashed into her. She turned and brandished a finger in his face. "If there's an emergency and I need you, you better haul your ass out of bed. We take care of each other out here."

"A concept I'm accustomed to," Theo said. His voice was deadpan, face blank. As if he had somehow managed to lock down the upheaval of a few moments ago. Maybe she should follow his example; she could still feel her face burning with a riotous mix of surprise, fury and...well, there was something else there, but she sure as shit wasn't about to put a name on it.

Despite herself, Jazz couldn't tear her eyes away from him as he looked around, taking in his new surroundings. It was almost as if a ghost had returned to life before her.

What happened to you?

The words clawed at her throat, ferocious as demons in their need to escape.

Where did you go?

She wished to know with a curiosity that left her as hollow as if she were starving. She didn't want to know with an adamance that left her legs itchy with the need to run.

"Good," she said instead, finally in a delayed response.

Turning, she pushed open a door in the main hallway. "This room is yours. You have your own bathroom and are welcome to use the kitchen. Go anywhere you want on the grounds, but upstairs is my space. I better never catch you up there."

A sharp nod. "Understood."

They stood there momentarily, facing each other, neither speaking despite the storm of unsaid words swirling between them.

"Did you... did you join the military?" Jazz couldn't believe she asked, but the evidence was in his posture and the clipped tone of his answers, and *fuck it*. She wanted to know. His father had always pushed for it, and she knew how Theo had dreaded going home. He'd told her once that he thought his father had them brainwashed, under some mind control.

"I did."

"Your father?"

"Yes."

A sharp ache of sadness for Theo punched through Jazz's chest. They bonded all those years ago over their shared experiences with verbally and sometimes physically abusive fathers. The Theo, whom Jazz knew then, was gentle and kind, passionate about music, and always had his MP3 player loaded with the latest hits. Sometimes, when she met him by the river, he glowed with excitement, antsy to show her some new song he'd discovered. He'd always made her smile, running through the trees, attempting to befriend squirrels. They'd spent hours wandering in the woods in those days, usually on his Uncle Ted's property. Jazz never dared bring Theo to her father's ranch. She didn't want to risk sullying Theo with Jerry Reynold's poison. He'd shone with a sweetness back then that Jazz could tell by looking into his eyes was now absent. That empathy and innocence were an enormous part of why she fell for him—why she lowered her guard and let him in.

Fat lot of good that did her.

Jazz's relationship with Theo Bridger drove home a fact she should have known, even when she was eighteen.

Trust no one with your happiness.

For the thousandth time since she nearly broke his face with the porch door, Jazz wondered what happened the day Theo left without a word. The question would eat her alive, but she would rather have hay splinters shoved under her fingernails than ask.

"Make yourself at home," she said after an achingly long moment passed. "I'll see you at dinner."

Chapter Four

THEO

WHEN JAZZ DISAPPEARED FROM the room, Theo sank onto the bed and pressed his face into his shaking hands until stars burst behind his lids.

Holy shit.

Jasmine Reynolds. She'd changed, of course; her body, all long, lean strength, had lost the softer swells of girlhood. Her hair was twisted into a tight, serviceable braid instead of the wild, tangled curtain that had always flowed to her waist, rippling behind her when she ran. Some, at a glance, would call it black, but Theo knew when the sun caressed those strands, they would shine with a rainbow of colours. There were new lines around her eyes, carved by long days spent outside and life's stressors, but the same ferocious, steely spirit shone from those hazel depths. He'd never met anyone like her and had given up hope that he ever would.

What the hell sort of fate brought this upon him?

The room spun, and Theo worried he would collapse if he stood suddenly. His heart was doing its best to pound its way out through his ribs.

Emotions boiled through him: joy at seeing her face again, fear over her hostile reaction, and anguish that it had been so long.

Even if the chance to explain why he'd left presented itself, Theo wasn't sure Jazz could forgive him. Of all the things his father had done, taking Theo from Jamieson Creek remained the worst–allowing himself to be taken as if he were a helpless child remained the biggest regret of his life. What he wouldn't give to go back in time. To stand up for himself, tell his bully of a father to fuck off.

With a shaky exhale, Theo forced his legs to lift him. He entered the small ensuite bathroom, relieved his unhappy bladder, and turned the faucet cold before splashing his face.

Feeling slightly more human, he looked around. The tiny room was clean and bright yellow as if painted with sunlight—a sprawling, rich green plant draping long tendrils around the top of the shower stall. Theo pinched one of the leaves, rubbing it gently between his fingers. It was real.

A mirrored cabinet hung above the sink; when Theo opened it, it was empty, and the shelves were clean. Sunrise Ranch, *this room*, was his home for the next six months. The realization struck him anew. He was here in Jamieson Creek with Jasmine—Jazz, he corrected himself. What the hell had he gotten himself into?

Whenever he blinked, Theo saw her *then*, her head thrown back to worship the sun as they walked their horses side by side. He felt the echo of his pounding heart as he snuck from his uncle's house and the crunch of gravel beneath the soles of his Converse sneakers as he ran down the long drive to crash into her arms. Theo heard Jazz's bike clatter to the road as he swept her up and consumed her Lip Smacker kisses and sunshine lemon scent. Jazz was the light in his bleak adolescence, her sarcastic humour and blistering kindness his fuel. Their fleeting months together were the prize that drove him through the winter months until summer rolled around, and he could return to Jamieson Creek—those years changed *everything*.

That *night* changed everything.

The moment his father's gruff voice snapped him from sleep. The rough hands that yanked him by the collar until it nearly strangled him, shoving him outside into the muggy August night. The much too familiar pit in his stomach his father's presence always caused—words from an older brother to a younger wielded violently and meant to wound.

"Boy is as weak as you are, Ted. It makes me regret ever naming him after you. God knows what he's learned being up here with you. You probably turned him as fruity as you. That would be just my luck."

When crushed under a thick-soled military-style boot, a cell phone made a distinctive crunch. Theo still felt the weight of that sound, as if the foot had come down on him instead. Jasmine's number was on that phone. He hadn't memorized it yet; she'd had to get a new one only a few weeks before. Her dad had borrowed it, left it on the tailgate of his truck, and then ran it over...*by accident.*

The onslaught of memories poked the ever-present coil of anxiety in Theo's gut. He imagined it as a snake waiting to unfurl and wrap him tight, choking the life from him. He closed his eyes, drawing three deep breaths in through his nose and then allowing the air to trickle from his mouth. He and Jazz had been so close. Maybe they could become friends again. Or, if not friends, at least work together peacefully during his stay.

Theo still believed being at Sunrise Ranch was the best thing for him. He'd spent the best days of his life in this town. If Theo could capture even a tendril of the joy he'd known before his dad showed up that night fifteen years ago, he would be happier and healthier than he had been since returning from his tour. He wasn't sure how much stock he put in fate, but surely it was no coincidence that he'd ended up here.

He needed to buck up and leave the room, get his bags from his truck, and settle in. He needed to face Jasmine—Jazz. The name would take some getting used to. She lived in his memories as Jasmine, *his* Jasmine. Thinking of her as anything else would be challenging.

The house was empty when Theo finally gathered the courage to leave his sanctuary. Crossing the kitchen, he pulled on his boots and then headed down the porch stairs to his truck, pausing at the sight that greeted him.

A huge white dog sat in the back of Theo's pickup, nearly a foot of pink tongue lolling from its mouth as it panted, face pulled wide in a humungous doggy grin. On the ground sat two other dogs, looking up at the white mutt as if he were royalty. At the sound of the screen door slamming, all three canine faces swivelled to look at him.

"Well, hey guys," Theo said, approaching slowly. He extended a hand to the first dog, a wiry-haired mongrel who, on closer inspection, was missing an eye. The dog gave his hand a cursory sniff, then a tentative lick, before turning away.

"Whatcha doin' up there, fella?" Theo asked the white dog, hoping the beast was as friendly as he appeared. Theo extended his fingers, and a flurry of excited wiggles and licks rewarded him. The third dog, a smaller breed with the colouring and ears of a Beagle but the shaggy coat of some collie, regarded him for a long moment, gave the ground two thumps with its tail, then strode away to flop down in the shade of an outbuilding.

"Alright then," Theo said. "Let's get you out of there."

He reached to open the tailgate, but the dog set his paws on the side of the truck's bed and leaped down, landing with a grunt.

"Sorry!" An out-of-breath voice came from behind him.

Theo turned to see Jazz rushing toward him, her braid in disarray and a slash of dirt smudged across one high cheekbone. The light played through the rich strands of the hair that curled around her face. She was fucking gorgeous.

"That's Titus. He has no boundaries and even less common sense. He's only a year and a half. The last owner gave him up because he was too big. Not sure what he expected from a Pyrenees, Newfoundland cross."

Titus circled Theo's legs, giving him a thorough sniff. The dog's head reached Theo's waist. As he smiled at the dog, Titus jumped without warning, and his colossal paws landed squarely on Theo's chest. Not anticipating the affectionate attack, Theo went down hard, landing on his ass on the driveway gravel. It seemed to be the result Titus had hoped for, and with grunts of glee, he commenced licking every inch of Theo he could reach.

"Ack!" Theo choked as he fought against the dog. The creature must have weighed a hundred and fifty pounds.

"Titus!" Jazz called, reaching to grab the dog's collar. Her face broke as she hauled the beast off and extended a hand to Theo. The first peal of laughter escaped her, and she clamped a hand over her mouth. "I'm so sorry," she gasped as he crawled to his feet. Jazz pressed the hand tighter, trying to quell the giggles. It did no good; they continued to bubble out of her, gaining momentum.

Theo looked down. Twin paw prints the size of dinner plates adorned his shirt, and he was pretty confident slobber dripped from his jaw. For a moment, Theo was stunned. He was a veteran, a fully grown six foot three, two-hundred-and-twenty-pound man, and a fucking puppy just flattened him in front of the woman he used to love. Fate sure was a cruel bitch sometimes.

"What is that thing?" he asked, his voice incredulous and much higher than usual. "Don't tell me that is a dog. That is not a dog. Did Falkor have sex with one of the horses, and *that* was the result? What sort of funny farm are you running here, Jasmine?"

Jazz was doubled over, gasping for air, breathless with laughter, and the sound was so *familiar* that something snapped in Theo's chest. He began to laugh with her. The sound came out rusty and hoarse at first, as if going unused for so long had disintegrated it.

"Your face." Jazz gasped. "I'm so... Falkor, oh my God."

Theo leaned his back against his truck, wiping dog drool, mud, and mirthful tears off his cheeks.

"Remember watching The NeverEnding Story that night, and it rained so hard you were stuck at Ted's with me?" The instant the words left his mouth, Theo knew he'd made a mistake.

The amusement drained from Jazz's face. She drew a deep breath, straightening. "Yeah, I remember," she said. Her jaw tightened, and she pinned him with a look, her rich, dark eyes unfathomable. "I remember everything."

Then, with a snap of her fingers that brought Titus loping to her side, Jazz spun and stalked off. Theo stared after her, retreating form, all the long-lost laughter draining from him as suddenly as it arrived.

Chapter Five

JASMINE

J AZZ COULDN'T PLACE THE emotion hollowing her
chest. What the hell was she doing, laughing with Theo?
They weren't friends. They no longer knew each other. They
didn't share inside jokes or secret looks. They were strangers
to each other.

Fifteen years ago, Theo Bridger crushed her heart, and she
could not allow herself to forget it again. Six months on the
ranch would fly by if she kept her head down and engaged
with him as little as possible.

Desperate to escape the cascade of memories and feelings
washing over her, Jazz entered the stables and snatched up a
saddle. She realized she was shaking as she removed a bridle

from the pegs on the wall and hooked it over the saddle's horn. With a growl, she hauled the tack outside.

Jazz swung the saddle onto the wooden rail at the paddock and whistled before returning inside to grab a curry comb and saddle pad. When she returned, Goliath, a sleek black Morgan stallion she'd spent her life savings on, stood at the fence waiting, not so patiently. Jazz had raised Goliath from a colt, and he repaid her handsomely in the way of stud fees—not a shabby deal for either of them.

At the sight of her with his tack, Goliath released an earth-splitting whiny, spun a few tight circles, and kicked up his heels. The sun glinted off the blue-black of his coat, and his long mane and tail caught the breeze and whipped it around him. Jazz's chest squeezed at the beauty of him, the power.

With practiced hands, she saddled him and swung onto his back. Between her legs, Jazz felt the hum of anticipation running through the horse. It took a firm hand to keep Goliath in a walk as they cleared the barnyard. Once they set foot in the open field, he danced and shifted. Jazz tightened her thighs around his thick body, urging him into a trot and then a barely restrained canter.

Finally, she gave them both what they longed for. When Jazz allowed the reins to slip loose through her fingers, giving Goliath his head, he hopped, then transitioned into a smooth-as-butter gallop. Jazz leaned low over his neck, relishing the bite of wind-summoned tears in her eyes.

The path was wide and flat; they ran it often, and Jazz knew it was safe. Stallions needed to run, and the surge of the muscular, perfect beast beneath her sent adrenaline and joy spiking through her, leaving no room for anxiety, no space for memories. If Goliath could run fast enough, they might escape the man who waited back at the farm.

Unfortunately, even a horse as strong as Goliath grew tired, and reality slammed back in with all the pleasantness of a gut punch. Once they made their way home and Jazz removed Goliath's tack, she rubbed him down, cleaning away each speck of sweat and loose hair until the horse's coat shone as inky as sun-caught raven wings. With a re-signed sigh, Jazz led Goliath to his paddock, put away her tools, and stretched her aching back. Time was up. Her stomach demanded she go inside, face the music, and feed herself.

Usually, Jazz would be relaxed and content after such a ride, looking forward to dinner and a long soak in the tub. But as she walked to the house, sparks crackled through her body, making her limbs electric with nerves. Pulling in several deep breaths, she shook her hands and went through the front door.

The clanging of pots echoed from the kitchen. When she entered, Jazz found her housekeeper and woman of all trades, Mrs. Abbot-but-call-her-Betty, starting dinner. Betty was a godsend and had been a part of the ranch for as long as Jazz could remember.

"Hello, my dear," Betty greeted, her round cheeks plumping under the weight of her smile, nearly obscuring her eyes. "How are things? I see the new one arrived."

Jazz released a long puff of air, blowing sweaty strands of hair across her forehead, and scrubbed a hand over her face. "Did he ever."

Betty cocked her head, sharp green eyes narrowing as her motherly instincts switched to hyper-drive. "Is there something wrong with the lad? He seemed pleasant enough when he came down for a snack."

Jazz peaked over Betty's shoulder, assessed the ETA on dinner, and then grabbed an apple from the bowl that always sat full on the counter. "There's nothing wrong with him, Bets, it's just—" Jazz lowered her voice and leaned close enough for Betty's familiar baby powder and vanilla scent to tickle her nose. "That's *Theo*."

It only took a few seconds for Betty's eyes to widen in recognition. Betty Abbott had worked on the Reynolds' farm since Jazz's mother had died twenty-five years ago. She was the closest thing Jazz had had to a mom since.

"Thee Theo?" Betty hissed, glancing over her shoulder in case his name passing over her lips had summoned him.

Jazz bit her thumbnail and nodded. "Yes, *thee* Theo. How many Theos could there possibly be?"

Betty narrowed her eyes, and Jazz waved a hand in apology. "Sorry," she said. "I think I'm still in shock. I couldn't believe my eyes when I opened the door, and he was standing there." It was more like when she almost smashed his face with it, but Betty didn't need a recap of *precisely* what transpired.

"It must have been quite the surprise after all these years." Betty turned to the stove, stirring the fragrant concoction bubbling happily atop it.

"Fifteen years, Betty! I thought my heart would stop," Jazz admitted before crunching into her apple. "Or that I would puke on his boots," she spluttered the words around the fruit, spraying a bit of juice and earning a glance of reprimand from Betty.

They were quiet for a few moments, Jazz chewing and Betty stirring, entirely at ease in each other's company.

Finally, Betty *tsked* audibly and shook her head. "I can't wrap my mind around it. Perhaps this is fate, and the two of you should start up again."

Jazz snorted, almost launching a chunk of fruit into her nasal cavity. "Bless your romantic, insane heart."

Betty shrugged. "All I'm saying is the lord works in mysterious ways."

"So does the devil," Jazz muttered.

"It's a little early to give me nicknames, isn't it, Jasmine?"

This time, the apple succeeded in its quest to choke her. The bite she'd been on the verge of swallowing lodged in her throat, and Jazz started to cough. Crossing the room in two long strides, Theo laid a hand between her shoulder blades, ready. Grey eyes searched her face, assessing, making sure she was alright, the same way he always had.

Before he disappeared and broke her heart.

Jazz gave herself a firm mental shake.

"I'm alright," she gasped after a few more coughs.

Theo needed to stop touching her. A tingling circle of heat was blooming from where his palm lay, nothing but the thin cotton of her t-shirt separating it from her skin.

Memories of the first time she experienced the magic of his touch bubbled to the surface, flashing behind her lids when she blinked. She'd never been with a man since who incited such a reaction in her body. Or her heart. Not even Blair, in the eight years of their marriage.

Her face was growing hot, and Jazz shook off Theo's hand and accepted the glass of water Betty held out to her.

"Spending too much time with those horses," the older woman grumbled. "You're starting to eat like them."

Betty finished preparing dinner and excused herself to head home, claiming a headache despite Jazz's pleas for her to sit and have dinner with them. Betty's husband, Jim, had passed away two years ago, and Jazz hated the thought of Betty going to her small, empty house and eating alone. They ate together most nights, laughing and gossiping long after their plates were empty.

Jazz stared after the other woman's back with narrowed eyes as Betty gathered her things and bustled out of the kitchen. She didn't know what Betty was playing at, but Jazz was suspicious. Betty didn't have the air of someone suffering from a headache and needing her bed. Heart sinking, Jazz turned back to the table and the man patiently sitting at it.

With a sigh, she pulled out her chair and dropped onto it, forcing herself to look at Theo and give him a weak smile.

He looked tired. Blue bruises pillowed his stormy eyes, and thick, dark stubble coated his cheeks. "She's amazing," he said, angling his chin toward the door Betty had disappeared through. "You've known her a long time?"

"Twenty-five years," Jazz said, pushing her fork through the fettuccine sauce on her plate, her ravenous appetite suddenly in hiding. "My father hired her after my mom passed. She was supposed to take care of me. He didn't want to bother. Betty ended up doing much more, though. She was sort of a Jill of all Trades. When I took over the ranch, it was a given that she'd stay to help me."

Theo nodded, brow creasing as he focused on wrapping a noodle through the tines of his fork before spearing a chunk of chicken.

"You two seem close," he said once he chewed and swallowed his first bite.

"We are. She's known me most of my life."

"Mrs. Abbott," Theo said, snapping his fingers as the memory hit him. "You never used to call her Betty."

"No, I didn't. But she wasn't my friend back then." That was the closest Jazz was willing to get to discussing the past.

"Does she know who I am?" Theo's voice dropped low, almost into a whisper. Nearly as if attempting to stop the flow of words, he shoved a significant bite of food into his mouth.

"She does."

Theo straightened, dropping his fork with a clatter that made him wince. "Jazz, when I left—"

Jazz started shaking her head before he could finish, desperate to stop him from talking. She didn't want the truth of why he'd left without saying goodbye. She didn't need it. Not now. Her life was full of things she needed to address; an age-old quarrel with her first boyfriend wasn't one of those things.

"It's all in the past. We aren't kids anymore. Let's get through these six months. Then we never have to see each other again."

Theo closed his eyes, swallowing hard enough that Jazz heard it from across the table. "Alright," he whispered.

Face down on the table, Jazz's phone vibrated, nearly launching itself over the edge. Slapping a palm over it, Jazz flipped it, her heart plunging into a free fall of anxiety when she saw the name on the screen.

"You can get that if you need to," Theo said.

"I know that," Jazz snapped.

Ignoring Theo's questioning glance, she tucked the phone under her thigh and returned to her food.

Neither of them spoke again as they finished their meals.

Chapter Six

THEO

EXHAUSTION TURNED THEO'S LIMBS lead-heavy, but sleep eluded him. He'd been staring at the ceiling, counting the timber beams bisecting it and starting over each time he reached the wall. Still, even that technique did nothing to entice slumber. Sleepless nights were typical, and soul-deep exhaustion had become a much-loathed companion to Theo. He was so accustomed to it now that he wasn't sure he would know what to do with himself after a good rest.

When he managed to sleep, more often than not, memories masquerading as nightmares ripped him back to consciousness. Sweat-drenched and shaking, he would claw his way up from the trenches of the dream into wakefulness.

Theo could never go back to sleep after and would begin his day at whatever time it was. Running helped banish the demons and clear his head. So did his music. Since his father's death, Theo had slowly allowed himself to return to playing.

Gregory Bridger had acted as if a musical son was the worst fate in the world, looking down on Theo when he brought home class awards for music or caught him singing. When Theo excitedly announced he wanted to attend a music college after high school, Gregory stood from the dinner table and left the room without a word. Then, he'd arranged for Theo's enrollment in the military academy without telling Theo. The military was what Bridger men did, and Theo wouldn't break tradition to become a *musician*. Not on Gregory's watch.

Sighing, Theo banged his head against his pillow a few times, resisting the urge to turn and scream into it. His guitar was still in the truck, shyness having crept in at the thought of Jasmine seeing it. In the two summers they spent together, Theo never told her about his love of creating music, his gift for it. But finally, at thirty-four, he gained the confidence to recognize and name his talent for what it was: *a gift*. His mother loved it when he sang and played for her. But when his father belittled Theo, she never defended him. Now that

Gregory was gone, Theo was working on forgiving her for that. There was a lot of forgiveness that needed to happen in his family.

Theo threw back the quilt with a groan and stalked to the bathroom to douse his face in cool water. Then, pulling on his jeans and a zippered hoodie, he crossed the unfamiliar room. When he slipped through the bedroom door, Theo nearly tripped over the giant, prone form of a sleeping Titus, who opened one brown eye and grunted when Theo stepped over him.

Outside, the old, one-eyed dog lifted his head and thumped his tail, so Theo squatted and scratched behind his ears. A tag on the worn leather collar jingled, and Theo squinted at the little disc, trying to read it in the golden glow of the porch light. **Odin.**

Theo laughed and gave the dog one more pat on the head before standing.

The only sound in the farmyard was the crunch of Theo's boots as he crossed to his parked truck. A crescent moon floated in a star-pierced sky, offering a dim glow to the sprawling buildings.

Moving as quietly as he could, Theo retrieved his guitar, shut the truck door, and paused, wondering where to go. He didn't want to disturb Jazz or the animals while he played, but he had yet to explore the property enough to know a good spot to hide away.

Finally settling on a direction, Theo walked down the driveway until he came to a path that cut through the ditch and snaked off toward the treeline. Ducking, Theo slipped between the fence wires, wincing when a barb hooked his shirt with a slight tearing sound. He attempted to twist enough to survey the damage but only succeeded in loudly cracking his back. With a sigh, Theo reached over the fence, grabbed his guitar case from the post where he'd leaned it, and loped down the path.

Theo hadn't gone far when the sound of rushing water reached him. Slipping through the trees, he found a shallow, rocky creek. For a second, Theo paused, listening as the water filled the night with its own music. The cool air was crisp with the earthy scents of moss, wet rock, and clean water. Some tension eased from Theo's shoulders as he stood, breathing greedily. A small bench sat at the creek's bank in the centre of the clearing as if set there to wait for him. Theo went, lifted his guitar from the case, and sat.

Fingers seeking the familiar companionship of the strings, Theo formed the cords to a melody that had run through his head as he drove earlier in the day. He strummed, switched an A for an E Minor, strummed again, and smiled as the beautifully eerie chord floated into the darkness. That would do nicely. He had no lyrics yet, but those would come. Theo knew it with a bone-deep certainty. The song bubbled up from his soul; it would make itself whole in time.

Theo mulled over his situation as he played, his fingers moving with minimal prompting from his brain. He could leave the ranch now that he knew Jazz was its proprietor and how she felt about his presence. But the thought of packing up and once more saying goodbye to Jamieson Creek almost as soon as he arrived left a sour sting in his throat. He came back here for a reason. Was he willing to allow Jasmine Reynolds to chase him away so easily?

When did she change the name to Sunrise Ranch? It had been the Reynolds' Ranch, and people muttered the name with an undercurrent of acid distorting their tones. Jasmine's father, Jerry Reynolds, was not a well-liked community member. Memories of Jasmine showing up at Ted's with tear tracks on her cheeks and her wrists ringed in blue-black bracelets made his gut twist.

Whenever Theo saw Jasmine hurt, he longed to march over to her house and kick the older man's ass. But he'd been a coward—a kid. And then, in a blink, he'd been gone.

There'd been countless times Theo considered returning and looking Jasmine up. Only once did he crack and type her name into a Facebook search. It was not long after he was back from training. After he'd called for the millionth time only to hear the number he remembered wasn't in service. The only thing he found, after spending far too much time digging, were pictures posted by Jasmine's best friend Valentina. They'd shown the woman standing as a maid of honour to Jasmine, who gazed up at her new husband. A man Theo couldn't even bring himself to look at in the photo. What drove the spike of anguish home was the date on the post, only three months after the day Theo's father removed him from Jamieson's Creek. After he took Theo's phone and smashed it, he told him he wasn't to contact anyone in the "god damned hick town again."

But Jasmine hadn't waited for him. Theo had thought that if he could get through his training, there would be a chance to go back and talk to her. Maybe if he could see her face to face, he could convince her it had all been a mistake.

Maybe...maybe...maybes were for idiots.

He'd slammed the laptop closed and never entered the name Jasmine Reynolds into a search bar again. There were years in between then, his deployments, and when he discovered therapy, that had not been good. It made Theo sick in his gut to think what might have happened if he hadn't decided to seek help. And now...here he was. Full circle, for better or worse, back in Jamieson Creek with Jasmine Reynolds.

Theo lost track of how long he sat, strumming, singing quiet words, adjusting, trying new chords. When his eyes grew too heavy to keep open, he laid his guitar across his lap and leaned his head against the back of the bench, intending to close his eyes for a moment before he returned to the house.

Chapter Seven

JASMINE

WHERE THE HELL WAS Theo?

Jazz growled as she flung the hay bale over the fence and slipped through the wires. Pulling her knife from her belt, she cut the twine and kicked the sections apart, spreading it for the cattle in that pasture. Henry and his bovine friends grew fat on spring grass at this time of year, but Jazz had to cycle the fields to give them time to develop. If she didn't, the greedy animals would destroy them. Hay wasn't cheap, though, and the dwindling supply in the barn was making her sweat. But then, what financial thought didn't make her sweat these days? The mere thought of money made her stomach cramp like she'd eaten clams at Patty's pub.

Jazz's unique way of running the ranch worked well for all parties involved, except perhaps the bank. She was proud of Sunrise and what it stood for. Jazz didn't shell out for hefty salaries. Still, she gave the people who came to her a lovely room, a beautiful setting, delicious food, and the sort of hard work that left the body exhausted and the mind mellow.

"Too bad friggin' Theodore Bridger couldn't appreciate that," Jazz muttered under her breath as she slid back through the fence and brushed off her jeans.

"Talking to yourself again, Jazzy? You really lost it once we broke up."

Jazz screamed and whirled, swinging a right hook at her ex-husband's head.

"Fuck!" Blair rocked back on his heels, the blow missing his nose by millimetres. "Dude!"

Jazz braced her hands on her knees, breathing hard as she struggled to regain her composure. "You. Scared. The. Shit. Out. Of. Me," she panted.

Blair flashed her the dimpled, devilish grin that had once been enough to take her knees out. Then he patted her on the back hard. "Sorry, I didn't realize you hadn't heard me drive up."

"What the hell is the point of having all these dogs if they can't even warn me who's coming up the driveway!" Jazz's voice rose to a shout as she pointed at Titus, who swooshed his huge flag of a tail, and then Odin and Loki, who lay curled butt-to-butt in the shade of the barn, snoring. "Gruff is a better guard animal than any of you sorry excuses." As if in agreement, the billy goat lifted his head and bleated before returning to the pile of kitchen scraps Jazz had brought him.

Blair only laughed and rubbed his knuckles across the broad expanse of Titus' head when the dog came to lean against his leg. "Where's the new grunt? Don't you usually make them do this stuff while you sit in the shade and sip lemonade?"

Jazz snorted. "As if that's ever happened." She released a long sigh, braced her hands against her lower back, and stretched. "I don't know. He didn't show up this morning, and there was no answer when I knocked on the door."

"Did you check inside... make sure he didn't—" Blair winced as he allowed the words to trail off.

Jazz stared at him momentarily, horrified at what he was implying. Pushing past him, she strode toward the house, her heart pounding in the base of her throat. The thought that

Theo may have done something to himself hadn't occurred to her, but now fear crackled through her limbs.

People came to Sunrise because they had problems. Violent offenders weren't allowed in the program. Some of her guests had a criminal past, but more often, they were battling with addiction or working on their mental health. She didn't know Theo's personal brand of demon, but he was guaranteed to have one. She took the porch stairs two at a time, banged through the screen door, and strode down the hall to Theo's room, muddy boots and all. She pounded on the door, and when there was no answer, Jazz sucked in a breath and pushed it open.

The room was empty. The bed was rumpled and messy but vacant. Coming up behind her, Blair exhaled in relief. Jazz's shoulders loosened. She didn't know where Theo was, but at least he wasn't dead in her farmhouse.

"Maybe he went for a wander and got lost or something," Blair said, trailing her into the kitchen. He grabbed his favourite coffee mug from the rack, filled it, and leaned back against the counter.

"You couldn't suggest that first before bringing up—" Pressing her mouth tight, she shook her head.

"Yeah, that was a bit extreme. He probably got lost." Blair studied the fingernails of his free hand while Jazz considered throat-punching him.

With a sigh, she shoved her hands through her hair, completely fucking up her braid. "He better not have." Jazz grabbed her own fresh mug. She was tempted to add a slug of whiskey to the cold, sludgy brew waiting in the pot. "I don't have the time to go look for him."

"I can help out." Blair's handsome face twisted into a grimace as the coffee hit his tongue. He left it sticking out momentarily, like a particularly squashed piece of roadkill and set down his cup. "If you really need me to."

Jazz narrowed her eyes, studying him. Then she whipped her head around to look out the window with a gasp of exaggerated shock. "Did you see that?"

Blair craned his neck, trying to see what she was looking at. "What?"

Jazz settled back against the counter and sipped nonchalantly. "After you offered to help, I could have sworn I saw a pig fly by the window."

Blair cast her a flat look. "Har har," he deadpanned. "How will I ever stop laughing at that hilarious joke."

Boots pounded up the front steps, saving Jazz from having to come up with a retort. The screen doors crashed shut, and Theo careened around the corner, skidding to a stop at the sight of them. Sweat beaded his forehead, and he had a white-knuckled grip on a guitar case.

"Jasmine, Jazz... I'm so sorry. I—" he panted. His eyes looked a little wild as they darted back and forth between her and Blair.

"You're late," Jazz said coldly. "I thought you said you would have my back. Then, the first day, you ditch me to do the chores alone. Do you even want to be here?"

Theo dropped his gaze and scrubbed his free hand over the back of his neck. Blair cleared his throat and glanced between Theo and Jazz. Then he levered off the counter and sauntered to the sink, depositing his cup inside. "I have to... well, shit, I don't have an excuse. This is fucking awkward, and I want to leave. Good luck, buddy," he muttered to Theo as he passed him on the way out.

Once Blair was gone, Theo tried again. "I'm sorry. I had trouble sleeping, so I took my guitar to the creek."

"And then what? Decided you didn't have to bother coming back until you damned well pleased?"

A red flush spread up his neck. "I fell asleep," he said, his voice low. "On the bench down by the creek."

"Not so much trouble sleeping after all, then," Jazz spat. Instant guilt suffused her. Theo was clearly exhausted. Blue half-moons cushioned his eyes, and his broad shoulders slumped as if weighed down by the world. Maybe they were. She didn't know what he carried each day.

Try asking him. Jazz shoved the little voice away. *I don't care. It's not my job.*

She tipped her head back and forced out a long exhale before standing straight and looking Theo in the eye, "I understand it can take a few days to get used to the routine around here. You're in a new place, and that's never easy. But don't let it happen again. Please."

Theo nodded once, sharply. "Yes, ma'am."

He held her gaze, neither willing to be the first to break eye contact. As Jazz's irritation ebbed, she found herself admiring him. Age had been kind to Theo, as it so unfairly was to many men. The sprinkling of greys at his temples gave off vibes of maturity and wisdom. Wouldn't be the same for a woman, Jazz thought resentfully. On her they would give off *time to go to the salon* vibes. Not that she went to the salon or gave two shits about what anyone thought of her hair. People who worried about that sort of thing clearly didn't have a ranch to run.

Theo broke their unofficial stare down, allowing his gaze to drop to the floor, but for an instant, so quickly that Jazz thought she may have imagined it, they fell to her lips. When his own parted slightly, the tip of his tongue darting out to wet the curve of the bottom one, a spike of heat shot through Jazz. She flinched. To cover her discombobulation, she clapped her hands together sharply, causing Theo to jump.

"Alright," she snapped. "Get dressed to work. You've slacked off enough." Spinning on her heels, Jazz stomped out of the kitchen.

Chapter Eight

THEO

HOW THE HELL HAD he fucked up on his first day?

In his room, Theo tugged on a pair of jeans and a worn, long-sleeved Henley thin enough at the elbows to be nearly translucent. In the tiny bathroom, he brushed his teeth with vicious speed, then combed his hair. He knew he would work twice as hard to make up for his rough start. The last thing he needed was to stay on Jazz's bad side for the next six months. Theo knew all too well she could hold a grudge.

When Theo met Jazz outside the barn, she refused to meet his eyes. Maybe he hadn't imagined the crackle of electricity jumping between them earlier in the kitchen. Chemistry had never been an issue between him and Jazz. Their teen hormones had flamed out of control the second they'd met. Even in the fifteen years since he last saw her, Theo never forgot the taste of her, the clench of her body as she climaxed around him. He'd never put his mouth on someone who tasted as good as her.

"This fence needs to be repaired."

The crack of Jazz's voice snapped Theo from the past. He swallowed hard and nodded, wishing he'd worn looser jeans. He needed to stop thinking of Jazz as anything but his boss. At least her refusal to look at him meant she wouldn't notice his semi-hard cock pressing uncomfortably against the fly of his jeans.

"Yes, ma'am," he said.

"I'll be planting in the garden if you need me."

"Yes, ma'am."

"Stop calling me ma'am. I'm younger than you."

"Yes, Boss." Theo held her gaze until Jazz whirled away and stalked across the yard; only when she was a safe distance away did he allow the small smile to escape.

The rest of the day passed in a blur. Theo only caught the occasional glimpse of Jazz. He fed animals, brushed horses, filled troughs and collected eggs. That was only in the first half of the morning. By the time Jazz whistled from the porch to signal it was time for dinner, Theo was ready to drop from exhaustion. She hadn't been lying in her brochure when she claimed she gave her 'guests' backbreaking and meditative labour. Though Theo's entire body ached and he longed for a shower with every fibre of his being, there was a peace inside him he hadn't experienced in years... or possibly ever.

Theo found Betty in the kitchen, humming as she ladled bowls full of a stew so fragrant he wanted to drop to his knees and weep.

"I didn't know there were angels named Betty," he said, peering over her shoulder and sniffing.

The older woman flashed him a dimpled grin. "There are angels with all sorts of names, my boy. Are you hungry?"

"I'm not sure I've ever been this hungry."

Theo's stomach let out a furious growl as if on cue, and Betty laughed. "It's nearly ready, just pulling out the biscuits."

Crossing the room, Theo took a glass from the dish rack and filled it to the brim with cold water from the tap before draining it in four long pulls. He'd spent weeks in the desert in fatigue gear, and still, he wasn't sure he'd ever been so thirsty.

"Wash your hands and sit. Tell me about your first day," Betty said as she bent to retrieve a pan of perfectly round and golden biscuits from the oven.

Theo groaned when the scent drifted across the room to seduce his nostrils. He lowered himself to a chair and would have excitedly bounced like a kid as Betty moved the food to the table if he hadn't been so exhausted.

"It was... well, it was hard," Theo said honestly. "And I was late, so I'm afraid I'm already in Jazz's bad books."

Betty clucked her tongue, setting a steaming bowl in front of him. "Our girl is a cactus, prickly on the outside, squishy on the inside. Try not to worry too much about it. She'll come around."

Theo found it odd that she'd described Jazz as 'our girl' and wondered if Jazz had shared their history with Betty. She would have witnessed Jazz during the midst of their love affair and her heartbreak once he left. The thought turned Theo's hunger sour in his gut.

He opened his mouth to respond when footsteps came from the hall, and Jazz appeared. "That smells amazing, Bets, I'm famished."

Her long, blue-black hair was unbound and wet from the shower, the thick, glossy ropes reaching her waist. The star pattern of freckles across her nose and cheeks highlighted the mossy hazel of her eyes.

Though Jazz was only six months younger than him, and her life had been anything but easy, Theo was stunned by how youthful she looked. Seeing her fresh-faced and glowing made him feel like an ogre sitting there, dirty, stinking, and scarred. He'd never been good enough for Jasmine Reynolds, and that hadn't changed in the last fifteen years. The realization was a stone sinking in his gut, tugging him toward a blackness he was all too familiar with. Theo lowered his head over his bowl and attempted to fill the yawning void in his soul with stew.

Theo plunged into sleep the second his head hit the pillow. He could not know how long he slept before the memories surfaced, masquerading as dreams as they invaded his unguarded consciousness.

The first explosion rattled the world. It shook the overturned truck Theo huddled against, jarring each bone in his body.

Every grain of sand in the endless barren landscape spreading about him shuddered. The next boom mushroomed out, mingling with screams to form a hellish symphony.

Sweat drenched Theo, streaking rivulets through the dust that coated his face. They had been on a peace mission. No one had seen the attack coming. He could smell the stench of fear oozing from his pores. A body landed in the sand beside him, and Theo could hear them praying relentlessly below their breath—Sophia. Oh shit, please let her be safe.

Theo turned, catching her lovely brown eyes seconds before a bullet erupted from between them, just under the brim of her helmet. It had come through low, angled up, catching her with a freak shot that would have been nearly impossible to replicate. The sound of Theo's bellow rose above the gunfire. The sheer anguished rage rang in his ears as the hot iron tang of Sophia's blood bloomed on his tongue and blurred his vision. Her blood, the force that pumped through her, giving animation to her plentiful jokes, the infectious, raucous laughter that used to permeate the camp at night. Sophia, who'd flirted shamelessly with him over tin plates of rock-hard biscuits and rehydrated beef. Her body was still warm and supple when it slumped across Theo's lap, but her eyes...they were empty.

Theo shot upright, gasping for breath as he wrenched himself free from the tortured sleep. His heart thrashed against his ribs. Stomach acid burned his trachea and the backs of his nostrils.

Swinging his legs over the bed in case he had to run for the bathroom, Theo wrapped his arms around his middle, bending forward as he breathed. Fight the nausea, calm the heart, and shove the memories back into the box where they snuck from.

Through his nose, deep and measured, then an exhale.

Theo let the air trickle from between his lips. He hadn't had an episode in months and knew the disruption in routine was the cause. The nightmares were worse with stress. The last event that set him off was his father's death.

Only a few months after his discharge, Theo got the call that Gregory Bridger had dropped dead on his morning jog. The man who trapped Theo like an ant under a jar for his entire life was gone in a blink. The emotions had been explosive and confusing–a Molotov cocktail of grief, giddy, shameful joy, and disappointment. Disappointment in that things could never be better. He would never have the father other people had, hell–the father Oliver and Chris seemed to have had, the father Theo dreamed of sharing with his brothers.

His *father* was gone, and he died thinking of Theo as a weak, sorry excuse for a son, no matter the lengths Theo had gone to try to make him proud.

A flash of light caught in the corner of his eyes, and Theo glanced up in time to see a shadow move beneath the door and disappear. A second later, a stair creaked, and he caught a muffled curse.

Jasmine.

Another bolt of queasy panic erupted in his gut. Had she heard him? What sort of noises had he made? The last thing he needed, the last thing he thought he could stand, would be pity replacing the aloof irritation in Jazz's familiar gaze when she looked at him. Theo sucked in a shuddering breath. He had to get out of there.

Slipping out of bed he grabbed his guitar. The bedroom door creaked on its hinges as he opened it and he winced, glancing to the stairs. To his relief, the house remained quiet. Holding his breath, as if that would somehow make him more silent, Theo headed out into the night.

Chapter Nine

JASMINE

JAZZ'S HANDS SHOOK AS she clutched the quilt across her chest. Theo's scream had pierced her sleep and sent her heart racing around her chest wild as a bolting rabbit. Shoving her blankets off, Jazz was out of her room and down the stairs before she stopped to consider what she was doing. Her first instinct, which still burned through her, was to wake him from whatever haunted him. As her feet creaked across the bare, chilly floor, she thought she heard him groan a word—*Jasmine*—but the sounds had stopped when she got to his door. She paused, holding her breath until she heard the creak of bedsprings and the sounds of meditative breathing.

Again, Jazz wondered what Theo had been through. The people who came to the ranch had an addiction to a substance, mental health issues, or both. They weren't criminals; that would be a whole other stack of paperwork, but each needed time away from their regular lives. Or a roof over their heads while they regained their footing in the world. Jazz never asked for their stories; it wasn't her place to know, but by the time their six months were up, most felt close enough to Jazz to share.

Theo was the sixth person to come to Sunrise, trusting what she offered might help banish their demons. Some left just as tortured, hating Jazz and the experience, but some loved it and thanked her for what she did for them. A couple had become dear friends and returned to visit her and Betty, staying in touch via social media or sending Christmas cards.

Jazz leaned closer, sure for a second she heard the choked rasp of a sob. Her fingers moved toward the doorknob, pulse pounding in their tips, but she forced them to settle against the wood. It was not her place. She would never have dreamed of going into the room of the person staying with her, and that should be no different now because it was her Theo.

Theo! Damn it. Just Theo.

Would the ranch help him? Jazz wondered as she forced her legs to turn and carry her back up the stairs. She hoped so. Despite their past, six months tended to speed by when someone was as busy as she was. Jazz needed to allow her memories to dissipate. Theo deserved peace as much as the others.

Their days didn't take long to fall into a quiet rhythm. Jazz assigned Theo tasks around the ranch for the day, then went about her business. Unless he had questions or needed more work, she rarely saw him until dinner. She left the house before him, and when he joined her outside, sexily dishevelled from sleep, Jazz would scramble to escape as quickly as possible.

So, Jazz was surprised when she found Theo hunched over a bowl of oatmeal in the kitchen a few weeks into his stay. He clenched a spoon in one hand and had a death grip on a coffee mug with the other. The sharp morning light illuminated his pale, drawn face, accenting the blue bruises beneath his eyes and turning his cheekbones to stark blades.

Jazz watched him power through a few sips and alternating bites before clearing her throat and walking in. At the sight of her, Theo's back snapped straight, and he wiped the look of exhaustion away, plastering on a smile. Jazz considered reminding him that she knew him too well to fall for whatever that look was, but she stopped herself.

"Good morning," she said, wincing at the rasp of her sleep-husky voice.

"Good morning." Theo sounded more awake than she did, though moments ago, she was sure he'd fall face-first into his porridge. "What's on the docket today, Boss?"

Jazz scrunched her nose at him, moving to the coffee pot. "Don't call me boss. It's weird. And don't talk to me until I have at least one of these in my system." She waggled a mug at him. Theo's head dipped, and a grin, real this time, flashed across his mouth before he returned to his food.

Neither spoke while Jazz clutched her cup and sipped, but the silence wasn't uncomfortable. To her surprise, it was close to companionable, and she had to force herself to enjoy it before her brain thought to ask *why* it felt that way. Once the caffeine entered her bloodstream and worked its miracle, Jazz sighed and sat back in her chair.

"We need to head out to the far pastures and do repairs."

Oh, okay. She hadn't planned on saying that.

Theo looked up from whatever he was reading on his phone. "Alright."

Jazz assumed she was committed now. It looked like Theo was going to the far property with her. "It's going to take a couple of days. Do you remember how to ride a horse?"

Theo flashed her a crooked grin, and she had to tell her stomach not to erupt in butterflies. "If it's like riding a bicycle and you don't forget, then I should be okay, but I foresee an extremely sore ass in my future."

Jazz snorted into her cup, and Theo caught her eyes, his twinkling. A moment zinged between them, a flash of what they'd once shared. The old friendship rearing its head.

"Are we camping?" Theo asked once Jazz managed to break her gaze from his.

She nodded. "Yeah, I'm going to guess two nights."

"Who will take care of the animals?"

"I have a friend, Joe. He owns the farm on the other side of town and comes to help if I'm gone."

Theo seemed to digest that for a moment, then he nodded and asked around a bite of oatmeal, "Can Titus come?"

Jazz nearly choked on a sip of coffee when she spluttered a surprised laugh. This was the Theo she remembered, animal-loving and genuine. The glow of heat below her sternum, kindled by his grin, was dangerous. She'd much prefer him to stay aloof, a stranger to her now.

"I'm afraid not. Titus is a livestock guardian dog. His job is to stay here and protect the animals. He isn't great with long rides. He gets too tired and hot. Plus, we'd have to carry food for him, and he eats *a lot.*"

With a chuckle, Theo nodded. "I could see that."

Rapping her knuckles on the table, Jazz pushed herself from the chair. She had to get out of there before he said anything else endearing. "I'll meet you outside in ten minutes."

"What's this guy's name?" Theo asked, patting the glossy chestnut flank of the horse he was saddling. Jazz reminded him of a few technical points as he put on the tack, but ranch life seemed to be coming back to him. His history of working at his uncle's place made her life easier. Many people she hosted at Sunrise had never set foot in the country. She spent hours teaching them simple things, such as how to mend fences and clean the chicken coop. At first, she'd assumed shovelling shit was self-explanatory, but they had quickly proven her wrong.

"That's David," Jazz said as she swung her saddle onto the broad grey back of her horse, Ghost.

Goliath, affronted by the loss of his friends and Jazz's abandonment, whinnied from his paddock, then threw his head in the air and cantered along the fence before settling back to stare at them again.

"I'm sorry!" Jazz called to him. "Joe will take care of you!"

"Why does he have to stay?" Theo asked, narrowing his eyes in a dangerously cute way as he struggled to knot the cinch. Jazz had to look away when the tip of his tongue poked out of the corner of his mouth.

"Basically, he's too much of a pretty boy," she said, staring at the stallion. As if he knew his adoring public was looking on, Goliath tossed his head and did a few hops as if he wanted to rear but decided it wasn't worth the effort.

"Ah, benched because of his looks," Theo said, pulling the leather tight with a sound of triumph and earning a side-eyed glare from David. "An insult I'm all too familiar with."

Jazz snorted, slipping a halter over Ghost's ears and held an O-ring bit to his lips. The horse sighed as if he bore the weight of the world and accepted it, clacking it between his teeth a few times until he'd worked it into position. "Goliath is one of the few things on this ranch that makes us money. I can't risk anything happening to him. I ride him, but only for pleasure." She stroked a loving hand over Ghost's neck. "This big guy takes good care of me when we're working. Nothing spooks him."

She put a flattened palm to her brow, blocking the morning rays as she looked back at the stallion, who let out one more pitiful nicker. "With my luck, that bugger would see a bird, throw me, leave me for dead, and bust a leg on the way home."

Theo absently ran his fingers through David's mane as she talked, and Jazz lost herself in the motion. His hands were beautiful with long, capable fingers framing broad palms. There was a spiderweb of scars over the back of his right. An image flashed of Theo, his fingers, less lined, less scared and calloused, slipping through the strands of her own hair.

I love you, Jasmine. I don't want to leave.

"So, basically, you deal in semen."

Theo's words penetrated the unbidden memory, effectively destroying it, and Jazz shook her head, barking out a laugh. "Excuse me, what?"

"Semen; Henry, Goliath...I'm sensing a pattern here, and I'd like to state for the record I'm not willing to part with any of mine."

Jazz opened her mouth, closed it, and found herself mortifyingly incapable of doing anything but staring across at him for a few heart-pounding seconds. Then, with more audacity than Jazz thought him capable of, Theo threw her a wink and turned back to the horse.

A soft *meow* sounded from the pile of hay bales, and a large orange cat appeared and began winding itself around Theo's ankles. He let out a noise of excitement that did unfair things to Jazz's heart and squatted down to greet the feline. "Who is this?"

It took Jazz a second to realize he was talking to her. Because...of course, he was. What the fuck was wrong with her? "That's Catrick...Catrick Stewart." She rolled her lips together but couldn't keep her laughter contained when Theo looked up at her.

"I love the weird ass names all these animals have," he said, his words tinted with amusement.

"I know it's ridiculous." Jazz shook her head. "When my mom was alive, she always gave them quirky names, and I guess I kept it up. I always figured that was something she'd appreciate, you know?"

Theo nodded. "It makes you feel connected to her."

Jazz bit her lip but nodded. "I think you're right. I have little of her, but those memories are invaluable."

They were quiet as they finished the last of their preparations, swung onto their saddles, and turned the horses toward the mountains. Jazz glanced back a few times, ensuring Theo had control of the horse, though she told herself she didn't need to worry. He was an experienced rider, even if it had been years, and David was docile and calm. A quarter horse who'd spent years in rodeos doing roping competitions, David had yet to encounter anything that fazed him. His temperament was why she'd chosen him as a companion to Goliath, though when she heard his name, she knew it was fate.

A peace settled over Jazz as her body swayed to Ghost's familiar gait. The birds were out in force, trilling their joy over spring to the sky, trees, and anyone else who would listen. A long, lonely whinny rippled out from the barnyard—Goliath, heartbroken over his abandonment.

After a few moments, she twisted in her saddle. "So, we will ride the perimeter of the ranch. I do it once in the spring and once in the fall, looking for any spots where the fence line has been compromised. A lot of the wires and poles are old. My grandfather was the one who put it up. It took him years. We've been replacing it as we go."

Theo was nodding, looking blissed out as he bobbed along in time to David's steps. "That must have been a huge undertaking."

"It was. There are places where the line stops and then starts: the property line at the base of the ridge. The cattle can't climb that. And the river. I've had a few go across, but it takes a real ambitious cow to bother."

Once the chore was done, Jazz could give the cattle more room to roam until the fall. She and Theo had a few gruelling days of hard work, hard riding, and rough sleeping ahead of them. It was not usually a chore she would take clients on, but she knew Theo could handle it. She chose not to consider the part of her that seemed to harbour an ache of longing for his presence. She would just have to do her best to ignore how natural he looked in the saddle, his faded jeans stretched taught over the long, corded muscles of his thighs.

The situation only got worse when David barged in front of Ghost, determined to be the first horse on the trail. From that angle Jazz had a clear view of Theo's ass, cupped in the saddle, flexing as he used his legs to guide the horse.

What horny devil has possessed you? She wondered. It was as if her libido, average at best for most of her life, had suddenly popped out of hibernation with a whip and a bottle of viagra, ready to do business. If she was going to keep Theo at arms length, she really had to get her head out of the gutter.

Chapter Ten

THEO

DESPITE THE HARD PHYSICAL work he'd been doing daily on the ranch for the past couple of weeks, every muscle in Theo's body felt the effects of the long ride as they set up their camp. He kept all complaints to himself, however. Jazz was the strongest person he had ever met, and he didn't think he could stand her thinking of him as weak. As far as he knew, his father was the only one who'd ever thought that about him, and Theo preferred to keep it that way. Together, they worked with quiet efficiency, and it wasn't until Theo turned to Jazz with a frown that either of them spoke.

"Where is the other tent?" he asked, glancing around at the pile of supplies at his feet.

Jazz cast a sideways scowl at him from where she was bent over, laying out a pile of kindling to start a fire. "It should have been with the stuff on your saddle."

Theo turned back to the pile of tack on the ground, sorting through the bedrolls and tightly bound mattress pads to ensure he hadn't missed it. Then he remembered.

Titus.

"Shit," he muttered, a stone weight of anxiety sinking through his stomach.

Jazz straightened with a slight wince before narrowing her eyes at him, lips flattening in suspicion. "Shit, what?" she asked, drawing the word out as if she didn't truly desire the answer.

"Titus was trying to get me to play... grabbing things and running off."

Jazz's head flopped back, and a groan seeped out of her. "Are you telling me this—" she swept her arm at the minuscule one-person tent she had erected, "is our only shelter?"

Theo winced, scratching at his chin. "Yes. But—" he brandished one finger in her direction. "Let's focus on what is important here. It's Titus' fault, not mine."

Jazz squeezed her eyes shut, inhaling deeply a few times in a way Theo felt was a tad on the dramatic side, before turning her back on him as she continued, silently, building a fire.

"I don't mind sleeping on the ground. It wouldn't be the first time," Theo said after a moment. "I can keep the fire going." The spot where they'd made camp had a spongy layer of soft earth and leaf matter. It would suck, but this ground would be softer than plenty of the places he'd slept in his life.

Jazz didn't turn around, but he saw her shoulders relax.

Once they'd eaten the hot dogs that Jazz had stabbed onto a stick and roasted over the flames. Theo stretched out with his back against his saddle, extending his aching legs in front of him with a groan.

"This reminds me of the old westerns Ted and I used to watch," he said, tucking his hands behind his head. The night air brushed cool fingers along his face, and he relished the silk touch against his overheated skin. Despite how much his ass hurt and the debacle with the tent, Theo couldn't remember the last time he'd felt so content.

"I don't think they had Oscar Myers back then," Jazz remarked. "Beans straight outta the can for those cowpokes." She stretched her back with a grimace, the first sign that the long day had affected her. When she reached back for her braid and began unwinding the thick strands, Theo watched helplessly, mesmerized by the waterfall of inky curls unfurling around her. Neither spoke and if Jazz felt his eyes clinging to her, she made no indication. It surprised Theo how easy it was to be quiet and comfortable in her presence, even after their history, even with the way she continually pushed him away.

After a few moments, he said, "You love this place, don't you?" The words weren't so much a question as a statement. Reaching out his leg, he knocked the toe of his boot against hers, dislodging a clump of dirt. It didn't truly count as touching her, yet a thrill still moved through him at the contact.

"Yes," Jazz answered plainly.

"Have you ever thought about leaving? Trading it all in for an easier life?"

"No."

Theo chuckled. "Gregarious, as always," he drawled.

One side of her mouth lifted in a flash of a smile that was gone as quickly as it came. "I left for a while," she said. "I lived with Blair and went to school. Pretended my father and this place didn't exist."

I pretended you didn't exist.

Theo could hear the words hanging there as clearly as if she'd spoken them out loud.

"When... when I looked you up on Facebook, I also looked at Valley's profile. She had made a post about helping you move to Cascade Creek. That's why I thought you didn't live here anymore."

Jazz chewed at her lip, nodding. "I wondered."

"What did you go to school for?" he asked, desperate to keep her talking, to chase back the veil of the past that threatened to creep in.

"Horticulture," Jazz said, the grin jumping across her face when he barked with laughter.

"You did a great job distancing yourself, hey," he teased.

Jazz shrugged. "What can I say? I love what I love; this ranch is in my blood." She leaned back on her elbows, tipping her face up to catch the last dregs of spring sunshine. "My great-grandfather bought this land," she said. "He and my great-grandmother spent years saving the money for it, and they were among the first people to settle here. They practically founded Jamieson Creek. My grandfather, father, and I were born in that house. Sometimes, I let myself imagine—" her words trailed off, and she pulled her bottom lip between her teeth, biting at it.

"Imagine what?" Theo pressed after a moment.

"Just... maybe doing what I do, but on a larger scale. I'm not sure what that looks like or how I would manage it, but I can never shake the feeling that this place has magic." She paused, her eyes wandering the horizon she probably knew as well as her reflection. "When I wake up, I see the acres rolling off to meet the mountains. They're green in the spring and gold in the summer, the veins of creeks and treelines pumping it full of life." She drew a deep breath, settling deeper into herself and the ground she sat upon as if she were part of the land. "There's nowhere else I'd rather wake up. No other view I want to open my eyes to." Her voice broke, and embarrassed, she scrubbed at her face.

Theo was silent for a long moment, digesting her words, his eyes travelling the path hers had taken. "It must be amazing," he said. "To have such a deep, lasting connection to a place."

His uncle's ranch had been the closest he'd ever come to feeling like he belonged, even though that had never truly been his home.

"It is. And it makes me all the more terrified I'll be the one to fail it."

Theo looked at her, letting his eyes linger on the sharp edge of her cheekbones, relishing the glow of her honeyed skin under the loving touch of the dusk light. Her eyes held him captive, electricity spiking between them, until Jazz squirmed under his scrutiny, pulling her eyes away.

Theo was quiet for a second, then he spoke, his gaze travelling along the silhouette of the mountains. "Remember when Scott said you couldn't climb to the top of that big oak outside the bar?" Theo shook his head, breath hissing from his nostrils in a disbelieving hiss. "You were tipsy, and yet you scampered up there, quick as a squirrel. I was sure I'd have to scrape you off the sidewalk. You're the most stubborn woman I know, Jasmine. Why would you fail?"

For a moment, he thought she would tell him, crack herself open, and spill her truths as she'd done when they were young. They hadn't kept a thing from one another back then. Theo had ached for that quality of connection over the years, but he'd never found it again, not with anyone but Jazz.

She didn't open up to him, though. Instead, she pushed herself upwards, crawling to her feet. "I'm tired. I'm going to wash up. You can put your sleeping bag in the tent, but if you snore or fart, I'll suffocate you with my saddle pad."

Theo opened his mouth to argue again but paused. He had to ask himself when he'd ever won an argument against her. He'd slip out and sleep on the ground if they couldn't fit in the tent. It wasn't as though she could haul him back if he did.

"Yes, ma'am," he said and did his best not to stare as she dusted off the ass of her worn Levis while she walked away.

Theo opened his mouth to argue again but paused. He had to ask himself when he'd ever won an argument against her. He'd slip out and sleep on the ground if they couldn't fit in the tent. It wasn't as though she could haul him back if he did.

"This isn't going to work," Theo said. "I'll sleep outside. It's fine." He and Jazz stood side by side, staring at the tiny canvas dome in front of them. The sun had fully set and the air was gathering a significant chill.

"It's supposed to get cold." Jazz chewed at her lip, the colour in her cheeks suspiciously high as she dipped her head to peer through the door.

Theo shrugged. "I'll keep the fire burning."

"I'll feel bad if I know you're out here freezing your nuts off."

Theo cast her a playful sidelong glance. "Why thank you. It is uncharacteristically kind of you to be concerned about the temperature of my nuts."

"Come on," Jazz said, exasperation tinting her voice. "Get in. I will be fine. We're both so tired, we'll pass right out."

Theo was not passing out.

The warmth from Jazz's body seeped through their layers of sleeping bags and clothes straight into Theo's soul. It seemed possible that his entire body might burst into flames. Twisting his hips, he attempted to ease the ache in his back and the uncomfortable press of his insistent erection against the fly of his jeans. His cock did not seem to understand why he would not roll over and ravish her already.

How did she smell so good after a day on horseback?

Jazz's breathing hitched, and she rolled toward him in her sleep. The movement brought her even closer since there was barely a molecule of space between them. Theo ground his teeth, stopping a groan of frustration before it escaped. The soft gusts of her breath washed over his face. Fucking hell he wanted to turn those soft sleepy inhales into gasps of pleasure.

Damn, Titus.

Theo would make a rug out of that dog when they got back to the ranch. This was all the mutt's fault.

Chapter Eleven

JASMINE

J AZZ OPENED HER EYES and blinked, trying to pinpoint what had pulled her from sleep. A thin screen separated her from the inky sheet of star-strewn sky. Then it came again, the sound that woke her; Theo, a growling whimper of agony resonating from somewhere deep inside him.

Wiggling onto her side so she faced the broad expanse of his back, Jazz listened. They were pressed so close in the tiny confines of the tent that his violent trembling shook her as well. Unsure what to do, she reached out a palm and laid it in the space between his shoulder blades, rubbing in small circles. Theo twitched under her touch but didn't wake.

Jazz was losing the battle against her heavy lids when Theo jerked so violently that Jazz feared he might accidentally strike her in the confined space. Scooting backward as far as the tent would allow, she watched the muscles of his shoulders, visible through the thin shirt he wore for sleep, flex and jump as if he were fighting. Maybe he was fighting, battling whatever demon plagued him.

When a heart-wrenching cry tore out of him, Jazz couldn't take it anymore.

"Theo," she whispered. He moaned louder, head thrashing back and forth on his makeshift pillow of rolled-up sweatshirts.

Jazz touched his shoulder. "Theo?" Another fit of unresponsive thrashing greeted her touch. She thought she remembered something about not waking someone during a sleep episode.

"Fuck it." Gritting her teeth, Jazz pressed against him, narrowly avoiding a blow to the face when Theo's elbow jerked back. She wrapped her arms around Theo's waist and pressed her cheek to the flat spot between his shoulders, holding him in as tight a grip as she could. "Shhh," she whispered. "Shhh, Theo, you're not alone."

It took a long time for his breathing to steady. Jazz allowed her grip to relax when it did, but she didn't let go. His warmth and outdoorsy male scent surrounded her, lulling her back to a state of sleepy half-awareness. This was right, holding him, sleeping side by side. Why hadn't they been doing this all along?

She didn't know when she fell back to sleep, but neither stirred again until the sun poked exploratory fingers into the tent at dawn.

The rasp of a tent zipper sliding open sounded behind Jazz as she was mixing the instant coffee into two mugs of hot water.

"Uncanny timing," she commented without turning. "Just like my ex. Blair always knows exactly when the coffee is ready."

She forced herself to turn to him when Theo still didn't speak. He stood shirtless, watching her through lowered lashes as he buckled his belt. The early morning light made his bare skin glow, highlighting the long, lean muscles cording his body. Jazz clenched her fists around the mugs she held, trying to squeeze away the urge to touch him.

"I dreamed again, didn't I?" Theo said, his voice rough with sleep.

Jazz nodded, raised her cup to her lips, took a long swallow, and then fought not to wince when the liquid burned from her esophagus to her stomach.

"I'm sorry I woke you."

"It's fine. Don't worry about it." Holding Theo's eyes, she passed him the other cup. "Here. It's not great, only instant, but it will keep the caffeine headache at bay."

"Thank you." Theo accepted the drink, wrapped it in both hands and stared into the depths as if the murky liquid held the universe's secrets.

Silence stretched between them, tenuous as a cobweb. "There's a section by the creek we should start on first," Jazz said after a moment. "Some deadfall took out the top two wires."

"Alright. Just let me—" Theo jerked a thumb toward the trees.

"Of course, sorry." Heat pooled in Jazz's cheeks, which was ridiculous. "I have some protein bars for us. We can break later for a better meal."

Theo nodded once, then turned to set his mug on the stump they'd been using as a table before walking away. Jazz didn't know if he remembered her holding him during the night, but she wasn't about to ask him. Trying to ignore how the morning sun shone on his bare back, she turned back to her saddlebags, riffling through them for the bars. Hopefully, they weren't too squished; that would do nothing to improve their appeal.

When Theo returned, some of the strain had eased from his face, and he seemed more alert, if only slightly. When she tossed him the protein bar, which was flattened, he fumbled it but managed to keep hold.

"We'll leave the horses here to graze. The section that needs repairing is over there." Jazz jerked her chin across the pasture.

"Lead the way," Theo mumbled around a mouthful of the bar. Jazz narrowed her eyes at him and turned away. She wasn't sure why, but she was fighting a smile.

They moved through the high grass for a few moments, bird song and the faint rush of the river punctuating the morning.

"It doesn't always happen," Theo blurted. "But they're always worse when I'm stressed, or in a new situation... or both." Something about the way he said it made Jazz think he'd been rehearsing the words to himself. It took her a moment to realize he was talking about the nightmares.

"What are they about?" Jazz asked. At the look on his face, she wished she could take back the words as soon as she spoke them. The question was too personal, especially when she sought to maintain a professional space between them, and it was clear from the flash of pain he didn't much want to talk about them.

"Afghanistan," was all he said—one word laden with meaning.

"I could never picture you going into service."

"I never wanted to," Theo said, his voice thick with regret. "My father forced my hand. I was sort of under the impression for a long time that I had to do what he said. I learned later that he had all the classic traits of a narcissist. He had my entire family under the same spell. My brothers were fine with the life he chose for them. I was not, but I didn't understand there *was* a choice at the time. We served our country. That was what Bridgers did, and the tradition wasn't about to stop with me." The words came free, straight and deadpanned as if they were something he had heard a hundred times.

Jazz snorted. "What a load of toxic masculine bullshit."

"I agree."

"Do you want to tell me more about the dreams?" Again, the question slipped out against her better judgment. She should have utilized her doctor friend and asked Valley if there was a vitamin to reinforce her verbal filter.

Theo remained quiet for so long that Jazz thought he might not answer. Perhaps he was marvelling at her inability to mind her business.

"I don't think so. At least, not right now," he said at last, flashing a smile that looked forced but was an apparent attempt to banish the heaviness between them.

"Alright, well, I'm here with two working ears if you ever need to vent," she said.

"Thanks, Jazz." The smile reached his eyes this time, sending fine lines fanning from the corners. They should have aged him, but instead, those lines lent his serious face a boyish air.

With a groan, Theo stretched his arms toward the blue expanse of the sky. "It's too beautiful a day, and we're in too beautiful a place to bring that all up anyway," he said. "I want to enjoy this."

"Good luck," Jazz said as they drew to a halt. She dramatically swept her arms toward the tangled mass of wire and dead branches awaiting them. A laugh nearly escaped her when Theo took one look at the mess, and his shoulders slumped.

"Fuck," he muttered as Jazz dropped her bag and began pulling out tools.

Jazz woke before Theo, shedding the last clinging tendrils of a dream that had featured his head between her thighs, with a sigh. Her body was aching, pulsing with need so sharp that it was almost painful. In her sleep, she'd pushed a hand down into the waistband of her jeans, far too close to taking matters into its own hands for her liking. Gritting her teeth, Jazz tried to ignore the licking flames of the climax burning just beneath her skin. With a shaky sigh, she rolled away from the intoxicating heat of Theo's body and wriggled out of the tent. She felt wobbly and off-centre after two nights jammed into a tent with Theo. The urge to touch him was growing stronger instead of fading with proximity. And why did he have to cry out in his sleep until her heart ached to soothe him?

Zipping the tent closed as silently as possible, Jazz went to her saddle bag and retrieved the small, microfiber gym towel she'd shoved inside. Then she stood, stretching the kinks from her back and looking over her ranch. The beauty of the land and her pride in it never failed to clog her throat with emotion. She thought of her family, working the land for nearly a century, the people who shared her blood and passion. For a moment, Jazz wondered what her grandfather would think if he knew what she had done with Sunrise and what she hoped to do with it in the future. She thought maybe, even if it varied from his original dream for the land, he'd approve of her helping people.

She and Theo had chosen a spot near the river for their camp last night, tucking their tent and fire under a rocky outcrop that overlooked a small meadow. The river curled along its bottom, but Jazz cut across, heading for the tree line on the other side. The tall pines would give her a modicum of privacy in case Theo woke up.

Reaching the river's edge, Jazz stripped out of her clothes and laid them flat on a rock, hoping the sun would warm them. She found a spot where the sandy bottom rolled quickly away to deep green. The less time it took to walk in, the better. Moving swiftly, Jazz did her best not to focus on the bite of the water. Holding her breath, she took four long strides and plunged below the surface. She could only manage a few seconds before she burst back up, spluttering and trembling.

"Fucking, fuck fuck." Jazz's throat spasmed with the urge to scream. She'd been jumping into this water all year around for as long as she could remember, but if it wasn't summer, it was akin to torture. Hopefully, it would drown her flaming libido. Teeth chattering, she pushed through the water toward shore. Only her calves and feet were still submerged when the loud snap of a breaking branch caused Jazz to freeze.

An animal? Was it one big enough that she should worry about it?

The thoughts had barely flashed through her cold-numbed brain when Theo stumbled out of the trees, shirtless, his hair in disarray from sleep. They registered each other at the same moment. Theo's eyes went wide, and he crashed a hand over them with a sharp slap.

"Fuck, Jazz, I'm so sorry!" he choked.

"There's an entire river!" Jazz yelled, attempting to cover herself while not losing her footing as she rushed out of the river. The last thing she wanted was to slip and end up back in the drink. "Don't look, or I'll castrate you!"

"I'm not!" Theo yelled. He stood a few metres away, hand clamped over his eyes.

"What are you doing?" Jazz snapped as she struggled to pull her jeans over her damp legs. "Did you follow me?"

Theo let out a sharp, indignant sound. "Of course not. I was going to jump in. I stink and didn't think you wanted to smell me."

She noticed his smell that morning, but it hadn't been unpleasant. It had reminded her of home—of the place she loved so much and hard work—with the undertone of male that kindled a longing in her she didn't want to fuel. Without thinking, she snapped, "I should get to see you naked then!"

Why the fuck had she said that?

"I didn't see anything," Theo said.

Jazz pulled her shirt over her head, then grimaced as she freed the sodden rope of her braid. "Really?"

Theo's lips folded in on themselves, and then he sighed and shook his head, still keeping the hand tight. "No. I'm lying. I saw your entire body. You look amazing. I'm sorry. It was only for a second. Except—"

"Except what?" Jazz growled.

"Except I will definitely see it each time I blink for...maybe forever? And I don't know how to fix that."

"Arrgg!" Jazz flung the boot she was holding, hitting Theo in the stomach.

"Ooof." He doubled up with a grunt, finally letting his hand drop, though his eyes were scrunched incredibly tight beneath. He looked so ridiculous, with his cheeks nearly touching his eyebrows, that Jazz laughed.

"Open your eyes and toss me that boot," she said, hiccuping on giggles.

"Why should I?" Theo grumbled, but he did as she asked. The boot landed in front of her with a thump. Jazz retrieved it and pulled it onto her socked foot. When she straightened, Theo was using one hand to work his belt free of his jeans.

"What are you doing?" she squeaked.

Theo gave her an entirely cocky grin, and Jazz didn't appreciate what it did to her stomach. She wasn't sure she knew he was capable of such a look.

"I was trying to even it out," he said, shrugging one bare shoulder. "Fair is fair, Jasmine."

"I was... distraught. Please don't take your clothes off."

"You showed me yours..."

"I didn't *mean* to show you mine!" Jazz had to wrench her eyes away as she made a break for the trees. She had to get out of there before she did something stupid. Her greedy body was already suggesting she walk right over and help him get the belt the rest of the way off. "I'm going to camp," she called over her shoulder right before she tripped on a stick and stumbled, catching herself before she totally ate shit.

Theo tipped his head back, letting out a rolling laugh that followed Jazz halfway back to camp.

Chapter Twelve

THEO

T HE CLOSER THEO AND Jazz got to home, the thicker the air of exhaustion and irritability between them became. Jazz and Ghost rode in front along the single trail, leaving Theo and David plodding behind. Theo watched the swing of her braid and the sway of her hips, mesmerized, nearly too tired to blink. He couldn't wipe away the flash image of her coming out of the water that morning. It was like looking at a lightning flash; it stayed with him even when he blinked. He didn't know what had possessed him to tease her the way he had after, but the furious red that stained her cheeks as he began taking off his belt had made whatever ire she directed at him now all worth it.

A cacophony of barking greeted them when they crested the hill of the field nearest the ranch yard. A few moments later, the dogs swirled around the horses' feet, causing them to nicker grumpily. Even they were ready for some downtime in the barn.

They were dismounting when an entirely too cheerful voice called from the barn. "Hey!" A lanky man with thinning blond hair popped out of the double doors, grinning at Jazz. Using his forearm to swipe at his brow, he came forward. "Glad you're back. Goliath has been in a real tizzy."

"When is he not in a tizzy?" Jazz remarked dryly, switching Ghost's bridal for a halter. "Joe, this is Theo, my current resident."

Joe extended a hand, grinning. He was missing a canine tooth on the left side, and Theo had to force himself not to stare at the black space. "Nice to meet you," he said, clasping Joe's hand. Joe was still smiling, unnervingly happy. Leaning a bit closer, he gestured a dirty hand back and forth between their bodies.

"We're practically name buddies," he said, releasing a hissing laugh. Was this guy drunk? Theo wasn't sure he should be looking after Jazz's prized animals.

"Oh?" he said, forcing a polite smile onto his face, though all it wanted to do was crumple into a frown.

"Yeah, Joe, Theo, they rhyme!"

Theo extracted himself and released a fake laugh. "Ah, yes. So they do."

"Well, I better get moving." Joe smacked both hands against his thigh, causing David to snort and toss his head. When his ears went back, Theo pulled him away and set to work loosening the cinch. Joe had the air of a slow leaver, and Theo didn't have the patience for multiple goodbyes.

"Thank you for keeping an eye on things, Joe. You know how much I appreciate it," Jazz said, smiling warmly at the man. Theo realized he must be close to the same age as they were, but the years had not been easy on the poor guy.

"Not a problem, Jazzy. Let me know the next time you need an extra hand." His gaze swivelled to Theo, and his heart sank. He'd hoped that his part of the conversation was fulfilled. "Isn't likely that it will be anytime soon with this big hunk of meat around, am I right?" With a wink and a cackle that made Theo want to knock another tooth out of his head, Joe turned and headed off.

"I can deal with the horses if you want to go shower," Theo said once Joe was out of sight. As soon as he saw the way

Jazz's back stiffened, he longed to suck the words back into his mouth like a spaghetti noodle. She turned with ominous slowness toward him, giving each hair on his body a chance to stand on end.

"Excuse me?" she said, her voice going flat. "Are you implying that I smell?"

Theo shook his head hard enough to self-inflict a whiplash. "No, Ma'am."

"Oh, so you think I'm a weak female who can't take care of her shit?"

Good god, what had he done?

Theo shook his head again. The exhaustion must have addled his brain. Deciding it was best to keep his mouth closed, he kept standing and shaking his head like a deranged idiot.

With a snort of disgust, Jazz wheeled away. Moving to the barn door, she stuck her hand inside and turned back, holding a ring of keys.

"Here," she tossed them to Theo, who, to his relief, caught them.

"Take my truck and pick up some burgers from Patty's. Betty is still at her sister's, and I sure as hell ain't cooking tonight."

"Yes, ma'am." He pocketed the keys and turned back to David.

"*I'll* finish the horses," Jazz said. "I'm perfectly capable. The faster you go, the faster we can eat."

"Alright." Theo bit down on his lip to prevent himself from saying anything that would make the situation worse.

"The ranch's company card is inside the knife sheath in the glove compartment. Use it." Her tone broached no argument.

Managing not to wince, Theo stepped away from David and gave Jazz one more nod. Since he no longer had a death wish, he would say nothing about her keeping a credit card inside the truck.

When Theo pulled open the door of the rusted blue Chevy with an ear-splitting squeak, Titus' giant head popped up over the back of Theo's truck. With a grunt, the dog jumped out and sauntered over, hopping into the cab of Jazz's truck without so much as a by-your-leave from Theo. He narrowed his eyes at the dog. "Wait a darn minute, I have a bone to pick with you." When the dog cocked his head, Theo chuckled. "Yeah, I heard it." He shrugged. "Alright, fella. Come on then, I forgive you."

Theo was a few kilometres from town when the deer bound up from the ditch and streaked across the road in front of him. "Fuck!" The brakes of the old truck shrieked as Theo hammered on them.

Titus flew forward, and, on instinct, Theo flung out an arm, attempting to stop the animal's momentum. His gut reaction didn't account for the fact Titus weighed about one hundred and twenty pounds. The dog slammed into the dashboard, pining Theo's hand and forearm between his body and the dash. Growling out a curse of pain, Theo steered the truck one-handed off the road and flicked on the hazard lights.

"*Ouch*," he growled, shaking out his throbbing hand. "You okay, big guy?"

Titus met Theo's eyes with a doleful sigh. Then, with a feat of flexibility that baffled Theo, the dog turned around in the footwell and climbed back onto the seat. As soon as the pressure from Theo's arm and Titus' body was off it, the glove compartment thumped open, disgorging a landslide of contents, including a large knife sheathed in leather. With a groan, Theo let his head fall forward to bounce against the steering wheel. The day was welcome to end whenever. After allowing himself a moment to wallow, Theo leaned over and began scooping up the detritus. With a stack of envelopes in hand, he paused. They were all from Jamieson Creek City Hall. Holding one up to the late rays of the sun, Theo squinted at it. He could make out bold red letters: PAST DUE. He held up another, the same thing. With a long exhale, Theo lowered the pile to his lap. Jazz's words from their first night in camp came back to him.

I just hope I don't fail.

Was Jazz in danger of losing the ranch? The thought made his stomach curdle. What would she do without it? Sunrise was her home. It was an integral part of who she was. He pictured the way her eyes lit up when she talked about the place. She was brave and good, giving strangers a place to heal while receiving very little in return. There was no way—absolutely no way—Jasmine was losing her ranch.

"Not on my watch," Theo muttered. Stuffing the envelopes back into the glove box, he slammed it shut and put the truck in gear. Titus stretched out on the bucket seat and laid his head on Theo's lap, letting out a grunt of what he assumed was agreement. He wasn't sure how he could help her. Lord knew she was too stubborn to take money from him, but there was a way, and he would find it. When Theo pulled up in front of Patty's Pub, an idea bloomed and grew.

Chapter Thirteen

JASMINE

As soon as Theo drove away down the road, Jazz dropped her head against Ghost's neck with a sigh. "I'm such an asshole," she muttered to the horse. He'd only been trying to help. To be nice to her because he knew she was tired and sore.

Once she'd finished getting the horses settled, checked the henhouse for eggs, and unloaded the tools from the packs, Jazz was ready to drop. Her stomach growled louder than Odin's when he smelled a squirrel, and she was battling the inexplicable urge to burst into tears. A sharp, hot pain had taken up residence low on her left side, along with a wash of hormones and an aching need that proximity to Theo all weekend had only exacerbated.

Damn, the timing of her biological clock.

Her baser self was demanding fertilization, and it was fucking with her. A glance at her watch told her Theo would be back soon with their food, but Jazz couldn't fathom the idea of waiting a moment longer to shower. Stepping through the screen door, she inhaled, pausing long enough to allow the scents of home to wrap around her, welcoming her back. Then she trudged upstairs, peeling off her dusty jeans and shirt and throwing them into the basket.

Dressed in her underwear, Jazz stood before the mirror, unwinding her hair. When the black mass hung around her in ropey waves, Jazz studied herself. Her body was long, lean and muscular but not lacking femininity. Her tawny gold skin and sharp cheekbones were a gift from her Indigenous grandmother, and her mossy hazel eyes were the only features that marked her as her father's daughter. They were as tumultuous as she was, shifting from green to brown depending on her mood, the lighting, and clothing.

She wasn't conventionally pretty, but that never bothered her. She attracted the gazes of more men than she cared for. It was the strength that radiated from her, the fact that, at five foot eight, she could look plenty of them in the eye. Men noticed her. They wanted either to conquer her, or they genuinely desired strong women. The former was the most common. She could blame her strength for the hollow gut-ache of loneliness that sometimes threatened to swallow her. What attracted men to her ultimately drove them away. Jazz had only gone on a few dates after her divorce from Blair. They'd been enough to dose any tiny flame of optimism she'd fanned into existence.

Jazz's split from Blair had been mutual, and they had remained close. Some people—*Valley*—might say *too* close. Ultimately, she and Blair were too good of friends. When it came down to staying together and hating each other or retaining that friendship, they decided it was time to end the marriage and save what mattered most to them. But fuck, she missed being touched. She missed having someone *want* her.

Theo wanted her.

The thought crept across her mind in seductive, misty tendrils. She hadn't dreamt up the thick hardness pressing against her ass that morning. She'd pretended to be asleep when he rose and slipped from the tent, jeans clutched in his hand, but she'd peaked, and...*oh.* All morning, she'd pictured it. The monotony of pulling wires until her muscles screamed had left far too much time for her imagination to run rampant.

The memory sparked a fever in her limbs. Holding her own gaze through the glass, Jazz slipped her hand into the waistband of her panties. She was soaked and swollen. Swallowing against the lump in her throat, Jazz blinked hard. With a few tight, vicious circles, she came against her hand, but it did little to ease the throbbing. She longed to be bent over and filled, brought to the brink over and over. Theo would know what to do. His rough fingers would sink into the flesh of her thighs as he pounded into her. Then, she wouldn't feel so empty. With a sob, Jazz tore herself away from the sight of her brimming tears, yanked off her underwear and stepped into the shower.

When Jazz descended the stairs forty minutes later, Theo was putting a heaping pile of fries onto two plates containing a tantalizing fat burger each. Jazz groaned at the sight.

"I hope you still like all the fixings," Theo said, placing the plates on the table.

"You remember that?" Jazz asked, crossing the room to pull open the fridge.

There was a loaded tick of silence, and she was sure Theo was going to say *something*, but finally, he murmured, "Yeah." Settling himself into a chair, he said nothing more.

Jazz grabbed two beers from the fridge and held one out toward Theo. "Are you okay with this?"

Theo swallowed the fry he'd popped into his mouth. "I am, yes."

"Want one?"

"I would love one."

"So," Jazz popped the caps of both drinks and brought them to the table. "Booze isn't your vice then?" As soon as the words were out, she could have kicked herself. She'd never said that to her other residents, and she had no right to treat Theo differently.

Theo seemed unfazed. He took a long drag of the beer, grinned at her, and shook his head. "No, I'm not an alcoholic. And, since I know how your mind works, I'm not a recovering addict, either."

Jazz picked up a fry and broke it in half to have something to do with her hands. "It isn't my business," she said.

Theo shrugged. "I'm here, alone with you on your property. You have a right to know what is going on with me."

He was giving her an opening, and Jazz recognized that. She could ask now, and he would rip open his old wounds and spill his story to her. As much as she yearned to know what had brought him back to Jamieson Creek and Sunrise, Jazz knew now wasn't the time or the place. So, she said, "You took a while in town."

"The pub was busy, and I ended up chatting with Patty. He remembered me from before." He quirked a smile at her. "From the times we used to sneak in and he 'didn't know' we were underage."

Jazz snorted around her bite of burger. "Even though we always hung out with his son, who was the same age as us." Once she'd chewed, she cast Theo a narrow look, her eyes sparking with mischief. "Are you going to pretend we also didn't go to that party Scott threw when Patty was out of town?"

Theo made a sound like he had a chunk of burger lodged in his windpipe. "Oh, god." He pressed a hand over his mouth to shield her from the view of his chewed food. Swallowing, he shook his head ruefully. "The night where you kissed me senseless, and everyone saw how... er... excited I was about it?" Grabbing his beer, he took a long drink, but Jazz didn't miss how pink his cheeks had gone. "Oh, and then—" he set the bottle down and tapped his chin as if trying to recall an illusive memory. "People called me Boner Bridger for the rest of the summer? Is that the one you're talking about? Because that party rings a bell..."

Jazz laughed. "Doesn't seem *that* memorable." But those sun-soaked days had been the best of her life, and she knew they lay tucked in a little box in her mind. All she would have to do was open it, and they would be as clear and sharp as if they happened yesterday. All the more reason to keep that box shut tight. She didn't need more reasons to remember why she had fallen in love with Theo.

Jazz was acutely aware they'd hardly spoken of their shared past besides the brief mention of The NeverEnding Story. She knew that had been her decree, but it was becoming increasingly difficult not to casually toss out "oh, remember when" statements daily. After spending three days in his company and two nights sleeping beside him, she struggled to remember why she'd been so adamant about keeping him at arm's length. Tonight, with her nerves loosened by cold beer and her hunger satiated with delicious, greasy food, it was hard to remember why she shouldn't also ease the ache of loneliness with Theo's familiar presence.

"I always thought your uncle would leave you the farm," Jazz said after they were nearly finished.

A shadow of sadness moved over Theo's face, wiping away the peace of the moments before. Jazz experienced a stab of regret for ruining the levity. Shifting in his chair, Theo leaned back and pushed away his plate.

"He would have, but it was foreclosed. The bank auctioned it off after he passed. I had no idea he wasn't paying his taxes, or I would have tried to help. Ted's ranch was the only place that ever truly felt like home to me."

Jazz's mouth turned sour at his words. She pushed away her plate and swigged her beer, forcing down the glob of fries that had turned to sawdust in her mouth as Theo spoke.

"Want another?" she asked, pushing to her feet.

"Please," Theo said. The grave, borderline sad expression he had worn so often since arriving was back in place. Jazz was suddenly desperate to see him smile again.

"Should we take them out to the porch?" She gestured with her chin to the French doors leading to the back deck.

"Sure, sounds great." Theo stood, gathering their plates.

"Leave them by the sink. I'll make sure to load them before Betty gets back tomorrow."

Theo ignored her. Scraping their plates, he piled them in the sink, squirted a healthy pump of blue soap across them and turned on the hot water. Jazz shrugged and gathered the discarded napkins and bottles, disposing of them. Then she leaned a hip against the counter, studying Theo as he worked. Frothy bubbles slipped along the corded tendons of forearms that bunched and flexed as he worked. She imagined those arms braced on either side of her head as he pushed inside her.

Nope.

With sheer force of will, Jazz shoved the thought away, but her body was already flushed with ferocious heat.

Did he have someone at home with whom he regularly spent evenings like this? Someone he ate across from, tidied up with, and then took upstairs to bed? Surely he wouldn't be here if he did. It wasn't so easy to leave a partner for six months. Everyone who'd come to the ranch so far had been single.

There was so much she didn't know about him. After so many years, their lives had moulded them into alternate versions of their teenage selves. They weren't the same people anymore. She knew that, so why did it feel like no time had passed? This moment, right now, felt... and Jazz was sure this was the beer talking, but the thought made her eyes sting... it could have been the life they'd been meant to have—the life they'd been supposed to share.

"Jazz?" Theo asked without turning away from the sink.

"Yeah?"

"Did I do something wrong?"

Jazz blinked, surprised by his question. "No. Why?"

Theo set the dish on the rack and turned, wiping his hands on his jeans before bracing them against the counter at his back. Jazz forced herself not to stare at how his faded t-shirt hugged his chest and lean stomach.

"It felt like you were attempting to use the power of your stare to flay the skin from my back."

"Sorry," Jazz mumbled, heat rushing up her neck. "You didn't do anything wrong, now or this afternoon. I'm sorry I was such a bitch before."

Theo chewed at his lip but didn't speak. Jazz watched the swell of flesh slip free of his teeth and, without thinking, took a step closer. Raising a finger, she pressed it to that tantalizing swell. Theo shifted on the balls of his feet, a half movement as if he were going to move closer and lean into her, but he stopped himself.

It would be so simple to step into his arms. They'd been good together once, even as teens. They discovered and educated themselves with each other as their muses. They'd shared all their firsts. His touch would dispel the nagging sliver of loneliness wedging at her heart. Hell, it would dispel the throb of her body—too long denied its most base desires.

Jazz took another step, close enough that a deep breath would have her breasts brushing his chest. Her heart thudded against her throat, and she swallowed.

"Jasmine," Theo breathed. The single word was rough as nails in a can, full of warning, but more; desire also resonated through it. Jazz felt the echo of that need throughout her entire being.

"Theo."

"If you keep looking at me like that, people will start using that nickname from the party again."

Her eyes didn't wait for permission from her brain. They plummeted straight to the front of his jeans, not caring if he noticed or giving one fuck about propriety. The denim did nothing to hide the bulge straining his zipper. Holy shit.

Jazz swallowed hard. "Maybe that wouldn't be so bad?"

Theo drew a shaky breath and shrugged. "It was pretty embarrassing the first time; I'm not sure I'd care for a second round." His tone was faux casual, and his eyes dropped to her lips before he finished speaking. "Though I suppose I'm older now… much tougher skin." He sounded out of breath.

Jazz pulled a shaky breath; then she took a long drink of the beer. Her hand was cold and damp from clutching it so tightly. She leaned past Theo to set it down on the counter, relishing the shudder that racked him at the contact of her body against him. Fuck her fickle heart for its unwillingness to cooperate with what her mind knew was best.

"I was thinking, maybe…" her voice trailed off as her nerves wavered.

Theo squeezed his eyes shut briefly, pulling in air through his nose before he opened them again and pinned her with a stormy stare.

"You've no idea how much I want to hear the rest of that sentence, Jasmine. But I don't think it would be a good idea."

Without waiting for her to answer, Theo pushed away from the counter and slipped far enough away from her that she couldn't easily touch him. Jazz never took her eyes from his face, fighting tears of humiliation, anger, and disappointment but refusing to look away. With a shaky sigh, Theo dipped his head and brushed a kiss across her cheekbone; then, he walked past her and out of the kitchen. A few seconds later, Jazz heard the door to his bedroom click closed—a period at the end of their night.

Squeezing her lids shut, Jazz allowed a few tears to slide hot and free over her cheeks. Then she stared at the ceiling, blinking to clear her vision before brushing the rest away with the back of her hand. After a moment's hesitation, she grabbed her drink, then the one she'd opened for Theo, before heading out to the porch. A cacophony of thumping tails mingling with an orchestra of night bugs greeted her. The hum of crickets and frogs was so loud that the sound made it hard to think. That was fine. Jazz was so fucking tired of thinking. Of worrying. She wanted one night of silence from her raging mind. She wanted a reprieve from the loneliness that was becoming her constant companion.

With a shaky sigh, Jazz stared out over the land—her land—and relished the swell of fierce love she always experienced at the sight of it stretching out around her. No matter what else was happening around her or inside her, she had this place, which had the power to sustain her in a way nothing else could.

Shoving back a niggling of unease that was sure to resemble regret in the morning, Jazz pulled her cell from her pocket and tapped out a text, hitting send before she could rethink.

Hey, you up?

Chapter Fourteen

THEO

THEO LET HIS BACK hit the closed door, his head thudding back against the wood panelling. He'd turned down Jasmine.

What the hell was he doing?

All he'd wanted since arriving at Sunrise and seeing her again was to hold her, feel her lips against his, and rediscover the joy they had once shared in each other.

"Fucking hell," he murmured, cupping one hand around his aching cock in apology. He could barely think with the ferocity of the need pulsing through him. It had been a long time since he'd been with anyone, add on the fact he had never met a woman he desired as much as Jazz, and he was one big ball of horny.

From the kitchen, he heard the clink of bottles followed by the thud of the sliding door closing. She'd gone out onto the deck rather than outside. Waiting a few moments, Theo fought for control over his thudding heart and protesting body. When the fist that had a death grip on his lungs eased, he grabbed his guitar case from beside the bed. Careful not to bang it against anything, he slipped from his room and out the front door.

No dogs appeared to greet him, and the raucous serenade of the frogs and crickets was nearly deafening. From the barn, he heard Gruff's sleepy *meeehh*. Moving with the quiet speed born of military training, Theo was down the stairs and slipping into the night within seconds. He was halfway across the field when a vehicle turned up the drive, the high beams cutting a swath across the property, nearly blinding him. Theo paused, resisting the urge to duck into the long grass as Blair's familiar truck rumbled past.

A wash of hurt moved through Theo, shocking as a bucket of ice water over the head. Turning her down had wrung every ounce of willpower out of Theo. All it took was one look from her. *That* look, coupled with the attitude with which she crossed the room, and his cock had been at full attention. He wanted Jasmine with a ferocity that scared the shit out of him. Apparently, she hadn't been feeling picky, however. Jazz hadn't wanted him. She'd wanted *someone*. To Theo, that made a world of difference.

A sour taste invaded his mouth, and he swallowed hard. Turning away from the sight of Blair parking in front of the farmhouse, Theo jogged toward the creek. If only he could outrun his brain's cruelty. Images of Jazz tangled in her ex's arms flashed through his imagination.

Blair had been married to her. He probably knew how to make her moan and squirm the way Theo once had. She'd been a fiend for oral—loved having his mouth on her, his tongue slipping and flicking that tiny, glorious bundle of nerves. And the taste of her... fuck. The way she would tangle her fingers in his hair, pulling with no heed to whether she hurt him, too lost in her pleasure. The heat of her orgasm against his lips.

"Fuck," Theo snarled. Breaking through the trees into the clearing where the creek meandered along its mossy banks, he came up short, breathing hard. The peace in the clearing was such a juxtaposition to his furious thoughts and raging body that, for a second, Theo feared his mere presence would taint the place. Setting his guitar by the bench, he paced a few laps of the clearing, shoving his fingers through his hair and yanking. It did nothing to dispel the memories.

With a groan, Theo slammed his back against the nearest tree, relishing the bite of rough bark. Reaching for his belt, he fumbled it open, wincing as the metal banged his bruised knuckles. He took himself in hand with a pained hiss, loathing mixing with animalistic need as he squeezed, unable to deny his body release any longer.

Two nights in that ridiculous tent. Two nights of smelling her, waking up to her body close enough to touch. Bathed in the heat rolling off her, but knowing he could not bridge the feather of space between them. It had been torture. That morning when he woke with her ass pressed against him and his cock so hard he feared he would come in his sleeping bag like an adolescent if she moved. And then the river...Holy Hell, the river. Theo was sure the sight of Jazz rising from the sparkling green water, rivulets running over her lean, tanned body, and her nipples pulled tight from the cold would live in his brain for the rest of his life. His balls clenched painfully at the memory, and he groaned. In a few strokes, he was on the brink. Throwing his head back with a grunt, Theo spilled himself onto the leaf-matted ground.

Theo was tossing fragrant sections of hay into David and Goliath's feeder when Blair sauntered onto the porch. With a steaming coffee cup in hand, the fucker looked far too at home, considering he'd never actually lived at the ranch.

"Morning," he called down to Theo. "Coffee is ready. Want some?"

Damn it, why did the guy have to go and be *nice*? That was the problem with Blair. He was so fucking likable, even Theo, who at the moment was writhing in an inferno of jealousy, couldn't summon any hate for the man.

Theo dusted his hands on his jeans and forced his head to nod appreciatively in Blair's direction without making eye contact. "Thanks, man, I'll just finish up here."

When Blair did not move to return to the house, Theo glanced up again, using his forearm to block the morning sun's assault on his retinas.

"She told me about you," Blair's tone was casual, but he squinted across the fields, refusing to meet Theo's eyes while he lifted his cup and sipped. "I was never around in the summer when we were kids. My dad lives in PEI, and we spent the holidays there, but Jazz and I have been friends since we were in diapers."

Theo, sensing the other man was going somewhere, moved to lean against the porch rail. "I wondered why we never met."

"Yeah, felt like I knew you, though. Jazz never fuckin' shut up about you, especially after that first summer." Blair chewed his lip, bobbing his head several times before opening his mouth again. "I came back, and my best friend was...different. She'd... bloomed. I know that's a sort of poetic nonsense, but I can't think of any other way to put it." Finally, Blair turned and met his eyes. It surprised Theo to see the tumult of emotion in their blue depths. "Then you left. But, even though you were gone, you still haunted our marriage."

Theo winced, unsure what he was supposed to say. At last, he settled on, "I'm sorry. I wouldn't have wanted that."

Blair bobbed his head, then shrugged. "Not your fault. If I know Jazz, she probably haunted you, too."

Theo let out a snort. "Got that right."

Blair sipped from his mug, making a faint slurping sound while Theo stared out over the paddock bars at the horses. Their coats shone satin smooth in the morning sun, and he suddenly longed to be on one of their backs and racing away across the fields.

"Are we pathetic?" Blair asked after a few moments of semi-awkward silence.

Theo looked at the other man, his mouth quirking in a sardonic smile. "Nah, Jasmine is an amazing woman. We'd be fools not to be haunted by her."

You got further than I did.

Theo stepped up onto the porch and followed Blair inside.

You did what I only dreamed of. You married her.

Chapter Fifteen

JASMINE

J AZZ PUSHED HER FACE into her pillow and groaned as though she were dying. Which, to be fair, she might have been. What the fuck was she thinking? Getting drunk and...Oh God. Memory sucker punched her in her already churning gut, and she released a long, muffled scream into the bedding.

Blair.

Poor Blair. She'd used him last night. There was no other way to phrase it. Jazz texted, knowing he wouldn't deny her, not the way Theo had, and she'd been right.

Claws ticked across the hardwood floor, and Jazz rolled her head enough to see Loki's head resting on the mattress.

He was staring at her with his blue and brown eyes. "How did you get in here?" she croaked. The dog's feathery tail swooshed across the floor, powered by the joy of being noticed.

"Come on." Jazz patted the bed beside her, wrapping an arm around the dog when he bounced up and stretched alongside her. Nuzzling her face into his soft fur, she inhaled. He smelled of hay, dog, and home. Jazz blinked against a rush of tears. She needed to apologize to Theo and Blair. But all she wanted in the world was to lie there, wrapped in the quilt her grandmother had made, and cuddle with her dog. She was sure she could sleep for a week if she allowed herself.

With one last moan for good measure, Jazz blinked hard and rolled onto her back. "Can you do it for me?" she asked Loki. He gave her a side-eye stare, grunted, and pushed his nose into the blankets.

"Fine," Jazz muttered. "I'll be an adult."

Sitting up, she pushed the blankets back and slid her legs off the bed. Feet firmly planted on the floor, she paused, letting the cold wood seep into the bare soles of her feet and ground her. She also worried standing up too fast might have her running for the toilet. Her stomach eased up on its turbulence at last, and Jazz stood.

After using the bathroom, brushing her teeth, and drinking as much water as her furious stomach could hold, Jazz was pulling on a pair of jeans when she heard voices outside the partially open window.

Frowning, she crossed the room and peered out. A large truck was parked in front of the barn. Theo was in the bed, throwing bales down to... Blair? A few feet away, the driver, a young man from the farm down the road, rolled on the ground in the midst of a wrestling match with Titus.

"Shit..." Jazz drug the word out, letting her head thump against the window frame. The alfalfa hay she'd ordered for the horses. She forgot about the delivery. The ever-present tally of bills scrolling through her brain adjusted itself, the amount due rising alarmingly. With one last longing look at Loki, sprawled fast asleep in her still-warm bed, Jazz gathered her hair into a messy pile on her head and went downstairs.

Jazz followed the rhythmic thumping of the axe to the woodshed, where she found Theo splitting and stacking firewood. The grey T-shirt he wore stretched over his back muscles and was soaked through with sweat. Jazz had to resist the urge to sit down and watch him work.

Gathering her courage, she called his name. "Theo?" Jazz jerked her head when he looked up, beckoning for him to come over.

"What's up, boss?" he asked, pulling off his worn leather gloves as he walked over. He looked... tired. Exhausted even, and Jazz wondered if he'd slept at all last night.

"Can I talk to you for a second?"

He nodded, coming to lean on the paddock fence beside her.

Jazz pushed her hands into her pockets to hide their shaking. She felt like a child who'd suffered a reprimand. "I owe you an apology." She forced the words out around the lump in her throat. "I shouldn't... I shouldn't have come on to you. It was unprofessional and inconsiderate of your feelings."

"Jasmine—" Theo winced. "Jazz," he corrected. "I think, given our past, a little unprofessionalism is bound to happen here and there. Don't worry too much about it."

Jazz shook his head. "No, you're here on the ranch to heal, not fend off unwanted advances."

Thro scrubbed a hand over his face and let out a wry laugh. "Not exactly unwanted." He lowered his hand and pinned her with a look that threatened to melt her bones.

"You do not know how hard it was to say no to you, Jazz. Or how many times I've cursed myself since last night."

Jazz dug her fingers into the flesh of her thighs through her pockets to stop herself from reaching for him.

"About Blair," she said, fighting her tremulous voice into submission. "I'm also sorry you had to—" her voice broke, and she cleared her throat with a loud tearing sound. "I know seeing him must have been uncomfortable." She squeezed her eyes shut and blew a gust across her lips. "I plan to apologize to him, too, just so you know."

Theo stared at his boots, then sucked in a breath so deep, it endangered the buttons on his shirt. Finally, he met her eyes. "What are you apologizing for?" He pushed away from the fence in a fluid motion. "Blair is here every morning. I doubt the guy knows how to make coffee."

The words were nonchalant, and the tone casual. But as he walked away, Jazz saw from the flash of pain on Theo's face that he knew what Blair was doing there. What she'd done last night had hurt him, whether or not he was willing to admit it.

A hot fist of guilt squeezed Jazz's belly. "Wait," she called before he got too far. "Do you want to go to the fair with me tomorrow?"

The smile Theo gave her didn't quite reach his eyes, and an eternity passed before he nodded. "Yeah," he said finally. "Sounds good."

Chapter Sixteen

THEO

A BARRAGE OF LIGHTS spilled across Jazz's skin, staining it with streaks of colour. The rainbow illumination made her ethereal compared to the chaos around them. There were still moments when the shock of having her reappear so suddenly in his life made Theo's head spin.

When she looked up and caught him staring, she frowned. "What? Is there mustard on my face?" she asked, lifting long fingers to her lips. Theo pictured leaning forward and sucking the digits into his mouth, tonguing each slowly before letting them slide over his teeth. He shivered at the wave of desire that burst through him at the thought. Need and embarrassment over being caught staring sent a flush through his body.

"No," he stammered belatedly. Then, he opted for the truth because he didn't know what else to say. "I was thinking how beautiful you looked with the lights dancing on your skin that way."

Jazz stared at him for a second, blinking. "Oh... uh, thank you," she said at last. "Let's get tickets." She jerked her head at the little booth nestled between high fences.

Theo followed her, protesting when she pulled out her wallet to pay for both passes. She rewarded him with a glower that nearly scared his balls back up inside his body. Theo extended his wrist without another word so the teenager inside the booth could attach a neon paper bracelet.

"I get a discount since I'm on the local agricultural board," Jazz admitted as they walked away.

"Alright," Theo said, not about to argue with her.

Jazz led Theo toward the barns, and the plethora of smells reached him long before they arrived. Manure from various contributors, hay, and woodchips, all heated by the day's lingering sun and floating about to mingle with the pervasive scents of popcorn and hot dogs. Theo wasn't sure if he should feel hungry or nauseous. He had never been a fan of busy events. As soon as he was old enough, he'd even opted to stay home while his family attended the Vancouver PNE.

This section of the fairgrounds was quieter. At least, people's voices were lowered in deference to the livestock, and the raucous noise of the midway was diluted to a tolerable level by the distance.

"I'm a sucker for the small animal barn," Jazz said as they neared a squat building that was likely once red but had long since faded to the rusty shade of old blood.

"What's in there," Theo asked. He'd never been at his uncle's for the spring fair, but Jazz had often regaled him with tales when he'd arrived shortly after. He'd asked his father once if he could leave a week earlier to attend since school would be nearly wrapped up, but Gregory had scoffed and told Theo that diligently presenting himself at school was more important than watching a bunch of rednecks argue over whose bull had the biggest balls.

"Chickens and other fowl," Jazz said as she turned and gave him a mischievous grin, unaware of his mental foray into the past. "But mostly—" she said, lowering her voice to a playful whisper, "I come for the bunnies."

As soon as she said the word *bunnies*, her step quickened as if she could no longer contain her excitement, and Theo didn't hesitate to follow her. He'd follow her anywhere, and that knowledge made his shirt collar feel too tight. Jazz paused once they were through the doors as if she were taking it all in. Theo had to bite his tongue to contain his smile. However, it escaped anyway when Jazz turned to him, hands clasped against her chest, dark eyes shining, and hissed, "So. Many. Bunnies."

"You're so fucking adorable," Theo said, laughing. He grabbed her hand before she could stop him, tugging her further into the barn. "Come on, let's go snuggle some bunnies."

Jazz's arms were overflowing with a Flemish giant when a woman approached them. In her thirties, with roughly a meter of blonde braid hanging over her shoulder, she stopped, put her hands on her hips and gave Theo a slow, blue-eyed sweep of appraisal before turning to Jazz.

"They will notice if you stick that thing under your shirt, missy. If you plan to commit grand theft bunny, you're better off with a dwarf breed."

Jazz stopped crooning to the beast she cradled and glanced up, a breathtaking smile spreading over her face at the sight of the woman. "Hey, you didn't tell me you were coming tonight."

The blonde tucked her hands into the back pocket of her jeans and leaned a hip against a cage-covered table. "Oh, you know, spring fair as usual. Overeating and going on enough rides to make the kids happy, but not enough to waste the money I spent on food by having it reappear too soon." She flashed a dimpled grin. "It's a fine line."

Jazz was still smiling, her rich eyes alight with excitement. That joy had been missing from her, Theo realized. It had been the thing that had rendered her the most changed from the girl he'd known and loved. Tonight was the most relaxed Theo had seen her since he'd been back. "We should have planned better. We could have all met up."

Jazz's friend cast Theo another sideways look. "Seems we aren't telling each other a lot of things these days because you failed to tell me about this guy—" she jerked her chin toward Theo. "Lesbian, I may be, but a dude who looks *that* good is worth mentioning."

Theo's cheeks heated as both women's gazes swivelled to his face. He resisted the urge to shy away from their appraising looks. He knew exactly who Valley was, though they'd never officially met. She'd always been away with her family during the summer when he was in Jamieson's Creek.

"I'm Valley," the blonde said, extending her hand to Theo. Her sharp blue eyes flashed as she appraised him. It was glaringly apparent that she was not a woman who missed much.

Theo placed his hand in hers. She had a strong grip, and there was a row of callouses at the base of her fingers. A rider, like Jazz. "Theo Bridger." The hand squeezed tight.

"*Thee* Theo Bridger," Valley squeaked, dropping his hand and spinning around to pierce Jazz with a loaded look.

Jazz was running the rabbit's huge ears through her fingers. "The one and only," she muttered without looking up. "I've been meaning to call you... I just... haven't."

"I'm pretty crushed you didn't call the moment he arrived." Valley's sharp gaze returned to him, and Theo resisted the urge to squirm. "I can't believe you're here—why exactly are you here?"

"I'm Jazz's latest work in progress," Theo said. "Neither of us knew about the other's involvement until I arrived, though."

"I can't believe it," Valley murmured.

"Join the club," Jazz said, refusing to meet either of their eyes.

A pimple-faced teen chose that moment to approach them, his entire being oozing unenthusiasm over the situation he found himself in. "Ma'am, there's a lineup of children waiting to hold Amelia Earhare."

Theo couldn't help the bark of laughter that shot out of him. Then, once he started, he couldn't stop. He wasn't sure if it was the bored, flat tone with which the kid managed to deliver the name *Amelia Earhare* or the look of abject horror on Jazz's face, but it culminated in a sudden bout of hysteria on his part.

When Jazz hugged the rabbit to her chest and gasped out an affronted, "Don't call me ma'am!" it nearly did him in. Valley was laughing now, too, and Jazz glared at them as she deposited Amelia into the teen's waiting arms.

"Are you two finished?" she snapped, pushing past them and stalking toward the exit. Valley straightened, wiping her face, and followed Jazz. Theo hurried to catch them. "Come on, boss," he said as he reached past Jazz to open the door. "I'll buy you some cotton candy."

Chapter Seventeen

JASMINE

WHILE THEO GOT IN line for food, Jazz led Valley to a round pen where a young woman was lunging a beautiful palomino. Leaning her forearms against the top rail, Jazz steeled herself, knowing her friend was about to grill her about Theo.

"He's stunning," she remarked, jerking her chin toward the horse when Valley leaned against the fence beside her.

"He is," Valley agreed, her eyes tracking the horse and his handler. The girl, who appeared to be in her early twenties, handled the big horse with a competent hand. It was easy to see the two shared a connection as the golden horse flowed around the pen.

"I know it isn't horses you want to talk about," Jazz said after a few moments.

"You are absolutely correct," Valley said.

Resting her elbows on the top rail, Jazz turned her face up to the last warm rays of the sinking sun and groaned. She'd known Valley would catch up with her eventually. Why had she kept Theo's presence on the ranch to herself? Since they were ten years old and Valley had moved to Jamieson Creek, they'd told each other all their secrets.

"You did not tell me your new hand was Theo Bridger, Jasmine." There was no small measure of annoyance in her tone and maybe even a touch of hurt.

Jazz's cheeks went hot. "I know," she muttered, refusing to meet Valley's shrewd gaze. This was the problem with having a psychologist as a best friend. A girl couldn't get away with anything.

"And why not?" Valley pressed her eyes, searching Jazz's face until she turned away. "How long has he been here?"

"A month," Jazz practically whispered, sinking her head into her shoulders to prepare for retribution.

Valley gasped. "I talked to you three days ago! I said to you, 'What's new?' and you said, and I quote, 'Oh, same old.' Did it not occur to you, at that point in time to say, well, you know what, Val, the craziest shit happened. The guy who annihilated my heart when we were kids showed up on my doorstep. He's going to stay IN MY HOUSE for six months."

"I know! I'm sorry." Jazz pressed her face into her palms and released a little scream. It was only a fraction of how loud she longed to yell. "I'm only just starting to wrap my head around it myself. It was such a shock, Val."

Valley was quiet for a few moments, and at the shift in energy, Jazz's stomach soured. She knew what was coming, and facing the question was another reason she hadn't told Valley about Theo's presence on the ranch.

"Have you told him?" Despite having prepared herself, Jazz still flinched.

"No," she said, letting her head sink forward to rest against the fence post.

"You need to, Jazzy. Him showing up this way may be the universe giving you another shot at doing the right thing."

Fuck. The lump was globbing up in her throat as it always did when she thought about telling Theo the truth. "But it doesn't change anything," she whispered.

"No, but he deserves to know."

Tears prickled the backs of Jazz's eyes, and she swallowed thickly. She would not cry about this. Not now. "I know."

Valley tipped her head forward, forcing Jazz to meet her gaze. "You know I'm here for you, day or night."

"I know," Jazz said again. A sudden rush of love for her friend intensified her urge to cry.

A throat cleared roughly, making both women jump. They turned to see Theo, arms laden with food and drink, standing a few paces away.

"I feel like I'm interrupting something," he said, his straight black brows dipping in. Jazz took a deep breath, forcing her shoulders back and chin up. She'd come here for a fun evening. A night she and Theo could spend mending fences, figuratively this time.

"No, you're fine. Thank you for grabbing all that. Let's go find somewhere to sit," she said, pushing away from the fence and battling a smile into place.

As they walked toward a cluster of picnic tables, Theo leaned closer to Jazz, bumping her shoulder gently with his. "Are you okay?" he whispered.

His concern pressed at her heart, a thumb to a bruise, and she gave him a brusque nod, not wanting him to see the emotion on her face. "Of course, why wouldn't I be?"

"Ugh." Valley used a wet wipe to scrub caramel off her fingers, then tossed it into the pile of garbage they'd amassed in the centre of the table. "I can't believe you let me eat that. It was the third one I had today. None of my jeans are going to do up tomorrow."

"Don't be ridiculous," Jazz scoffed, eyeing her friend's curvy form. "Fuck jeans, wear tights." They laughed, and Valley stood, coming around to hug Jazz.

"I can always count on you to say the right thing," she said. "I should go find Joan; she's probably cursing me for leaving her alone with those hellions."

"Such a loving way to speak of your children," Jazz said, laughing when Theo looked up from his burger in surprise.

"They know what they are," Valley said. Then she put her hands on her hips and eyed them both. "You two behave yourselves."

"Yes, ma'am," Theo said stoically. Jazz had to turn away to hide her smile. Once she was gone, they sat silently, watching as Valley melted into the throngs of people. Then Theo turned to Jazz with a frown.

"So, you're a genuine freak about rabbits, hey?"

Jazz let her face sink into her palms with a groan. "Can you believe its name?"

"Amelia Earhare," they said in sync before dissolving into laughter.

"You should have seen the look on your face!" Theo choked out, his eyes twinkling with mirth. "I'll remember it for the rest of my life."

"Oh, shh," Jazz wiped her eyes. The one day she'd put mascara on, it would be running down her face.

Theo was laughing harder again at the memory. "Hogging the bunny so a bunch of little kids couldn't play with it," he gasped.

"Shut up," Jazz said, throwing a balled-up napkin at him. "I can't even right now. I'll never forget you, Amelia Earhare."

"Who would have thought the tough-as-nails Jasmine Reynolds was a bunny whore."

Jazz quieted, digging her fingernails into a knot on the surface of the wooden table. "It's Joyce, actually," she said.

Theo stopped gathering their mess and glanced at her. "Joyce?"

"Jasmine Joyce. *Jazz* Joyce."

Silence un-spooled quickly as a fishing line between them. "Oh," Theo said finally.

"I kept my ex's name after we divorced," Jazz found herself explaining. "Didn't want to go back to my father's. Didn't see the point. It dies with me either way, and it wasn't much of a legacy anymore."

Theo bit his bottom lip, momentarily distracting Jazz when the plump swell disappeared between his straight white teeth. "That makes sense. Why would you after the way he treated you."

Jazz nodded. "Neither of us exactly won the lottery in the dad department, did we?"

"No, we didn't." Theo turned and strode the few feet to the garbage can. Jazz watched the sure movements of his long limbs. So many men strove for bulk when it came to their bodies, but Theo reminded her of a cat. Gone was the clumsiness of his youth. He was all fluid grace and lean lines. Wiry, but no less powerful because of it. The other day, Jazz rounded the barn and found him shirtless, tossing bales onto the truck bed. The pull of corded muscle and the flow of tanned skin working together in a perfect orchestra had mesmerized her.

Flushing at the memory, Jazz shook her head, bringing herself solidly back into the present, only to find Theo watching her. There was a shadow in his eyes as if he knew the road her mind had taken. A flush of heat crawled through Jazz's chest. She waited for him to comment or rib her, but all he said was, "Come on, let's play some games; I'll win you a stuffed rabbit."

Chapter Eighteen

THEO

THEO DIDN'T KNOW WHAT Jazz had been thinking about while she stared at him, but he recognized the flush staining her cheeks, the slight pout of her bottom lip, begging to be kissed. He could have been way off base, but the idea she may have been thinking of them together had him adjusting the front of his jeans.

When her dark eyes travelled over his body, they left a steamy path of memories in their wake. Kisses from years past rose invisibly to once more brand his skin. Theo was constantly aware of her, whether or not she was near him. Jazz was a floating ember, threatening to engulf his entire life.

Theo felt dizzy as he led her toward the midway, and not only from the lights and music that barraged his senses and made his soul long to curl up somewhere dark and safe. He was drunk on Jazz.

After passing four booths, each slightly different from the last, Theo found what he was looking for—a bright pink giant plush rabbit nestled in the racks of other garish stuffed toys. With a grin, he seized Jazz's hand and tugged her to the stand.

"Say hello to your new best fuuurriend!" he said, pointing. And simple as that, Theo won his own prize—the smile that bloomed across Jazz's face at the sight of the toy.

It cost him forty bucks and a sore throwing arm, but Theo finally handed the bunny to Jazz a half hour later. She grinned and hugged it to her chest, looking so much like the girl he'd so desperately loved that it caused emotion to prickle the back of his nose.

"Hey!" she exclaimed. "Want to make a bet?"

Theo narrowed his eyes. It may have been years since he'd known Jazz, but that wasn't long enough for him to forget her outrageous competitive streak. "What are the stakes?" he asked warily.

Jazz tapped a finger against her chin as she pursued their surroundings. Then she gasped and pointed to a booth with a line of plastic rifles holstered along the front. "Truth or dare. Whoever hits the most bottles in their turn wins."

Theo laughed. "You know I was literally in the army, right?"

Jazz cast him a narrow-eyed look. "You know I was literally raised on a ranch, right?"

"Touche," Theo said with a snort, loving her excitement. Relishing the feel of her hand on his arm, they hurried forward. God, he'd missed her. He didn't argue as she paid the man running the booth. When the attendant passed them each a plastic gun, a wave of goosebumps moved up Theo's arms, but he shoved away the unease. It was not real, only a game. A game he was playing with Jasmine. That thought centred him. The panic that briefly lifted its head settled back into its den to await the next opportunity.

"Okay, double or nothing," Jazz said, seizing Theo's arm. "Let's go lay a bet on the chicken races."

Theo's brain nearly broke from her words or the feel of her touch; he wasn't sure. He stumbled, letting out a surprised laugh. "I don't know what the hell a chicken race is, but I approve of the pun," he said. "Also, you know you won, right? You don't have to give me another chance."

Jazz snickered, and the sight of her long nose wrinkled with mirth filled Theo's chest with a bubble of something he didn't want to dissect. It nearly burst when she turned her face up to him, and her dark eyes turned kaleidoscopic with laughter and midway lights.

"Chicken races, my friend, are a Jamieson Creek tradition." Her golden voice was incandescent with sunny, good humour. She'd been this way often as a teen, despite all the crap she dealt with at home. Jazz always found something to laugh at in everyday things, or at least, she had.

She jerked her chin further down the wood-chipped path. Theo's gaze followed to where people lined up along a runway of portable plastic fencing. Jazz grabbed his hand when a cheer went up and yanked him forward. "Come on, we're missing them!"

Pushing their way through the crowd, they reached the fence as six hens strode nervously from a row of pet carriers.

"My money is on the red one," Theo said without hesitation. "I'm going to egg her on."

Jazz snorted. Slipping in front of him to make room for a boy trying to squeeze in to watch, she said, "That's a Grade A choice."

Someone bumped into Theo from behind, and on instinct, his arm went up, looping around Jazz's waist, steadying them both. She was tall. Theo could pull her back tight against him, lean forward to rest his chin on the crown of her head—he knew they would be a perfect fit. Battling back the urge to do just that, Theo said the first ridiculous line his mind supplied. "Those chickens look eggshausted."

Jazz's head tipped back as she laughed, and Theo could have drowned in the music of her happiness. Escaped wisps of hair blew back to brush the skin of his cheeks, tickling fiercely, but he didn't brush them away.

Theo tipped his head down, greedy for her scent, and it wasn't at all an accident when his lips brushed her ear as he spoke. "What do you get when you cross a chicken and a ghost?"

Jazz turned her head, eyes dancing as her gaze found his. She was so close he could see the tiny flakes of gold that made a halo around her pupils. "I don't know, what?"

"A poultry-geist."

The next wave of her laughter washed over his neck. "You are ridiculous," she said once she battled her smile under control. Shaking her head, she turned back to the race. Theo's fingers twitched with the urge to rise to her chin and turn her face back to his so he could brush his mouth against hers. He wanted to sample her smile, breathe her in, and sustain himself on her alone.

"How many chicken puns is too many chicken puns?" Theo asked as they watched the birds meander about. It was the most boring race Theo had ever witnessed, yet somehow, he didn't remember ever having more fun.

"You're close," Jazz retorted, casting him a side-eyed smile. "Maybe one or two more, and I think you've hit the max."

"I better not squander it," Theo said, tapping his chin. He didn't say anything else for a long moment, waiting until the first bird finally crossed the finish line to the ecstatic cheers of onlookers.

"Huh," he said. "I had no idea the people here were so egg-centric."

Jazz dropped her face into her palms, her shoulders quaking. "I had no idea your humour was so im-peck-able, Theo," she gasped before falling into giggles. Theo had to wipe tears off his face.

"We're the worst," Jazz said, using her fingers to wipe under her eyes. "I've never heard such terrible jokes."

"I mean, were they terrible? We're laughing, so I think that makes us comedic geniuses."

"If anyone else had heard that, they would have kicked us out of the fair." Jazz hooked her arm through his, steering him through the thinning crowd and away from the race. "Okay, naturally, you also lost the chicken races, so it's time to pay up, sir."

Chapter Nineteen

JASMINE

"WELL, TELL ME, WHAT'S my fate?" Theo asked Jazz fifteen minutes later as they both attempted to wipe sticky donut sugar off their fingers with dry napkins that shredded to sand at the slightest touch. "Truth or dare?"

For a fleeting moment, Jazz considered using the 'truth' to ask him what happened while he was on tour, what it was that haunted his dreams at night, but she dismissed the idea as soon as it spiralled into her brain. She couldn't do that to him. She'd never dream of asking such a thing of the other guests who'd come to the ranch. Then, as if some trickster god had placed it in her path, Jazz saw the sign... literally.

TALENT CONTEST.

An arrow pointed to a small stage where a handful of people milled about. Some stretched, some sang snippets of songs to warm their voices or tuned instruments.

With a gleeful laugh, Jazz hooked her arm through Theo's and began tugging him toward the information tent.

"I hope you have a talent ready!" Pulling her arm free, she spread both arms, indicating the sign. "Because I *dare* you, Theodore Bridger, to sign up for the Jamieson Creek talent show."

She braced a hand against one pleasantly solid shoulder and shoved him forward. "He wants to put his name down for the show," she said to the woman behind the table before Theo could say anything.

"Under duress, it would seem?" the woman said, grinning cherubically at Theo.

To Jazz's surprise, he flashed them both a mischievous smirk. "What do I get if I win?"

Jazz blinked, taken aback by the question. She'd expected him to protest. "Like, the entire contest?" she asked.

Crossing his arms over his chest, Theo cast a haughty look down his nose at her. "Yes, Jasmine. The entire contest. If I win, what do I get?"

"Hmmm," Jazz cocked her head studying him. He was relaxed. The tired lines he usually wore etched around his brow and mouth had eased, and his grey eyes shone with delight. "You're a lot cockier than I remember, Theodore Bridger." And fuck her if the words didn't emerge a tad breathless. At her words, his grin deepened, taking a dip towards lecherous.

Jazz rolled her eyes, sighing. "Fine. If, by some insane chance, you win this entire contest, I will allow you to pick a truth or dare for me in return." A strange expression flickered across Theo's face, and then it was gone as quickly as it appeared, making her wonder if she'd imagined it.

"Deal." Theo held out his hand, and Jazz placed hers against it, heat tickling her palm at the contact.

"Deal," she parroted, watching Theo bend and scribble his name on the sign-up sheet. She clenched her fists against the urge to reach out and brush away the dark curl of hair that slipped across his brow. Theo murmured something under his breath to the woman behind the table, and an alarming shade of pink surged over her cheeks.

Then, he was beside her.

"What did you say to her?" Jazz asked.

"Shhh, it starts soon," he said, cupping her elbow in one big palm and leading her to where a crowd milled around in front of the stage.

They watched a woman and her dog perform a series of impressive tricks, then a gap-toothed eight-year-old who told knock-knock jokes and managed a solid 50% success rate on the punch lines. They pretended, along with the rest of the crowd, not to notice when she improvised as best she could. It was adorable either way, and Theo's rich laugh enveloped Jazz. She wanted to stay wrapped in the sound of his happiness for the rest of time.

"Alright," the MC, another gangly youth who looked uncannily similar to the one in the rabbit tent, only much more animated, took the stage. "We have a talent show virgin here, brought to us by a good ol' fashioned game of truth or dare. Let's give Theo Bridger a hand."

Without looking at her, Theo rolled his shoulders, sucked in a deep breath, and headed for the stage. Bounding up the stairs, he stopped to speak with the kid for a moment. With a nod, the host called something through the back curtain, and a moment later, an arm reached through, passing out a guitar. Theo called out his thanks, hooked a chair from the edge of the stage with his free arm on his way past, and walked to the centre of the stage.

There were a few catcalls and shouts of encouragement from the audience. Then, the hum of voices rose around Jazz again as people chatted amongst themselves. Theo lowered himself into the chair, situating the guitar across his lap. He strummed a few times, adjusted the tuning, then reached up and pulled the mic stand down in front of him. He was heart-stoppingly still for a moment, head bent over the instrument. Then he began to play, and Jazz's heart stopped.

As the first few chords rolled forth, the voices began dropping away until silence fell over the crowd when Theo's voice joined the raw sound of the unaccompanied guitar. And oh, Jazz pressed a hand over her mouth. Theo Bridger could *sing*. His voice was magic. It was the heady buzz of stolen whiskey and first kisses, the hardest she'd ever laughed, the most she'd ever cried, molasses poured over gravel, rich, sweet, sticky, and gritty. She'd never heard a singing voice that came close. Goosebumps rose on her arms as his voice saturated the night. All sounds from the crowd, the midway, and the animals faded to nothing. Theo and his soulful rendition of *Broken Halo* was the only thing of importance.

Electricity crackled around Theo as he played. Jazz had assumed she knew so much about the man on stage. Still, she hadn't known *this*, hadn't known Theo had this inside him... not only was he capable of performing, but it was also clearly what he was meant to do. He wove a spell of notes that rendered watchers unable to look away, enraptured.

The song ended much too soon. The host came on stage, grinning as he retrieved the guitar from Theo. Jazz was reasonably sure, listening to the deafening cheers around her, that she now owed Theo a Truth or Dare.

The teen host grabbed Theo's arm before he could leave the stage, leaning forward to say something into Theo's ear. Theo nodded, clapping the kid on the back. Jazz bounced on the balls of her feet, trying to figure out what they were saying. Instead of leaving, Theo walked to the back of the stage and stood quietly waiting. When the host called a few more names back up, Jazz knew Theo was one of the finalists.

After a few moments of organizing, the host lined up a man who'd juggled while playing the harmonica, the little girl who told jokes, and Theo. When the juggler was announced the third-place winner, Jazz's heartbeat ratcheted up. The little girl was announced as second place, and Jazz pressed a hand over her mouth to contain her excitement.

"And, voted first place winner by unanimous decision—" The kid drew out the syllables like he was announcing a UFC fight. Jazz wanted to tell him to hurry the hell up. "Theoooooo Bridgerrrr!"

As the first-place winner, Theo received fifty dollars, which he promptly donated back to the fair, a booklet of ride tickets, which he squatted down to gift to the little girl, tipping precariously back when she flung herself into his arms in an unexpected hug, and lastly, a gift certificate for Patty's grill, which he pocketed.

Around her, people clapped and whooped. Jazz screamed, as excited as a groupie. After the three winners took a picture together for the local newspaper, another round of applause rang out. Hands smacked Theo's back, and he was encircled by smiling faces, all waiting to congratulate him.

"That was amazing!" Jazz threw herself at Theo when he finally jogged down the stairs. His arms came up, catching her, swinging her so her feet left the ground. When he released her, she slid down his chest, and her body thrilled at the contact.

God. He smelled so good.

Their faces hovered inches apart. The hypnotizing facets in Theo's storm cloud eyes trapped and held her. They fell lower, and the way they travelled across her lips was as sensual as if he'd actually kissed her. All she would have to do was lean forward an inch or so, and their mouths would be reunited. She craved the taste of him. Would it be the same? Mint, the smoke of pilfered alcohol and summer?

"Great job, man!" A hand came down hard on Theo's shoulder as someone passed by, making him jump and snapping Jazz from the spell of memories. Pulling away, she shoved her hands into the back pockets of her jeans as if she'd not been seconds away from kissing him.

Saved again. What the hell was wrong with her?

"You hungry?" Theo asked, still grinning. If he'd noticed the moment that stretched between them, he didn't acknowledge it. Had she imagined the way he'd looked at her mouth? She was fucking hungry, all right.

"Always," Jazz shot back, attempting to steady herself. She had to get a grip. Getting drunk on teenage memories never led to intelligent decisions in adulthood.

"Shall we go to Patty's? It's freeee." Theo pulled the certificate from his pocket and dangled it before her face like fishing bait.

Jazz raised a brow at him before spinning on her heels. She needed to get away from the excited happiness pooling around Theo before she slipped and fell in. "Yeah, come on, I'm in. Free food always tastes better."

"I won't tell Betty you said that." Theo laced his fingers through hers as if it were the most natural thing in the world and steered them through the dispersing crowd. Once they were clear, he didn't release his grip on her, and Jazz didn't pull away.

Chapter Twenty

THEO

"**D**ANCE WITH ME?" THEO came back from the washrooms to find Jazz leaning back in their corner booth, eyes half-lidded. She looked sleepy and content. It was the most relaxed he'd seen her since he'd arrived on the ranch. Without sitting, he held a hand out to her.

At his words, she blinked, pulling her gaze off the couples swirling across the dance floor and over to his face. "Why?" she blurted, then pursed her lips, frowning slightly as if the question escaped on its own accord.

"Because," Theo said. "You're watching them like you wish you were out there."

And I will use any excuse to get you in my arms.

"It's been a long time," Jazz said. "Blair and I used to come on Saturday nights. We'd share one beer and a plate of fries and dance until one a.m. We were always too broke to do anything else, but we had fun; it was enough."

"You guys never wanted to have kids?"

Jazz spluttered on the swallow of beer she'd just taken. Grabbing a napkin, she coughed into it briefly, then shook her head. "No. We... we weren't into the idea. Enjoying the honeymoon phase too much, I suppose."

Theo fought back a wave of acidic jealousy. He could have done without the mental image of Blair and his stupid, kind, handsome face smiling down at Jazz as he two-stepped her around the homey old bar and then made love to her. Shaking it off, Theo raised his brows at her instead, waggling his fingers in a 'come on' motion. Tonight wasn't right for heavy talk; there was no way he would risk ruining their evening together. He had no way of knowing if he'd get another. "Don't make me use my dare, Jasmine. I want to save that."

"Okay, okay." Jazz put her hand in his. "But only because we're celebrating your big win."

Theo laughed as he pulled her to his chest with a sharp tug. She landed against him with a gentle *oof.* "So if I weren't the illustrious Jamieson Creek Talent Show winner, you wouldn't give me the time of day?"

"Wouldn't even look twice at you," Jazz said haughtily, her eyes twinkling as she settled into his arms. They stepped in time to the country song, laughing at each other when they stepped on their toes and tripped over their feet. When the song ended, and the music slowed, Theo yanked Jazz close and refused to relinquish her. After a moment of struggle, she settled against his chest.

"We shouldn't be doing this," she said so quietly that the words barely reached Theo's ears over the song.

"Two friends can't share a dance?" He said the words lightly, though the sensations spiralling through his heart and groin were anything but friendly.

"I don't know if you and I can ever be something as simple as friends, Theo," she said, looking up at him.

"Then let's be more," he said on impulse. "Let me explain about the past. Let me make amends for what happened. And let's see where this takes us." Leaning closer, he allowed his lips to brush the shell of her ear. "I know I'm not the only one feeling this, Jazz."

Jazz was shaking her head before he finished speaking.

"Why?" he demanded, not caring when his voice cracked. "Why won't you let me talk about what happened?" He was pushing too hard. He knew she was going to revolt against his pressing, yet couldn't stop himself. A wire of tension snapped in his chest the moment he took her in his arms, and the ferocity with which he wanted to cling to her scared him. Jasmine was his. She'd always been his. Why wasn't she willing to see that? What did he have to do to make her see?

"I don't have time for a relationship, Theo," Jazz said, pulling back. For a second, his grip tightened, and then he released her, shoving both hands through his hair as she stepped away.

"I have a ranch to save. My divorce was only final about a year ago. And we have a history that's so complicated, I can't even bring myself to think about it too much."

"Jasmine—" Theo said, but she was already walking back to their booth and grabbing her purse. Theo wanted to roar with frustration. The furious swell of emotion rushed through his body, and he had to clench his fists to keep them from shaking. He was tired of fighting the way he felt for her. Why couldn't he stop loving her?

"Jasmine, wait." He snatched his jacket from the booth, threw a fifty on the table, and strode after her. Theo felt eyes on his back as he left the bar. They'd be the talk of Jamieson Creek tomorrow.

"Please!" The word snapped through the air, sharp as gunfire. Jazz jerked to a stop in front of his truck. She didn't turn, but the ridged set of her back and shoulders told Theo she was waiting. When he got within a couple of feet, she spun on him.

"What gives you the right?" she demanded, poking a finger into his chest, "to say that shit to me. *You* want a relationship. *You* want to explain yourself and see where this goes. That's great, but you're not listening to what I want!"

"Then tell me what you want, Jasmine!" Theo growled, pressing both fists against his brow.

"I want to go back to never having seen you again!" she cried. Her chin jerked up, tendons in her neck straining as she fought the urge to cry... or maybe to deck him. She didn't need to hit him physically. Her words were a right hook to his gut.

"What?" he rasped, stumbling back a step.

"I wish you'd never shown up at the ranch. Then I could have kept hating you." Her lip pulled back into a snarl. "And that was *if* I even thought of you at all. You'd still be a memory. The first boy I loved. The one who left. The one who marked the last time I ever trusted anyone with my jaded little heart. And that would be that. But, now I know you. Here—" she waved a hand back and forth in the space between them. "In this reality, I know you grew into a kind, loyal, handsome man. I know you have demons that torment you. I ache to hold you and help ease your pain, help chase those demons away. I *never* asked for any of this. I don't *want* any of this! I want to be free of every ounce of pain you ever caused me."

She was panting, her chest heaving like Goliath after a gallop. Theo's chest was a bomb about to explode. He wanted to cry, beg, smash something. To fall on his knees before her, cling to her, and tell her he would give anything to take away the pain he caused her. Finally, he did the only thing he could. Theo succumbed to the bone-deep desperation to *touch* her. He reached out, seized Jazz by the front of her jacket and pulled her against him.

Chapter Twenty-One

JASMINE

THEO'S LIPS CRASHED INTO hers. Pain and electric desire flared at the point of impact, and Jazz sucked a shaky breath. Strong fingers burrowed into the hair at her nape, callouses catching against individual strands. She squirmed, trying to get away and trying to get closer. Her body flared to life at the press of his. A seed stroked by the first hot rays of spring. She wasn't ready to grow. She wanted to remain hidden. She hated Theo for what he was doing to her—hated him as much as she loved him.

"God, Jasmine." Theo pulled back the barest fraction, his words scarcely more than a whisper, exhaled in reverence. "I've never stopped wanting you."

"You fucking bastard," Jazz hissed. The crack of her palm against his face rang through the empty parking lot. Then, she wrapped her arms around his neck and pressed closer.

"When I was on my tours, I'd wake up from dreaming about you and reach out into the dark. Then the years would crash back in, and I'd remember where I was." His fingers moved from her hair and slipped up and down her spine. She shivered against him.

Jazz couldn't bring herself to answer. To admit she'd woken in the throes of longing for him more times than she could count. She so carefully built the wall around her heart, erecting it tall and robust with bricks formed from the trauma and pain of her past. Though Theo was picking away at it, allowing that final crumbling of defence terrified Jazz. He had come so close to breaking her once, and life had followed in his wake to try to finish the job. She may be unable to control what Theo or anyone else did to her, but she could keep that protection siege-proof.

Those thoughts were a bucket of cold water flung across the raging fire of Jazz's libido. She rocked back on her heels, peeling herself from Theo's grasp. They stared at each other, panting. Theo's grey eyes were dark with need, but Jazz didn't miss the anguish that flashed through them as she pulled away.

"I'm sorry," Theo said, his voice snagging harshly. "I shouldn't have said all that. I shouldn't have tried to force you into something you've repeatedly said you don't want."

"It's fine," Jazz said, plucking at the bottom of her jacket with trembling fingers. "I just... we can't. You were right the other night when you stopped me. We can't go down that road again."

"Maybe though, if you let me tell you about the night I left, you'd be able to—" He trailed off, leaving the echo of despair as she shook her head. "Sorry, I'm doing it again."

"Why rip open scars when it will have no benefit in healing them?"

"But maybe that's the only way to ensure they properly heal," Theo said. "Take away the festering. Let it heal clean."

Jazz was shaking, perilously close to tears. Fuck, she didn't want to cry again. "Can you please take me home?" she managed to say around the lump in her throat.

Theo gazed at her for a long moment, the beams of street lights throwing splashes of illumination across the stark angles of his face. After an eternity, he nodded. "Of course." Jazz heard him swallow as he placed his fingertips against the small of her back and guided her to the truck.

Neither of them spoke on the short drive back to the ranch. Jazz watched the dark streaks of landscape through the blur in her eyes. She couldn't blink away. She should tell him to leave. That made the most sense for both of them, but the thought of him being gone made her feel hollow. After only a month of having done so, not seeing him daily seemed wrong.

Chapter Twenty-Two

THEO

J AZZ GATHERED HER THINGS and exited the truck, slamming the door before Theo could speak.

Fuck. He couldn't do this anymore. Something had to give, or his time at Sunrise was done.

"Jasmine," Theo called. "We need to talk about this. I know you think it won't change things, but I need to have my say." Despite her wanting him to, Theo couldn't let it go. "This is tearing my fucking heart out."

Jazz whirled, fists shaking at her sides. "Stop calling me Jasmine!" she yelled. "Jasmine was the before me. Jasmine was a foolish girl whose world fell apart time and again until she finally learned not to rely on anyone but herself. Now I'm Jazz, and that lesson is one I'll never forget."

"Jasm—Jazz," Theo stepped toward her, forcing words past the aching tightness in his throat. "You said it wasn't fair that I was trying to choose for you, but that's what you're doing to me."

Her chin rose, eyes sparking with flinty determination. "Fine. Have your say, Theo. Debride this fucking wound and be done with it." She practically vibrated with the determination not to allow what he said to matter.

"I didn't want to leave you," Theo said. "I loved you."

"We were kids. Our relationship meant nothing," she ground out the words, but they lacked conviction. Her body was rigid enough to break. Tendons stood out along her neck and forearms. There was nothing Theo wouldn't give to hold her. To feel the armour she'd built about herself soften and mould to him. But there was practically a force field radiating from her, keeping him away.

"It meant everything," he whispered. "You changed my life. I didn't know what love was before you, Jazz."

"I didn't know what heartbreak was before you," she spat back.

Theo squeezed his eyes shut, hiding the sheen of tears he knew gathered there as her words sliced through to the deepest parts of him. "My father took me," he said without opening them. "He literally forced me into the car in the middle of the night. I never saw Uncle Ted again. He died of a heart attack while I was on my first tour."

He heard Jazz swallow and opened his eyes, forcing their gazes to collide.

"I know," she said, her voice hard but not cruel. "I'm sorry. He was wonderful, and I know how much you loved him."

Theo pressed the heels of his hands hard into his eye sockets. He relished the stars that danced through the darkness because they were better than the tears. When the tightness in his chest finally eased, he dropped his hands and turned to her.

"I looked for you once I was back in Canada. I had this crazy idea, a dream, I suppose, that maybe you waited for me." This time, it was his voice that hardened. Theo allowed some of the old hurt, the betrayal, to creep back in. It was that or break down entirely. "But when I called your number, it came back disconnected. When I emailed, it came back as undelivered."

Jazz opened her mouth to speak, but Theo talked louder, drowning out whatever she was going to say. "Then I opened a Facebook page to see if I could find you."

Jazz's mouth closed, her chin tipped up defiant, tears brimming then spilling over the dam of her lower lids. She did nothing to hide them from him.

Theo shoved both hands through his hair, tugging at his neck, the base of his skull where the tension was gathering. "I couldn't find you. But I remembered your friend, Valley, so I looked for her. It took me a while to remember her real name. There's not a lot of Valentinas around, so once I did, I found her."

Jazz continued to stare at him. She refused to look away, though twin tears broke free and rolled down her cheeks and along the clenched muscles of her jaw.

"Guess what her profile picture was," Theo said, his voice barely scratching free—the slightest tremble to Jazz's lower lip.

"It was her, standing beside a bride. The most beautiful bride I'd ever seen—" Theo's voice broke, but he pushed on, unable to stop himself now that the words were finally breaking free. "The woman I'd imagined as my own bride, over and over again. The woman I wanted with every fibre of my being, even though I was only nineteen when I saw her last. The woman I was sure would still love me because, in my foolish youthful ignorance, I believed she was my soul mate."

A rush of wet heat tickled through the stubble on Theo's jaw, but he didn't move. He didn't care. The pain was one more piece of him, bared to her, whether or not she cared to have it.

"You didn't wait for me, though, Jasmine. You must have gotten with him within a couple of months of my leaving?" He swallowed, the sound loud in the quiet farmyard. "I couldn't believe you didn't love me enough to wait, just for a while. I thought you knew I would always find a way back to you."

Tears raced in streams down Jazz's cheeks, forming wet semicircles on the collar of her shirt. She licked her lips, her mouth so dry it made a clicking sound.

At last, she said in a voice scarcely audible. "I was pregnant, Theo."

Theo's entire body jerked, each word a blow as time turned syrupy. He stared at her, fighting to remember how to draw breath into his lungs. Jazz spoke again before he could form any coherent words.

"With your baby."

Chapter Twenty-Three

JASMINE

T HE BLOOD DRAINED FROM Theo's face until the shadow of his beard was a stain against the grey of his skin. He pressed a hand to his stomach as though he may puke.

"Pregnant?" The word ripped out of him, coming free by the roots and pulling each stringy, dangling emotion with it.

"Yes," Jazz forced the word from the barren landscape of her throat.

Theo stepped closer, one hand hovering in the chasm of space between them before it dropped, balling into a fist against his thigh.

Touch me. Jazz's heart shrieked. *Don't touch me.*

A scream seared the back of her aching throat. She missed Theo. She missed the boy he was when she plunged so foolishly into love with him. She ached to know the man he became, no matter how often she told herself *no*. The yearning to be comforted by him possessed her every cell, but Jazz would shatter if he so much as took her hand. His arms would be the only thing strong enough to keep the decimated parts of her heart together. Theo Bridger wielded a power that scared her shitless.

He left us.

She pulled the words over the smouldering love in her heart, dampening it, attempting to suffocate it.

He didn't know. You never told him.

The other voice inside her argued, and she wished it would stop.

You kept it from him; it isn't his fault.

The plucking hands of her subconscious tugged, trying to pull back the wet blanket of her fury and heartache in its attempt to let the love flare.

Pain. Blood. The most visceral fear she'd never known.

A violent shuddering began in Jazz's core and unfurled until it consumed her entire body. Seizing the length of her braid in her hands to try to quell the shaking, Jazz forced herself to continue.

"I found out three weeks after you left." Pulling in a shaky breath, she marrionetted her limbs into action, moving to the barn to lean against the wall. That was where her legs quit, and she slid down to sit with her back against it. Theo hesitated momentarily before folding his body to the spring-chilled ground beside hers. "I hid it for as long as I could. When I got too big, I finally told my father. I knew I'd need a doctor, vitamins, clothes."

"What did he do?"

"He freaked out and told me to take care of it, or he would. He said he'd been straddled once with a kid he didn't want, and he wouldn't go through it again."

Theo growled, digging his clenched fists into his thighs. Without thinking, Jazz reached out and placed an arm on his tendon-laced forearm, squeezing.

"Jazz, I didn't know," Theo choked. "I would have given anything to be there for you, *done* anything, consequences be damned."

She'd known that, hadn't she? Or some part of her had, and maybe not telling him, had been a way of protecting him, too.

"I wasn't going to get an abortion," she continued as if he hadn't spoken. "Not because I believe they are wrong or that people shouldn't have a choice; I do, but it wasn't the choice for me. I wanted—" her voice broke and she forced in an unsteady breath. "I wanted something that was part of you. I thought maybe if the baby had your eyes or your laugh, it wouldn't hurt so much that you were gone. Blair was my best friend, aside from Val. He has been since we were little kids. I told him everything. We got married a month later. He promised to take care of us, no matter what. He didn't care the baby wasn't his. We rented this awful shack on the edge of town, and both worked our asses off."

Blair had given her a rocking chair, and Jazz sat on the porch of their run-down rental house in the evenings, running her hands over the small mound of her belly, equal parts terrified and enthralled by what was happening to her. How many times had she imagined Theo's grey eyes staring up at her from a tiny version of him, one they created by loving each other?

"The picture," Theo whispered. "In that picture, you were—" He couldn't seem to force the word free.

"I was," Jazz said. "About ten weeks along." There was something to be said for regular periods, even as a youth.

Theo pulled his arm from her grasp and pressed both palms over his face, releasing a strangled gasp of sound. Jazz allowed him that modicum of privacy, pretending she didn't see his shoulders shake.

"What... what happened to—" Theo lifted his head after a moment. His eyes were stormier than she'd ever seen, red-rimmed, overflowing with pain and anger. Not at her, Jazz didn't think. But she hadn't told him the whole story yet.

"I did something I will never forgive myself for."

"Jasmine—"

Jazz hadn't talked about what happened since the day the doctors in the emergency room worked over her, trying desperately to save her and the baby. She'd locked that day in a vault and shoved it as deep down inside her as she could.

"I was working for Blair's parents, helping on their farm in Cascade Creek, working with the horses. I went for a ride, not thinking anything of it. The doctor said it was alright if I was careful and didn't continue into my third trimester.

I saddled up this younger horse, Cougar. I should have stuck with one of the older mares; to this day, I don't know what I was thinking." Jazz stared down at her hands. "Cougar needed exercise. I was young and stupid."

She picked her cuticles as she spoke, and a ribbon of flesh tore away, leaving a bloody groove. Wiping the crimson beads on her jeans, she continued. "A pheasant—a fucking pheasant—" she released a noise that wasn't a laugh, or a sob, just an empty, encompassing crack of sound. "It flew up and spooked him. He threw me and took off. By the time Blair found me, I was bleeding heavily. He rushed me in, but I suffered a placental abruption. They did everything they could, but it was too early. I was only twenty weeks along."

Tears poured free, running over her face to drip from her chin. Jazz stared at the dark puddles that formed on her jeans where they landed—black as the spots each painful memory left on her soul. The bruises remaining after her life pressed too hard.

"It's my fault, Theo, I killed him—" the words broke, detonating into a harsh sob. She wasn't prepared for the tornado of grief that rushed from her belly and ripped through her, pressing the air right out of her lungs.

For years, Jazz wondered if she should have tried to contact Theo and tell him what had happened. But he had never called, and only once did she fall far enough into despair that she allowed herself to enter his phone number. When she found out she was pregnant and Blair proposed, Jazz did her best to accept that he never would. She blocked his number, did her best to move on, and tried to focus on her new life. Valley insisted she try harder and that it was the right thing to do. She never wavered in her stance, but then the baby was gone, and Jazz reasoned it was too late; what would telling him accomplish?

She knew the truth, though. She'd been afraid. Afraid to hear his voice, to speak the words needed to carry the truth of all that had happened: the baby, the wedding, the losses that shredded her last strands of innocence. Somehow, it had been easier to wrap herself in the safety of the hatred she convinced herself she had for Theo and stay there.

"No!" The single word tore from Theo, ravaged and harsh. "It wasn't your fault, sweetheart. It wasn't. I should have been with you." He twisted, boots scraping in the dirt as he pulled her against his chest. Jazz didn't argue. Exhaustion and sadness rushed over her like a landslide. The ever-present threat of losing the ranch, the shock of seeing Theo, finally telling him the secret she carried as an ever-present weight about her neck. The physical exhaustion she experienced each day all culminated until she was drowning—until all she could do was cling to him and cry.

She fell apart in Theo's arms in a way she had never allowed. Not while bleeding in the hospital, clutching the still bundle in her arms. Not while the ink dried on the divorce papers separating her life from Blair's. Not over her father's grave. Jazz allowed Theo to hold all the jagged pieces of her soul together, for once too exhausted to do it herself.

Just for a moment. One moment, then she would be strong again.

Pressing her face into the hollow of his throat, Jazz counted the pounding of his heartbeats, the steady tempo a juxtaposition to her erratic sobs. Scorching, salty streams wet her temple, and Jazz registered how he shook. She lifted her laden arms and wrapped them around Theo's solid body, holding tight as the sobs shook him, too. They grieved the loss, fresh for one, an aching unhealed scab for the other, but shared all the same.

Jazz had no comprehension of how long they stayed that way. The moon was high, and the crickets had resumed their serenades when Theo released a breath that deflated his entire body. Jazz began to shiver with cold and adrenaline. Theo slipped off his jacket and wrapped her in it before he stood, extending a hand. Wordlessly, Jazz took it, allowing him to tug her to her feet. With the story at last told, she felt hollowed out, but there was a niggling of relief as well.

Once inside, Theo bent, gently pulling Jazz's boots off, then removing his own. Keeping a steadying hand laced with hers, he led her upstairs and, looking at her once for her nod of consent, to her bedroom. Jazz followed, dazed and more exhausted than she could ever remember being. She knew she should send him away but struggled to remember why.

Theo took his jacket from her shoulders and helped her shrug out of hers. "Take off your jeans," he whispered.

Jazz did what he asked without fuss. Shimming out of her pants, she pulled off her sweater, then reached around her back, unhooking her bra and pulling it out from under her tank top. Checking Theo's back, which was still turned, she crossed the room and slipped into the embrace of her bed.

At the squeak of the springs, he turned to her. "Can I make you some tea? Do you need anything?"

I need you. I need you to hold me. I need us to go back and never be separated. I need to have never gotten on the back of that fucking horse. I need a fifteen-year-old kid to come here and ask us questions and complain about his chores.

Jazz wondered what he would do if she said the words. But, even if she wanted to re-break his heart, the swollen, hot emotion in her throat wouldn't allow them freedom. She shook her head. "I'm alright."

Theo closed his eyes, standing still for a long moment, swaying slightly on his feet. Then he came to the bed and kneeled, his face only inches from hers.

"I'm so sorry you've borne this alone for so long. I'll be forever grateful that you had Blair and Valley, but I—" His voice broke, and Jazz watched his face crumple as he lost the fight against the wash of tears that filled the grey sea of his eyes with more clouds. "I'm so sorry, Jasmine." He dropped his head against her shoulder, his breath stuttering, soaking her skin with grief and heated breath.

Her arm felt heavy as Jazz reached to push the thick hair off Theo's brow. "I'm sorry, too," she whispered.

Theo started to shake his head, but she squeezed her hand around the perfect curve at the back of his skull. Would their son's head have fit perfectly within her palm?

"Will you stay?" she whispered, hating the quaver in her voice. "Will you stay and hold me tonight?"

"Of course," he was already pushing to his feet, wiping his eyes with his forearm, "anytime you need."

Jazz knew she wasn't the only one who needed comfort. Theo's features were etched with pain as stark as the scar that marked him. It aged him, bending him under a burden he hadn't born a mere hour ago. But she had, and now he carried half. Maybe sharing the weight would make it easier.

Pulling back her quilt, Jazz slid further back into the bed so Theo could join her. His lips folded against his teeth as he studied her, and then, dragging a hand over his face, he sighed. It only took a couple of seconds for him to undress. Jazz knew she should stop him, tell him she had changed her mind, and turn him away, but she didn't.

Chapter Twenty-Four

THEO

"THEO! THEO, WAKE UP."

Slowly, Theo rose toward consciousness, growing aware of cool fingers caressing his sweating brow. Air heaved in and out of his lungs, and his stomach roiled.

Fuck.

He hadn't suffered a nightmare in a week and had begun to harbour a sliver of hope that maybe they were gone. He focused on breathing, the whisper of Jazz's gentle shushing as her touch traced the crease between his brows.

Jazz's voice? Jazz was touching him. Was stretched out beside him, the heat from her body seeping into his skin.

The events of the night before, the raw pain her words had inflicted, slammed back, and Theo pushed his head deeper into the pillows.

Breathe. Don't puke on Jazz's bed; she'll never let you back.

"Are you alright?" Jazz asked after a few moments.

Theo forced his head to nod, hoping the tears pooling in his eyes wouldn't fall free. They'd both cried enough for now. The anguish and anxiety were a weight on his chest, however, pressing him down, strangling him.

"Yeah," he rasped after a few forceful swallows. "I'm sorry I woke you." To his dismay, Jazz's fingers fell from his brow.

With a sigh, she settled into the pillow beside him. "It's alright. It's time to get up anyway."

One of the roosters let loose an ecstatic cry from outside as if in agreement. Theo groaned and pressed a hand over his burning eyes.

"Do you... do you want to talk about it? It might help." Jazz's voice was a hesitant caress, uncharacteristically gentle for her. Maybe she hadn't yet donned her armour for the day.

Theo was silent for a long moment. He wasn't sure he wanted to bring more horror into the room with them. After last night, did they need to dredge up more pain? But... maybe now was the perfect time. He may have to share other secrets, but... those depended on what happened today. Tomorrow? If Jazz decided this was it for them, then he could save them for himself.

"I got this scar from a piece of shrapnel," he began, forcing down the burn of acid creeping up his throat. "It was a piece of the truck my friend and I were hiding behind. A bullet went—it went right through her, sent pieces flying." Theo was grateful he couldn't see her in the dim dawn light. He stared up at the ceiling, letting it tumble in. His emotions were so close to the surface that he could barely keep them reined in. "I don't dream about my injuries so much, though I thought I'd been blinded at first. But I remember her face. The feel of her blood splattering across my skin. The smell of... it *all*."

"Oh god, Theo." Jazz's warm hand wrapped around his, and she pulled it close, cradling it against her chest. "You shouldn't have had to go through that. No one should have."

"Yet people go through worse things all the time," he whispered. That thought sometimes crushed him, so overbearingly heavy he wasn't sure he could crawl from under it if he dwelled on it for too long.

Outside, the rooster crowed again, shattering the quiet. "I'll be okay," Theo said, squeezing Jazz's hand. "And, you may not want to hear this, but waking up beside you, in this soft, marshmallow light—" he rolled his head on the pillow to stare at her. She met his gaze, eyes shining. "It makes this morning special despite everything."

For a second, Theo thought he saw something suspiciously close to love flash across her eyes. He pushed the thought away as fast as it arose, not daring to allow even a sliver of such hope to wiggle into his heart.

"I'd like you to do something for me," he said after a moment of simply staring at each other. His heart rate ratcheted faster, matching the passing seconds. He was thankful for the heavy quilt covering him because his heart wasn't the only thing taking notice of Jazz and how devastatingly beautiful she looked in the glow of the sunrise.

Jazz's eyes narrowed slightly. "What?" she asked, drawing the word out, wary.

"I'd like you to stay here."

"Here?" she parroted.

"Yes, in bed."

"But, there's all the chores, and I was going to get all the materials ready to set up a table at the farmer's market this weekend—"

Theo reached out and pressed a finger over her lips, revelling in the dangerous flash of her eyes. For a moment, he thought she might bite him, and his throbbing cock jerked in anticipation. "I want you to stay in bed, sleep as long as you want, and have a long hot shower." Her eyes dropped to his mouth, and Theo bit back a groan. "And relax," he continued. "I will take care of things. And—" he raised his voice, cutting off her protest. "If there is anything I can't handle, I will call you."

Nothing but their heartbeats filled the space for a long, pulsing moment, and then, to Theo's surprise, Jazz nodded. "Alright," she whispered.

It's my fault, Theo, I killed him.

Him.

Theo's stomach roiled as he stepped into the dew-kissed morning air. Chickens scattered around his feet, frantic with the prospect of food. Henry, the Angus, raised his head from the water trough, twin torrents of water and green strands gushing from either side of his mouth, and lowed at the sight of Theo.

The place was teaming with life, but all Theo could hear were Jazz's words rattling in his skull like dried beans in a maraca.

It's my fault, Theo, I killed him.

Their love had created a son. And Theo had never known. Never knew he existed. Never knew he died.

Theo gasped, the sound too sharp in the soft morning. He couldn't breathe. A keen rose from his gut, so high it nearly lacked sound. Quickly, he clamped a hand over his mouth to make it stop, but that only made it harder to draw air into his screaming lungs.

Rushing away from the house, Theo stumbled for the dark embrace of the barn. Flinging through the door, he crashed onto a low stack of hay bales and ground his face into his palms. His ribs were going to shatter under the force of the pressing weight. The sob that exploded out of him was the only thing that relieved the pressure. He let them come again and again. Let the tsunami of pain obliterate him until he was barren and naked and new.

Theo wasn't sure how long he sat there before his breathing regulated. His head hung low, both arms dangling off his knees when something soft brushed against his fingers. A soft *meh* and another bump. Theo lifted his head to see Catrick Stewart studying him with golden orb eyes.

"Hey," he whispered. "Did I wake you?"

Meh.

"I don't speak, cat. I'm sorry. Cancelled my subscription to Rosetta Stone."

The cat rewarded his pathetic joke with another head butt. Theo straightened, patting his leg, and the cat hopped up. Placing tiny paws on Theo's shoulders, the animal gave Theo's chin and jaw a thorough rub with his own. Wispy hair tickled his entire face, but Theo didn't care. He hugged the little beast against his chest, scritching and scratching him until Catrick finally seemed tired of the affection. Theo smiled as he strolled away, serpentine tail high in the air.

"Thanks," he said.

Chapter Twenty-Five

JASMINE

J AZZ WAS METHODICALLY SHOVELLING oatmeal into her mouth at the table and attempting to wake up after the unaccustomed sleep-in when Blair slammed through the front door.

"Hey, isn't this your boy, Theo?" Crossing the kitchen in three long strides, he thrust his phone under Jazz's nose without bothering with any greeting.

"Good morning to you, too," Jazz said wryly. Blair wrinkled his nose and shook the phone in her face. She took it from his hand, eyes widening when she saw the image frozen on the screen. There was Theo poised over his guitar, the lights of the midway a rainbow smear behind him.

Jazz tapped the screen, and Theo's voice rose from the speaker. Blair leaned over her shoulder, releasing a low whistle as he watched. "He's really good."

"It's the talent show at the fair," Jazz whispered through the fingers she held pressed to her lips.

"He's viral." Blair pointed at a number in the lower corner of the screen. "Wait, it gets better."

Whoever recorded the video was close to the stage and had a perfect view of Theo. He sang with his entire body, and his voice was a gorgeous pairing of silk and grit. Dark hair fell across his brow, and his eyes drifted closed as he threw himself into the chords. Watching him, Jazz knew he'd been able to completely shut out the crowd and give himself to the music.

As verse two began, the video panned back, scanning the crowd, and Jazz nearly protested out loud, but then the camera came to rest on an elderly man holding the hand of a stooped, white-haired woman. She beamed up at Theo, clearly entranced, her face a roadmap of life and love. With a glance at each other, the couple made their way forward, people stepping aside to make room as they began to dance. The video panned back and forth, alternating between them and Theo.

When the song ended, Jazz handed the phone back to Blair. Her cheeks were wet, and she dashed at them hurriedly with the backs of her hands. "Send that to me, please. And come sit down. I need to talk to you."

Blair narrowed his eyes before easing a chair from under the table and settling onto it. "What's up?"

Jazz exhaled loud and long, fighting a shudder as she forced out the words, "About the other night."

He winced, suddenly taking a keen interest in the scarred surface of the table. "I figured this was coming. I'm sorry, Jazz."

Jazz jerked her head back, surprised. "Wait... *you're* sorry?"

Blair seemed to forget he didn't want to meet her eyes and looked up. "Yeah? Don't you want to give me shit for having sex with you while you weren't totally... well, with it?"

Guilt spiked through Jazz, and she reached out, placing a hand on Blair's wrist. "No. Is that what you thought? That I was mad at you for taking advantage of *me*?"

"I sort of did... and I've felt terrible about it since."

"Blair, sweetie." Jazz shook her head, struggling to understand. Blair had been feeling guilty about their night together. That was as unfair as her using him had been. He hadn't done anything wrong. "You summed up exactly what *I've* been feeling. I don't blame you at all. I'm the one who used you." Jazz sighed and rubbed her free hand over her face. Sudden bone-deep exhaustion was creeping in, making her sluggish. "It wasn't right of me to text you that night. You're not a booty call."

Blair remained silent for a long moment. Jazz thought he might not answer her when he finally said, "But I always said I'd be here, no matter what you needed."

Tears pricked behind Jazz's lids as she shook her head. "No. Not that. It wasn't right. You do not deserve to be used."

A memory struck her suddenly. The night they'd both known their marriage was over. They'd been fighting constantly about stupid shit. The relationship they worked so hard to build and maintain for eight years crumbled around them, a faulty foundation giving way. Blair was the first to break. Jazz couldn't even remember what they fought about, but he'd stopped... just *stopped*. Happy-go-lucky, easygoing and always eager to please, Blair stood before her, lost for words. His head hanging, and shoulders shaking as he sobbed.

Even now, two years later, the memory drove a spike of pain into her gut. She had loved him. She *did* love him so fucking much, but the problem was she'd never been *in* love with him. "How long will you punish me for not being *him*?" Blair had whispered when she went to wrap her arms around him. "I love you, Jazz. I love you too much to hate you, but I wish I could right now." And that had been it. They spent all night talking and filed for divorce the next day. Her dad was in palliative care, with only weeks left to live, and it wasn't long before Jazz was able to move to the ranch. She'd lost the last sorry excuse for a parent she had, blown up a marriage, and gained her lifelong home all in a matter of weeks.

Blair's long fingers were restless, picking at the cuticles on the opposite side. Finally, he blew out a weary sigh. "You've always been my person, Jazz. It isn't your fault I wasn't yours." He didn't meet her eyes as she spoke, and it was a good thing because, with his words, Jazz lost the fight against her tears. "Blair—" His name emerged on a ragged sob. God, damn it, she hated crying, and she'd been doing it far too much as of late. She blamed Theo for coming around and messing up the balance of things. "That makes what I did even worse."

Jazz made the mistake of meeting Blair's gaze, then. His lovely sky-blue eyes were bottomless with pain and suspiciously glossy. He'd always been so *good*. He was never afraid to be who he was. He didn't hesitate to show emotion, whether joy, sadness, or anything in between. Jazz would bet she'd seen him cry more often than he'd seen her. Why was she so afraid to be vulnerable? The act of opening herself up and giving herself to another person terrified her. It was as if she were arming them, giving them the weapon to destroy her.

"I'm weak," Blair whispered. "When it comes to you, I'll take whatever I can. I always have. Maybe I'm pathetic, but it's pretty late to change now."

A ragged sob escaped Jazz. Pressing her face into her palms, she fought against the stomach-turning guilt. Her head pounded with the force of the tears pressurizing inside her skull. With sudden clarity, she saw the harm she'd done, allowing the dependence she and Blair shared. She'd willfully leaned into their friendship and ignored that Blair's feelings did not mirror her own. With each laugh they shared, when they comforted each other and supported each other through anger or sadness, she passed Blair a lifeline of hope whether she meant to or not.

Heart splintering, Jazz twisted in her chair and held her arms open. Blair's jaw muscles jumped as he fought to contain his emotions. Pulling his chair closer, he allowed Jazz to wrap her arms around him. For a moment, they sat without speaking, the weight of a lifetime's worth of memories pressing down around them.

Jazz breathed against Blair's neck, letting the familiar lemony scent of his skin calm her.

"Blair—" she said, finally forcing herself to break the moment. His broad shoulders trembled as he inhaled.

"I know," he said, voice thick.

"You need space from me," she said anyway.

"I'm not sure what my life looks like without you, Jazzy," he said. With a sigh, he sat back and rubbed the back of a hand across his cheeks.

"Neither do I," Jazz admitted, struggling to keep her voice whole. "But I think it's time to find out."

With a sniff, Blair nodded. He looked so lost, so heartbreakingly dear, that Jazz feared she'd lose any modicum of strength she retained. "Go on, git now," she choked in a terrible Southern accent.

Blair spluttered out a damp laugh. "I love you, Jazzy." Reaching out, he cupped his hand against her cheek.

Jazz turned her face against it, allowing her eyes to close for only a second. "I love you too, Blaring."

"If you need anything—" His voice broke, and he stopped, jaw muscles jumping as he clenched his teeth.

Jazz pressed a hand to the large one, still cupping her cheek and squeezing, letting him know he didn't have to fight to get the words out. She didn't need them. "I know."

Releasing a long breath, Blair let his hand fall away. He opened his mouth, then closed it, giving his head a slight nod as he turned away. Jazz watched his lanky form duck through the kitchen entryway. For the first time in as long as she could remember, possibly her entire life, she didn't know when she'd see Blair again.

After Blair left, Jazz did something she'd never done. She crawled into bed and stayed there for the rest of the afternoon. Around four p.m., she received a single text from Theo.

> Still all good out here. I just wanted to make sure you're alive.

Theo had been so sweet that morning, and Jazz didn't want him to worry. She typed a quick answer.

> Yes. See you at dinner.

Theo didn't answer, and Jazz returned to doing what she'd done the rest of the day—alternating between crying and opening her phone to the last thing Blair sent her, the video of Theo. She couldn't stop watching it. Her phone began offering her other videos with similar elements, but none of them came close to living up to Theo's, and she quickly swiped them away. Each time she opened it, she checked the climbing number of views at the bottom of the screen.

She still couldn't believe she'd listened when he commanded her to stay in bed that morning. The memory made her pulse jump. She'd been incredibly close to kissing him. The moment he shut the bedroom door behind him, Jazz rolled over, seized her vibrator from the top drawer of her dresser, and came in record time before falling headlong back into sleep.

Theo was sitting at the dinner table when the scent of roasting chicken finally lured Jazz downstairs. His head was tipped back, the rich sound of his laugh permeating the room as he laughed at something Betty said. He didn't notice when Jazz placed her phone on the table before him.

"You hit eight hundred thousand views," she said without explanation.

Theo looked up, confused. "Sorry?"

Jazz dropped onto the chair beside him and reached over, hitting play on the video. Theo's voice rose to fill the room.

"What's this now?" Betty asked, drying her hands on her apron as she came over to watch over Theo's other shoulder.

"Someone recorded me?" Theo whispered, dark brows tucking into a confused frown.

Betty patted his shoulder with a smile that was a cross between matronly and patronizing. "Even as old as I am, I know everything is being recorded these days."

"Especially handsome men with guitars and voices that make angels cry," Jazz said, only half sarcastically. "Keep watching."

When the couple stepped from the crowd and began to dance, Jazz glanced at Theo. His eyes widened, then after a few seconds, turned glossy with emotion. Jazz pretended not to notice.

The video ended, but Theo continued to stare at the screen, looking flabbergasted. Then, the phone vibrated, and Ed Hamilton's name flashed on the screen.

Theo pushed the device across the table, but Jazz reached out and hit decline.

On Theo's other side, Betty, who hadn't noticed the call, sniffed and dabbed her eyes with the corner of her apron. "That was absolutely beautiful, honey." One chapped hand patted Theo's shoulder. "I had no idea you were so talented."

"Neither did I," Jazz said. "You really haven't seen this?" she asked Theo.

He shook his head. "I haven't. Did that many people actually watch it?"

"They did. And only one thousand of those views were from me today."

At that, he looked up, cheeks reddening when their gazes snagged. The shy smile that lifted one corner of his lips did unfair things to her heart. "Thank you for showing me. I don't even know what to say."

"I'm surprised you hadn't stumbled on it already."

The smile flirting at his mouth faded. "I don't do social media. It fucks with my mental health too much."

"That's fair," Jazz said. "I still can't believe I didn't know you could do this." She gestured to the phone. She'd always been so sure she'd known the *real* Theo.

Theo glanced at her, chewed his lip a moment, then looked down at his hands. "I've loved music since I was a kid. My mom would sneak me to guitar lessons and tell my dad I was going to Taekwondo. It was a good thing he was never interested in watching the classes or seeing what I'd learned. In high school, a music teacher talked me into joining the choir. They started giving me most of the solos. I was an awkward kid, skinny, terrified of girls." He smiled up at Jazz. "I filled out a bit before I met you... and the acne cleared up." For a moment, a world of unspoken memories floated between them, and a fizzing erupted in Jazz's gut as if she was once again a teenage girl with a crush on the summer boy.

Theo looked away, breaking the spell. Rubbing a hand up the back of his neck, he went on. "But when I was on stage, people looked at me differently. Like I was special—it was the way I always wished my dad would look at me. I'd seen him give my brothers that look... but I was never on the receiving end."

You are someone special. The words rose in Jazz's throat.

Theo swallowed hard. "After about a year, my dad found out. He ran into a parent who said something about how proud he must have been of me being the star of the show... something along those lines. My brothers Chris and Oliver graduated, and suddenly, Dad remembered he had another son. He showed up at the play. It was opening night, and I was the lead. I'd worked so hard for the part and was so happy when I got it. He barged in and dragged me off the stage, raging that no son of his was going to do something as 'girly' as singing and dancing for people like a trained monkey." Theo lifted one hand heavily, dabbing air quotes around the word 'girly' before dropping it back to his thigh.

"He enrolled me in cadets and made me attend the martial arts we said I'd been taking." He shrugged. "I didn't mind that much, but I didn't sing or pick up my guitar again until I was in Afghanistan. Waiting gets boring. One night, someone was singing, so I joined in without thinking about what I was doing. I didn't even notice when the other guy stopped or that the room went silent."

His cheeks burned scarlet, and he avoided both their gazes. "When I got back, I bought a guitar again." Theo studied his fingernails with interest before rolling his shoulders as if pushing a weight from them. "I hope you'll forgive how

243

dramatic this sounds, but that guitar saved my life more times than I can say." His voice tightened as if he were struggling to force the words free. "I'd pick it up whenever I thought about grabbing a razor blade."

Betty drew in a sharp breath, and before Jazz could move, the older woman had wrapped Theo up in her arms. Jazz heard him suck in a shaky breath of surprise, and her heart threatened to shatter. Tonight was one of the few times Theo had talked about his mother, and Jazz decided to try to learn more.

How unfair that both their fathers had held such power to wound their children and used it freely. Moulding and squeezing them both into the people they were. How different might they both have been with good men at the helm of their family homes?

"Well," Betty said, pulling back from Theo and pressing her hands to her apple-bright cheeks. "I think we could all use a glass of wine after that."

Jazz nodded her agreement, turning her eyes away from Theo to give him the peace to quickly rub his fingers below his eyes.

Chapter Twenty-Six

THEO

THEO LONGED TO ASK Jazz what was bothering her, but the air around her snapped with emotion, and he wasn't sure it would be wise.

"I'm heading into town once we're done today," he said. "If you don't mind letting Betty know I won't be around for dinner?" Theo said, pulling the knot on David's cinch with a jerk. The horse released the air he'd been holding with a resigned groan. Theo had figured out the gelding's trick of holding his breath while being saddled when he slipped right down onto the horse's side while checking fence lines. He'd dismounted without eating dirt, but it had been a close call.

"That's it, wily bugger," Theo said, patting the horse's thick neck. "Too smart for your own good."

Jazz cast him a narrow look over Goliath's back. The horse was dancing in place, vibrating with energy as he awaited his chance for freedom. "Remember, showing up late or drunk violates your contract," she said.

Theo resisted the urge to tell her he was not a child and forced a grin onto his face instead, refusing to rise to her grumpiness. "I remember, Boss. Besides—" he swung up into the saddle. "As I said before. I don't have a problem with booze or drugs. Not all addictions are to substances."

Theo could see how badly Jazz wanted to ask what he meant. She'd always been curious, and with the perspective that came with years, Theo could see how knowledge helped her feel in control. Something she'd had very little of in her life.

"I'll tell you," he offered. "One day, when the time is right if you want me to. But I promise you I'll be back and ready to work tomorrow morning. I know I messed up that first day, but it won't happen again. I've been good, haven't I?"

Jazz stared at him with her bottomless eyes for an uncomfortable moment, then nodded, returning to her horse.

"Whatever, Bridger. I'm not your keeper. I have a booth booked for the market on Sunday; I'd like help."

Theo bit back a retort and tugged David around, guiding him out of the corral. "Yes, Boss." Checking fence lines was on the docket for the day, and making sure the herd grazing out in the farthest pastures was fairing well. Jazz rented those fields to local ranchers, and they paid a premium to have her watch their cattle. It was one of the small ways she brought in money. Theo wondered why she didn't raise beef like many other farmers in the area did, but he didn't ask. He suspected it might have something to do with the tender nature of the heart she kept so closely barricaded.

Cactus indeed.

As they clopped out of the barnyard, Theo was excited for the ride and for Jazz's company, grumpy or not, on a beautiful late spring day.

<hr />

Theo's hands were shaking when he opened the Jamieson Creek city hall door that afternoon. He was being ridiculous; he chided himself. Why the hell was he so nervous? Pulling the sheaf of papers he'd taken from Jazz's truck out of his back pocket, Theo approached the desk. He'd packed each dollar he made in tips and gig fees and several thousand from his savings account into an envelope; the chunk of money he inherited from his father had been festering there. Theo wasn't using it at the moment, and though he knew he needed to figure out his next steps once his time at the ranch was up, he wasn't ready to think about it yet. There was also a sort of satisfaction in knowing how much his father would have hated him putting the money toward helping someone else. The amount he had wouldn't cover all that Jazz owed, but it would be enough for her to be secure for a while until she could figure things out. She would figure things out. Theo had no doubt about that.

An older man, glossy freckled pate shining in the fluorescent overhead lights, looked up and gave Theo a frazzled smile.

"Good morning. Can I help you?"

"Yes." Theo set the bills down on the scarred desktop and smoothed a hand over them before pushing them across. "I want to pay these."

The man stood, shoving the spectacles that dangled from his neck by a chain onto his nose. He riffled through the pages, then looked at Theo. "These are for the Joyce place?"

"Sunrise Ranch, yes. Jasmine sent me in to pay them." The lie rolled off Theo's tongue, despite his belief it was not the man's business. He was getting his money and the how and why of it should be of no consequence.

"I called Ms. Joyce about an hour ago, and she didn't seem inclined to pay anytime soon."

"She... had a few good days," Theo said, then fought back a wince.

Good days of what? Selling Goliath's semen?

The man's ruddy face creased around the eyes as he studied Theo momentarily. It seemed he was about to speak, but then he shrugged and went back to typing on his ancient keyboard. "The back taxes for the last four years." He glanced over the rim of his glasses. "Total is twenty thousand five hundred and five dollars." He clicked a few more times as Theo took the envelope of cash he clutched in his sweaty palm and began counting.

"Tell you what," he said. "I'll round it to an even twenty-thousand-five hundred for you."

"Oh, thank you." Theo struggled to keep any traces of sarcasm from his voice. The man genuinely looked pleased with himself.

Once he finished at City Hall, Theo stepped back out in the late spring sun. He didn't know whether to laugh or splatter his lunch across the sidewalk. Jazz was going to kill him if she found out what he'd done. But there was no way in hell he could ever let her lose her ranch. Jazz had lost enough in her life. As much as he hoped they could start fresh, form a new bond, a new relationship now that they'd laid the past to rest, Theo knew there were no guarantees. Knowing her home was safe would help him sleep at night, whether she was furious with him or not.

Chapter Twenty-Seven

JASMINE

"**T**HIS IS THE THIRD Friday night in a row Theo has left the ranch and gone somewhere mysterious," Jazz said, fighting the urge to drop her head onto Valley's white dining table and cry.

"Mysterious, hey," Valley said with a soft snort. "In Jamieson Creek?"

"Who knows if he's here? He could be anywhere."

"This seems to bother you an awful lot considering you 'don't care about Theo Bridger.'" Valley narrowed her eyes at Jazz before swiping an invisible crumb off the table's edge.

Jazz felt the first flickering of jealousy kindle in her belly. *Had he met someone?*

How would he have had time? She couldn't see how it would be possible, but what other explanation was there for his disappearing into the wee hours on the weekends? *He's probably sick of spending so much time with you.*

"You look like you're going to shit yourself," Valley said. "Tell me what you're thinking."

"Maybe he found a girlfriend—"

The buzz of her phone interrupted her. Yanking it from her pocket, Jazz saw Ed's name on the screen. She stabbed at the answer button. "What!"

"Jasmine, you can not keep dodging my calls." Ed's deep voice reverberated down the phone connection.

"I don't have the money." The near break in her voice alarmed Jazz. There was no fucking way she would cry on the phone with Ed Hamilton. She'd die before she allowed that. "Goodbye, Ed." She could hear the squeak of his faraway protests as she ended the call.

Valley chewed her lip and was studying Jazz when she risked a glance up. With one manicured nail, she reached out and tapped the table between their two coffee cups. "I've been thinking."

"That's ominous," Jazz said, narrowing her eyes. She hoped that by making a joke out of it, she could shift Valley's serious tone. Her best friend was having none of it.

"Shut it," Valley snapped. "Joan and I talked, and my practice is going well; the house is almost paid off. We want—"

"Nope. No way. No." Jazz pushed back in her chair, ready to flee if it came down to it. She knew exactly where Valley was going. "I'm not taking money from you guys."

The muscles in Valley's jaw clenched, but she kept her voice calm. "We have everything we want, Jazz. We have a home, a business, and a beautiful family. What I want now is to make sure my best friend doesn't lose what means the most to her in the world."

Tears burned the backs of Jazz's eyes, but she willed them away. "I can't," she whispered. "I can't take money from you guys." Her dad had borrowed money from every friend he'd ever made. There had been three people at his funeral. Jazz, the pastor, and Patty. She was thankful every day that none of them had come after her to try to get what they were owed.

"It would be a loan," Valley rushed on as if she'd spotted some kink in Jazz's armour to exploit and was launching her attack. "You could pay us back when you were able."

"I can't pay the bank, and they have the power to take my house," Jazz hissed, fighting to keep her voice low. "How the hell would I ever pay you guys back? What if I never could?"

"There'd be no rush. It could be years from now. I don't care, Jazz."

"So what, there would be this big *thing* between us whenever I saw you? I care! I could never have fun and enjoy our friendship V. I've already lost Blair. I can't lose you too. You mean more to me than money or the ranch—"

Fuck, fuck, fuck, she was going to cry.

Valley went still. "What do you mean you lost Blair?"

The dam broke, and the tears brimmed before spilling over her cheeks. Jazz swiped them away. "I sent him away," she wailed. "I told him he shouldn't come around anymore until he only has platonic feelings for me."

Valley lifted a hand, pressing two fingers against the centre of her forehead. "You sent him away? That makes it sound like he was a dog you didn't want anymore, Jasmine. What the fuck?"

"He needed to stop spending so much time with me. He wasn't moving on. I was worried I was leading him on." Jazz's voice broke, and she swallowed. She *had* been leading him on, hadn't she? She'd never admitted to Valley that she'd called

Blair over the night Theo turned her down. Shame squelched in her gut. She missed Blair's teasing presence lighting the mood at the ranch. He was such a constant in her life that the last couple of weeks had held a distinct Blair-shaped void.

"That's not your choice to make." Valley sounded genuinely angry.

Jazz looked at her, surprised. "He agreed with me!"

"Of course he did! Has he ever disagreed with you about anything?"

"What's that supposed to mean?"

Valley's chin jutted forward, her eyes flashing. Jazz had seen her friend mad plenty of times, but it had been years since Valley's ire was directed at her.

"It means," Valley ground out through her clenched jaw. "You would have bullied him into seeing your way, even if he disagreed. It means, *Jasmine,* that sometimes it's easier to agree with you than to stand up to you."

Jazz flinched, each word stinging as sharp as a slap. "That's not true," she whispered. She reached for her anger, for a rage that would bolster her and protect her, but all she found was a chasm of hurt and sadness.

"Blair loves you, and you pushed him away. Theo loves you, but you refuse to acknowledge it. I love you, for fuck sake, and you won't even entertain the idea of allowing me to help you. You won't let anyone past that goddamn wall you've built around yourself."

"Because I know better!" The words tore out of Jazz with more vitriol than she'd intended. There it was—a surge of incandescent fury. At last, it rose up, and she darted to hide behind it. "I know what letting people get close to you means. It means heartbreak, betrayed trust and loneliness."

"That's not what letting people in gets you, Jazz. That's what having a shitty parent gets you. It leaves scars. Even when you don't realize it, some wounds fester and refuse to heal without help. Look at you—" Valley waved her hand back and forth in Jazz's direction. "I have offered, begged, cajoled! I'm a licenced therapist, and you still don't let me help you. If I was a physician and you were bleeding out, would you refuse my help, too?"

"No, of course not. I—"

Valley didn't allow her to finish. "Theo explained to you what happened. And sure, maybe he didn't handle things the way he should have, but he was young and under the influence of a controlling narcissistic authority figure. Someone like that can be nearly impossible to disobey. Then, when he saw you were married, he thought you were happy and left you to live your life. I know what his leaving did to you, Jazz. I *know*. I was there. But that pain didn't happen because you allowed yourself to love. It happened because there are shitty people in the world, and shitty things happen."

"Yes, it did!" Jazz yelled. She couldn't seem to keep her voice steady. "It did because if I'd never loved him, it wouldn't have hurt when he left. It wouldn't have almost killed me."

"And what about the baby?" Valley said. "You've refused to talk about that night for fifteen years. You don't have to carry the pain alone."

Jazz shook her head so hard her braid whipped around and slashed her cheek. "No. It's in the past. Why do you always have to bring this up?"

"Silence does not erase the pain; it just means you bear it alone."

"I don't need to relive it. I don't *want* to. I'm over it."

"And what if you have another baby?" Valley's voice dropped low, and she reached out, snagging Jazz's hand and refusing to release it even when she struggled to yank it away. "What if you have another baby, born healthy and whole? Are you going to refuse to love it, knowing there is always a chance that something could happen to it?"

Jazz swallowed a sob. She'd never allowed herself to think about having more children. Not since the night the nurses took away the blanket-wrapped bundle and never brought him back. The thought sent terror rushing through her.

"Life has no guarantees, sweetheart." Valley leaned across the table, still holding Jazz's hand, refusing to allow her to pull her gaze away. "You can't deny yourself joy because pain may accompany it. There's always a push and pull, a balance. That's life, baby girl. You and I both know it isn't pretty. We have to seize the joy where we can."

Hanging her head, Jazz swallowed back the tears that seemed to spring from an endless well. "I'm so scared," she finally choked out. "I'm scared of what will happen with the ranch. I wish... I wish—" She couldn't finish the sentence, which was just as well. She wasn't truly sure what she wished for.

Valley jumped to her feet and came around the table. She held Jazz as she cried, and Jazz couldn't help but think this was twice now in as many months she'd allowed this to happen. Maybe Valley was right. Perhaps it was time to take down the wall. She didn't have to run a wrecking ball into the thing. Brick by brick would do. She could start by securing her home's future.

"I'll take the loan," she whispered against the familiar vanilla-sweet scent of Valley's hair. "But only if you'll give me some therapy sessions."

Valley barked out a laugh. "Not sure how much of a deal that is for me, but I'll take it." Chuckling, she pressed a kiss to the side of Jazz's head. "We're going to city hall in the morning, and tonight, you're coming to Patty's with me."

"Ed Hamilton will be ecstatic to take my number off speed dial," Jazz muttered, using the hem of her shirt to scrub her cheeks. "I don't want to go to Patty's. I want to make a blanket fort on my bed and hide from the world."

Valley patted her cheek. "Too bad. I'm the shrink, and I say we're going out. Buck up, princess."

Jazz flopped her head forward and groaned. She supposed she was going out whether she liked it or not.

Valley sipped from her frosty glass of Riesling while staring at Jazz over the rim. Her sharp green eyes narrowed, causing a tremor of unease to slither down Jazz's spine. She knew that look all too well. It was the second time she was facing down

Valentina Perrera in twelve hours, and she wasn't sure how she should feel.

"Why are you giving me your shrink face?" Jazz asked.

"I was wondering something," Valley said, lowering her glass and spinning it between her long, black-tipped fingers. The gesture seemed idle, as Valley meant it to, but Jazz knew her friend. She was about to pounce. All Jazz could hope was she had the wherewithal to fight her off.

"A question that has sparked many a debate," Jazz muttered.

Valley flapped a hand, emitting a derisive noise that resembled a leaking tire. "It's only that I'm curious—" she paused a beat, eyes laser-sharp, preparing to catch and dissect any flicker of reaction on Jazz's face, "to see how long you're going to deny having feelings for Theo."

Jazz curled her toes against the insoles of her boots, fighting to keep her face placid. "I'm not denying that because it's ridiculous. Theo is an old friend. End of story."

Valley settled back in her chair, eyes still narrowed. "Alright, *Jasmine.*"

"Alright, *Valentina.*"

"I have something to show you. Shouldn't be a big deal, considering your non-existent feelings." With that ominous proclamation, Valley slammed her ten-dollar glass of wine like Crown Royal in a cornfield, stood, and tossed a fifty onto the sticky tabletop.

Jazz blinked at her and then the money before she downed the rest of her beer with a sigh that rose from the weary depths of her soul. She had the sense she was going to need liquid courage. And what the hell was with everyone throwing around fifty-dollar bills? Had she ever had a spare fifty to chuck around?

Scarcely waiting for Jazz to get her feet under her, Valley drug her across the restaurant. It was the kind of establishment that had a separate bar area, and as they slipped down the hall, the volume levels rose.

"What the fuck?" Jazz muttered as they stepped through the old saloon-style doors. The bar section was packed. People milled and crowded in as tight as cattle in an auction yard. "What is going on?"

Jazz allowed Valley to haul her forward into the fray. Valley, a tiny, blonde force to be reckoned with, maneuvered them through the crowd with a combination of manners, brute strength, feminine wiles, and sheer force of will. When Valley grabbed her by the shoulders and shoved her forward, Jazz saw him, and every nerve in her body snapped to attention. Theo sat on the stage, a boyish grin that caused his scar to tug slightly on his eye decorated his face, the guitar tight to his chest.

Chapter Twenty-Eight

THEO

L IGHTS WERE FLICKERING TO life along Main Street as Theo parked outside Patty's and killed the truck's engine. He sat in the dim cabin for a moment, rolling his shoulders and attempting to draw deep breaths. He still hadn't relaxed after the stress of going to city hall. Now, the pounding of his heart ratcheted up to join the orchestra of ticking engines, pub crowds, and barking dogs. The pub looked busy, which did nothing to ease Theo's anxiety. It was a Friday night; cars filled the small lot and stretched down the tree-lined street.

Theo swallowed against the knot of trepidation in his throat. He forced it down. Summoning instead the memory of performing at the fair and how good it had felt to lose himself in the music. He thought of the response the video had received and the smiles on the couple's faces as they danced. *He* had brought them that joy... well, him and Chris Stapelton.

A giddy bubble of excitement rose in his chest, replacing the nerves. Some people may have even come here tonight *because* he was playing. Theo pushed open the truck door. He could do this. He was pretty sure it was what he'd been born to do.

Theo strummed the guitar, checking the tuning, then adjusted the mic stand before finally allowing himself to look up at the crowd. The place was a zoo, so full that the servers struggled to get to their tables.

What the hell was this?

He couldn't decide if it was a dream come true or a nightmare.

After Theo had played at Patty's twice, the old man approached him with the name of a friend who wanted to hire him for a gig. Theo played at Crossroads in Kelsie, and when Patty called him wanting him back that weekend, he'd readily agreed. He knew people enjoyed his music and voice, but he'd never expected a turnout of this magnitude. It had to do with the video Jazz had shown him. She'd mentioned a few times it had gone viral. Theo hadn't grasped what that meant, but now he was beginning to understand. People were starting to know his name and who he was... they'd come here to see *him*.

Swallowing a wave of nausea, Theo rolled his shoulders and settled the guitar onto his thigh. Silence rolled through the room as people noticed he was ready. Tipping his head forward, Theo spoke into the mic, fighting to keep his voice from shaking.

"Thanks for coming. I'm Theo Bridger, and I hope you enjoy the show." How surreal it felt to say *the show*. Was that what he was doing? Putting on a show? He guessed so. Theo wanted to drop his pick and pinch himself. A few whoops went up around the room as he strummed the opening chords to a Tragically Hip classic.

When he began to sing, the queasy rolling in his stomach ebbed. His voice emerged strong, and the hundred faces blurred, becoming insignificant. All that existed was the music, the heady joy of allowing it to boil out of him. The press of metal strings bit the pads of his fingers, grounding him with each vibrating cord.

Theo played song after song until his hands cramped, and his throat was so dry that his voice began to break. He mostly stuck to covers, though he sprinkled in a few he'd written. When he saw a few people singing along to his original songs, which he'd only been playing publicly in the last month, he blinked back tears.

When Theo set down his guitar, at last, the crowd groaned in disappointment. Theo grinned so hard he worried his face might rip. Leaning forward into the mic, he thanked everyone again and promised to return.

As people filed out of the bar or moved off to sit at tables, join friends, and order drinks, Theo noticed the guitar case to his left was full of tips.

"You're amazing," a server slipped beside him, passing him a huge glass of water, which Theo accepted with relief. She flashed him a dimpled grin. "I kept forgetting I was working and stopping to watch."

"Thanks," Theo mopped sweat from his brow with the hem of his shirt, noting how the girl's blue eyes flashed down to his exposed stomach. He quickly dropped his shirt back into place. She was pretty but looked barely old enough to be serving liquor.

"I'd better clean up," Theo said, jerking a thumb at the few things he'd left on stage. "Thanks again."

She took the water glass from him, disappointment flickering across her face, but she smiled, squeezing his arm with her free hand before heading back into the grey.

"So, what... you have groupies now?" The acerbic tone was tinged with amusement.

Theo spun at the familiar voice, heart taking a free dive into his stomach. "Jazz, what are you doing here?"

Valley shouldered her way up beside Jazz and grinned at him. "Well, a little birdy told me you were playing tonight, and I know my girl here has no clue what's happening in the world. Thought I would bring her out to the big city for the evening." There was a glint in the woman's eyes, and Theo wasn't sure if she was enjoying herself or was prepared to drop poison into his next drink.

"Why didn't you tell me you were doing this?" Jazz asked. The words were light, but there was a twinge of hurt in them.

"I... I don't know," Theo said stupidly. "I guess at first I was embarrassed. I didn't want to tell you and then have you come and be the only person who showed up. When it escalated, I... thought it was a fluke, I guess?" He winced, aware of how vague and wishy-washy his answer was. He planned to use the tips he was making to pay down her debts on the ranch, but how likely was it that she would guess that simply by knowing he was playing a few gigs?

Jazz shrugged. "Not a big deal."

There was something, though, in her posture, in how she stated it, that made Theo think it was more so than she was letting on. He would have to talk to her about it if he got the chance.

"You guys want to have a drink?" he asked, gesturing to where a small table had opened up.

"Sure, you two go sit, I'll grab them." Valley gave them a shove toward the table while they both protested. "My treat! We're celebrating your stardom." She flashed Theo a grin as she made her way toward the bar.

"Just sit," Jazz said. "I learned many years ago there was no point in arguing with that woman. She will literally do anything to be right and/or get her own way."

"Sounds like there are probably some stories there," Theo said, propping his guitar case against the wall behind them before slipping into the seat opposite Jazz.

"For sure. Though you're bound to collect a few of those after twenty years of friendship, I suppose, aren't you?"

Theo twisted his lips, forcing himself to meet her eyes. "I don't know. Besides my family, you're the only person I've come close to knowing that long."

"You don't talk to anyone from school? Or the army?"

"Well, there's my friend Dane, who I served with, but I only met him—" Theo paused, thinking, "Seven-ish years ago. He's probably the closest thing to a 'best friend' I have."

"How often do you talk to him?" Jazz asked. "It must be nice to have someone who has shared similar experiences with you."

"Once a month or so. He lives in Toronto, so it's a long jaunt for a visit. But we've gotten together a couple of times. He was in the Vancouver area for work. I went that way for a basketball game... that sort of thing."

"You're a big enough Raptors fan to fly to Toronto?" Jazz asked skeptically.

"No, but I wanted the experience and needed an escape. It wasn't long after my dad died."

Jazz chewed at her bottom lip. "I see."

"Here we go," Valley appeared, expertly balancing three glasses. "Another disgusting IPA for you—" she slid the beer in front of Jazz. "And I got you a lager because I have no idea what men like, and that seemed a safe bet."

"How very sexist of you, thanks." Theo smiled, and Valley threw him a wink.

"What are you guys talking about?" Valley asked, giving Jazz a look that, to Theo, an outsider, seemed uncomfortably long.

Jazz stared right back. "About how long I've been putting up with your crap," she said mildly before sipping her drink.

"I see." Valley settled back, swirling her wine around her glass. "Amazing how neither of us has aged in all that time."

Theo sipped his drink, relishing the slow creep of warmth it brought to his limbs, and listened as the women bantered. How different would it be if he'd never left? Would he have stories to share about the two of them? Would he have a friend who'd weathered life's storms come and join them as well? Theo knew there was no point in his musings, but he fell into the trap of doing so all the same. The past didn't hold those things for him, but maybe if he was careful and got things right this time, the future would.

"Jazz, will you dance with me?"

Valley had left the table to use the washroom, and Theo hadn't missed the flash of longing that moved across Jazz's face when an old Johnny Cash song started to play. She looked at him, dark eyes wide and unsure. Theo couldn't help but think of the last time they'd been in almost this same situation. The revelations that came after would never leave him. He was so surprised when she nodded in consent that Theo realized he hadn't expected her to say yes.

Grinning, he stood and pulled her up, leading them off across the dance floor. Jazz's laugh rose over the notes of the song, and Theo wanted to languish in their music forever. They were both breathless and grinning foolishly by the time the song finished. Theo tightened his arms around her, hoping she would stay, praying she would ask to dance again. But she pushed off gently.

"I should get back. I don't want to leave V sitting there alone."

Theo glanced up. Valley was talking to a group of people, seemingly engaged in conversation. He would almost have believed she hadn't noticed them dancing, but Valley caught his gaze and winked as he turned to lead Jazz off the floor.

Chapter Twenty-Nine

JASMINE

J AZZ'S HEAD BUZZED THE exact right amount when she and Valley left Patty's. The plan was to walk the few blocks to Valley's, where Jazz had left her car, and wait until the booze wore off or the sun rose, whichever happened first.

They were stepping onto the sidewalk when Theo's voice rose above the noise from the still raucous bar.

"Jazz!"

Jazz turned, waiting as Theo jogged toward them, admiring how his thighs bunched beneath the worn denim of his jeans. Shit, maybe she was drunker than she thought.

"What's up?" she asked, seizing the end of her hair and tugging, hoping the sting of pain in her scalp would wake her good sense.

"You're not driving, right?"

Jazz narrowed her eyes. "No, I am not driving."

Theo lifted both hands defensively in front of himself. "I didn't mean for that to sound insulting. I wanted to make sure. Can I give you a ride home?" He glanced over his shoulder at the bar. People were trickling out of the doors and heading their separate ways. Laughter and singing punctuated the warm evening air. A group of young men clapped Theo on the shoulder as they left, complimenting his performance.

"Oh, grab a ride," Valley said, giving Jazz a little shove in Theo's direction. "You know you never sleep well on my couch."

Damn the woman. Could she never keep her mouth shut?

Jazz clenched her jaw, resisting the urge to smack her friend. Valley was right, but Jazz didn't need to be pushed in Theo's direction at every turn. She was conflicted enough about their situation.

"Alright," she finally consented. "I'll jump in with you." She really did want to be home. She felt worn thin from the emotions of the day.

"Meet me at the truck. I'll be right back." Theo spun and jogged back to the bar. And fucking hell, he looked good. Jazz watched his ass until it disappeared inside.

"He's bossy. I like it," Valley said, grinning, digging one elbow into Jazz's ribs. "I bet he'll tell you you're a good girl."

"Fuck off."

"You know what they say, Jasmine... fuck on, you'll get better results." Valley released a maniacal cackle that echoed through the night air.

Jazz couldn't help the snort that ripped out of her. "Pretty sure no one has said that since high school in the early 2000s."

"Wisdom is timeless."

"Shouldn't you be getting home?" Jazz gave Valley a shove, turning her in the direction she needed to go. "Off you go, boozer."

Valley stumbled over her feet but started off in the right direction. "Fine, fine. I'm going."

Crossing her arms with a sigh, Jazz watched Valley walk away. She swayed slightly and began to loudly sing an off-key Shania Twain song. Jazz wondered if she should have helped her home. Then, at the flash of light that illuminated her profile with an eerie glow, Jazz realized Valley was looking down at her phone screen.

"Don't text and walk!" she yelled. Valley lifted a particular finger high in the air and continued.

Jazz walked to Theo's truck, but when she tried the door, it didn't open.

"Not a local, yet," she muttered. Going to the back, she opened the tailgate and hopped up. Laying back with her legs dangling over the edge and arms hooked behind her head, Jazz stared up at the expanse of star-strewn sky.

Why hadn't Theo told her he was performing here? She would have thought he wouldn't be shy about it after the big deal she had made with his win at the talent show.

Maybe he didn't want you here. A mean little voice chimed from the recess of her brain.

She was drifting, lost in thought, the sprawl of stars and an alcoholic buzz when a hand touched her knee. Jazz screamed, bolted upwards, and kicked her legs out.

"Oof." Theo's long body slumped forward with a grunt. "Christ, woman, I said your name twice!" The words were barely more than a drawn-out hiss of pain.

"Fuck." Jazz jumped off the tailgate and grabbed Theo's arm. Doubled over, he clutched the last place any man wanted to be kicked—especially with a pair of steel-tipped riding boots.

"Are you alright?" Jazz struggled to help steady him, cupping her free hand around his cheek.

Eyes squeezed shut, Theo merely grunted in acknowledgment of her questions.

"I'm so sorry," Jazz said, pushing the hair off his brow. It felt sweaty. "You scared me."

"Noticed," Theo wheezed. "Need... sit... down."

He sank onto the pavement right where he stood. Jazz kept hold of his elbow, steadying him as best she could before lowering herself to the ground beside him.

Groaning, Theo leaned his head against Jazz's shoulder. She tried to ignore the spike of affection that shot through the guilt she felt, but it glinted too brightly. Her past feelings for Theo and the emotions rising in her now were swirling together like cream into coffee, blending until they were indiscernible from each other.

"Are you going to be able to drive?" she whispered after a few moments. Without her giving them consent, her fingers rose, brushing through the strands of dark hair that had fallen across his brow. Theo groaned and pressed his face into her hand, his breath tickling the overheated skin of her palm.

"Eventually," he whispered without opening his eyes. "It wasn't a straight shot, thank God."

"You were amazing in there," she said, trying to distract him. "You could make something of this if you wanted."

"Thanks." It was all he said, and Jazz wondered how he was feeling about his sudden fame, small though it may be.

"You've been doing this for a while now?"

He nodded.

"Why didn't you tell me?"

He remained quiet for so long that Jazz thought he wouldn't answer or that he hadn't heard her question. Did getting kicked in the junk affect a man's hearing?

"I'm not sure, to be honest. I wanted... to make sure I could do it before telling you." Even in the glow from the street lamp, Jazz could see the colour stain his cheeks. "I suppose I wanted to impress you," he said finally.

It was nearly an hour before they made it back to the ranch. Whatever buzz Jazz enjoyed when they left Patty's was long gone, and Theo had been quiet on the drive.

"I'm sorry about your balls," Jazz said as they entered the house.

"They'll forgive you," Theo said. "Eventually."

When he cast her a rare grin over his shoulder, Jazz knew he was feeling better.

"I don't do well with being scared," she murmured, studying her feet. One toe peaked out of a hole in her left sock. "I almost broke Blair's nose the last time he snuck up on me."

"I want to say, once more, for the record, I did not sneak up on you. I have always made it a habit not to surprise women in parking lots at night." Theo leaned back against the entryway that separated the main hall from the kitchen. His long, strong body nearly filled the space. "What's Blair up to, anyway? I haven't seen him in a few days."

Tears instantly filled Jazz's eyes. She hadn't texted him after her fight with Valley. She still wasn't sure what the right path was, but she knew she missed him. "We had a bit of a thing. He's staying away for a while," she said finally. Her voice strained around the words. She hoped Theo wouldn't notice, but, of course, he did.

"You guys fought?"

"Not really? No. It's a long story." Damn it. She would not cry. Not again.

Theo was studying her, his teeth methodically working at the swell of his bottom lip as he thought. "The day you stayed in bed. That's when it was, right?"

Jazz nodded, then sniffed, nodded again. She would not cry about this, damn it.

Without another word, Theo stepped forward and wrapped his arms around her. It was the only permission she needed to break.

Jazz only took a few minutes to battle her tears back under control, but even after they stopped flowing, she didn't release her hold on Theo's waist. His heartbeat beneath her cheek was a rhythmic serenade that she wasn't ready to stop listening to. His fingers drew spirals against her back, burning a hypnotic path through the thin cotton of her shirt.

Finally, Jazz tipped her face up. Theo's mouth was so close. All it would take was a shift, her pushing up onto the balls of her feet, and she could taste him again. Lose herself in him, in the magic they created when they came together.

"Jazz," Theo breathed the word, soft as a prayer. "We shouldn't."

"I want to," she whispered. Her nipples pebbled against his chest, and she pushed closer. "I want to so fucking badly, and I'm tired of wanting what I can't have."

Theo groaned, resting his forehead against hers. "I didn't think I'd be able to get hard for days after what happened, but apparently, he will do anything for you."

A laugh tore out of Jazz. She couldn't help it. Theo raised his head and grinned. But when his eyes fell to her mouth, they both went still... silent. She wasn't sure who moved first, but with a tentative brush, they sampled each other.

A heady buzzing flooded Jazz's blood, and she threaded her arms around Theo's neck, drawing him down, deepening the kiss until he moaned into her mouth. The sound detonated pure need throughout her body.

"Come to my room," she ordered before forcing his mouth back to hers.

Theo stiffened against her, and Jazz was sure for a moment he would turn her down again. She wasn't above underhanded persuasion, however, and freeing one hand, she slid it down to cup the bulge pressing into her stomach.

"I'll be gentle," she promised in a whisper against his mouth.

Theo pressed his forehead against her neck, strands of hair dancing against her cheeks, caught in the gusts of his panting breath. Jazz resisted the urge to squirm under their tickling.

"You'll have to be," he said at last. "With my heart and my cock, please."

She drew back, eyes taking in his face. "If you'll be gentle with mine," she whispered.

One brow rose sardonically. "I know things have changed since we were together last, but..."

She leaned in and bit his lip before he could finish. Theo growled, his tongue darting past her lips to slip across hers, battling, tasting, teasing. A heavy pulsing had taken up residence between Jazz's thighs, and she pressed into him, seeking pressure and friction. She wanted to scream with the frustrating emptiness of her body.

"Take me upstairs," Theo growled into her mouth.

She was about to release him, ready to lead him to her room, when both his hands moved down her back, cupped her ass, and lifted. With a squeak, Jazz jumped, wrapping both her legs around his waist. "Hold on to me," Theo rasped against her ear.

"You're going to hurt your ba—" Her protest died at his first step when his erection pressed right against the ache between her thighs. With a hiss, Jazz buried her face in Theo's neck.

Theo was panting when he deposited Jazz in front of her bed. Jazz cast him a told-you-so look but couldn't maintain the facade when he seized the front of her shirt and tugged. Then, they were kissing again, and Jazz forgot about taunting him, at least not verbally.

"Pants off," she growled against his mouth as her fingers worked his belt buckle free, shoving the jeans off his hips. Dropping to her knees before him, she tugged at the denim.

"Fuck. Jasmine, wait." Theo's trembling hands tried to stop her, but when she pressed a kiss to the bulge of him through the fabric of his boxer briefs, they stilled, fisting in her shirt instead.

"Jazz," he ground out. "There's something... I need to tell you—" his voice fell away. Her fingers had found the scars—a grid of tiny ridges across the soft skin of his thighs. Frowning, Jazz leaned back on her heels, pushing his pants further down.

"Theo," she breathed. Hair-thin scars, all in varying shades of white and pink, created a cross-hatch pattern on his thighs. Jazz tore her gaze away and looked up at Theo. His head hung forward, eyes squeezed closed.

"I should have told you before you saw." His voice was quiet but steady.

"What..." Jazz trailed off. Then, a memory of his voice rose from her subconscious:

Not all addictions are to substances.

"I never told you. It started when I was a teen, and it got worse when my dad took me away. It was the last straw. I felt so trapped, and I was so impotently angry with no outlet. It felt as though I had no way to dispel it."

"We had sex that second summer. I never saw any scars," Jazz whispered.

"I was careful. I didn't want you to think... I don't know. There were so many things I didn't want you to think. *I* barely knew what to think." Theo drew a shaky breath, rolling his shoulders back as if trying to push off a weight.

Reaching down, he took Jazz by the arms and pulled her to her feet. "The anger at him blew me up, stretched my skin so tight I thought I would explode. This—" he waved a hand down at himself, "cracked me open so there was somewhere for the emotions to leak out."

Jazz stared up at him until he forced his eyes to hers. She could see he wanted to look away, fighting shame and grief. She needed him to know she wouldn't allow him to hide. He didn't need to hide ever again, and especially not from her.

"I cried once in front of him after he dragged me out of the play, the one I told you and Betty about. I showed him weakness, and he hit me. He slapped me right across the face and told me to be a man. I stood there, cheek burning, and I wanted to kill him. I saw it all playing out in my mind. Once he left me alone, I went into the bathroom. I stared at my face for a long time. I resemble him in looks. I always have, more so than my brothers. And it made me sick."

Theo met her eyes, a tempest of emotion roiling in the grey depths of his gaze, but he held the line of their connection steady. "I could see the individual marks of his fingers on my skin as though he branded me. I wanted to kill him," he said again. "And I smashed my fist into the mirror when I could no longer stand to look at myself."

Jazz gasped before she could stop herself. "Were you hurt?"

Theo nodded. "Cut my hand badly." He held up his right hand, showing her a web of scar tissue branching across the back. She remembered it, remembered asking about the pink marks, which were still fresh during the second summer. He'd distracted her, kissing her, maybe. The memory was fuzzy, lost amongst many more potent ones.

"I couldn't stop staring at the blood pooling in the sink. I took one of the shards of glass and pressed it against the inside of my wrists. To this day, I can't explain why. It was like watching someone else do it. I wondered if he'd even care if I was gone. Or if he'd be glad, but I didn't... I didn't want to kill myself. Then my mom banged on the door, yelling, 'Are you okay?' and I jumped so hard I cut right into my arm. It was so stupid, but there was this sense of easing when it happened.

My mom was banging and banging, freaking out. She'd heard the glass break. Finally, Oliver grabbed something to open the door with. It was one where you could push something into the hole to disengage the lock. When she saw me standing there, blood dripping off my hand, she shrieked. And I'm not exaggerating when I say that sound will haunt me forever. I couldn't believe I didn't think of her. Consider how she would feel. I was so caught up in the thought of punishing my dad with my pain that I forgot about the one person who actually loved me unconditionally."

"Theo." It was all Jazz could get out before further words failed her. Her throat crushed the rest in their tracks. Instead, she ran her hands over his cheeks and brow, brushing dark hair back from his eyes. His eyes slid closed, and his head bowed into her touch. Jazz took one of his hands in hers and guided him to the bed. She squatted before him when he sat, pulling the tangle of denim away and freeing him. Then, she crawled into the bed, pulled him down beside her and said, "Then what happened?"

Theo threaded their fingers together, studying the knot as he spoke. "I made up some bullshit story, but my mom didn't believe me. I needed a lot of stitches. She took me to the hospital and insisted I get a referral to a psychologist for assessment." He paused, swallowing audibly, and his voice came out deep and rough when he spoke. "She thought I was trying to kill myself."

The pad of his thumb worried at the ridges of callouses along Jazz's palms. "The doctors tried to brush her off. They said boys had accidents, and they were sure it wasn't a big deal. I told her I wasn't suicidal, but she refused to take no for an answer. She threatened to lodge a formal complaint if they wouldn't refer me. I remember thinking, why couldn't she stand up to *him*? Why couldn't she be the champion I needed? But I knew, even then, it was different. My dad controlled her, too."

They lay in silence, their mingling heartbeats and breath the only sounds. Jazz pressed a kiss to Theo's shoulder, and he pulled in a gulp of air as if she'd woken him from a trance.

"The therapy helped," he went on. "Then I spent my first summer here and found out who I was when I was away from my family. I met you..." His fingers tightened, and he brought their joined hands to his lips. "This may sound cheesy, but I think I understood what it was to be really and truly happy that first summer."

"And you didn't have to eat any Trolls to do it," Jazz whispered.

There was a beat of confused silence, and then Theo barked out a laugh. "Pardon?"

Jazz pressed her smile into his skin. "I'll explain later. Better yet, I'll get Valley's kids to explain it."

"You always were a weirdo," he said, one side of his mouth quirking up and his voice imbued with affection.

Jazz shrugged and nestled closer against him.

"Tell me all of it," she said. "All of it. Fill in the blanks for me."

And he did. Theo told Jazz about the horrible pressure from his father and brothers to follow them into the military. He told her about Sophia and how the cold, precise cuts of the razor blade gave him something to focus on, something to feel besides the hot splatter of blood and brain across his face. Theo told Jazz how the therapy and medications helped. How it took time to find the right combination, but he was feeling the best he had in as long as he could remember, and though Theo still suffered nightmares, he hadn't put a blade against his skin in two years.

"And then my therapist told me about this ranch she'd heard of because she remembered me talking about Jamieson

Creek. She said it sounded like a great place to clear my head, figure out what I wanted to do next and start building the foundation for a second chance."

Chapter Thirty

THEO

A WARM WEIGHT WAS pinning his arm to the bed when Theo slowly rose to consciousness. Turning his head a fraction, he wanted to cry at the proof last night wasn't a dream. Jazz was curled against him, her back against his side, her cheek pillowed on his biceps, and her hair a river of ink spilling around them both.

They must have fallen asleep talking. Theo said a silent prayer that he hadn't had another nightmare and shattered their peace.

Careful not to disturb her, Theo rolled so his body spooned around hers. She smelled of vanilla, horses, and fucking happiness. They were both dressed in t-shirts and underwear still, and though he felt lighter after last night's confessions, Theo's body was steadily making its unhappiness with a halt in procedures known.

Theo slipped his free hand under the loose hem of Jazz's shirt, biting his lip when his fingertips met warm, silky skin. Finding the arch of her hipbone, Theo worshipped the smooth stretch below with grazing swirls. The calloused tips of his fingers raised goosebumps over Jazz's arms. He watched as they came to attention, the blonde fuzz that rose with them. He knew he could drown in this woman and not bother to struggle.

Jazz let out a throaty sigh, shifting beneath his hand, needing his touch lower, even in sleep. God help him. Her firm ass fit against his aching cock, pressing, and Theo couldn't stop the hiss that escaped through his clenched teeth. Like sensing the crackle of lighting in stormy air, he knew the moment Jazz came fully awake, though she didn't speak.

Theo continued drawing his swirls upon the canvas of her skin, only shifting his body enough to press his lips to the strong column of her neck. Jazz hummed low and husky in her throat. The sound made his erection jerk against her, and Jazz giggled. The laugh morphed into a gasp when Theo replaced his lips with a grazing of teeth.

Jazz's cool fingers found his, wrapping around them, and Theo's heart plummeted. Maybe she had changed her mind after last night. Maybe the sight of his scars... But she didn't stop him. She drew his hand forward, cinching their bodies closer and guiding his touch to the waistline of her panties.

Theo squeezed his eyes closed, sinking into the joy of their tandem breathing and the synchronized pounding of their hearts. All the tiny nuances, the flashes of *togetherness* he'd never slowed enough to appreciate when he was young.

"Theo—" Jazz's voice rasped, a single sliver of sound packed with desire, hesitation, and more. Theo didn't dare hope for more, not now, not yet.

"I'm scared to move," he whispered against the seashell swoop of her ear. "In case this is all another dream."

Jazz's answer was to pull him further, pressing their joined fingers past the barrier of elastic to the heat of her core beneath. Theo groaned into her shoulder, thumb seeking out the tiny bundle of nerves that would bring her at least a fraction of the ecstasy he longed to lavish on her.

"It's not a dream," Jazz whispered, her voice a stretched-out rasp of sound. "Now, make me come before I lose my mind."

Theo pressed his forehead to her shoulder, body shaking with laughter, even as he began to worship her with delving strokes. "Still bossy as ever," he breathed against skin damp from the mingling of his kisses and the sheen rising on Jazz's skin as she moaned.

"Some things don't change," Jazz rasped, her hips bucking into his touch, making Theo chuckle again. "Oh fuck, Theo."

His chest was beginning to ache with the pressure of his happiness, but he couldn't allow himself to overthink it. He was well on his way to falling back in love with Jasmine Reynolds, and that knowledge would be enough to scare him senseless. Instead, he applied himself to her demands.

Dipping low into her, he slicked the wet heat he discovered up to the top of her slit, swirling, pressing until she whimpered.

"Theo, fuck, please—" She was becoming incomprehensible with the rising tide of her orgasm. He could feel it building already in the tiny tremors rippling through her body.

Suddenly, she flipped in his arms, slamming her mouth to his as she fumbled at the waistband of his boxers. Theo grunted at the less-than-gentle contact on his over-eager, over-sensitive cock.

"I want, I want—" She was trying to push his boxer briefs down, but they were stuck on his hips. Theo seized her wrists, and she writhed against his grasp. Fuck she was strong. His adrenaline flared, his body kicking into a new level of desire. A base need to conquer and fuck.

"Jazz, wait," he growled. Please, for the sake of his dignity, don't let him shoot off in his underwear like a trigger-happy teen. Hell, that had never happened when they were teens, so the embarrassment would double.

"No," Jazz said, trying to twist away from him. "I don't want to wait."

"If you brush against me one more time with that wet little cun—"

Her searching lips stopped his words, and Theo growled into her mouth when her hand closed around him. "Jazz—"

"Fuck me," Jazz panted. "Right now."

"Not yet," Theo ground out before biting the swell of her bottom lip. "I've been waiting too long to feel you clench that tight pussy around me again. I'm not rushing it now."

"Theo!" Jazz's voice was dangerously close to a whine, and the sound of her being so frantic for him was nearly his undoing.

"Don't worry," he whispered, pressing kisses to the corners of her mouth. "I never said I wasn't going to make you come."

Chapter Thirty-One

JASMINE

J AZZ WAS GOING TO suffocate Theo and his beautiful, filthy mouth if he didn't give her what she wanted. He was still holding her wrists and continuing the delicious exploration of her mouth. Once in a while, he would punctuate the kisses with a slow roll of his hips, pushing the hard bulge against her aching core.

"Patience, sweetheart," he murmured, but Jazz didn't miss the trembling in his hands, the way his breathing ripped and tore through his lungs.

"There's time for patience later," Jazz growled.

Theo snorted against her neck, pulling back far enough that she could bear witness to his smile. It was a wonderful thing to see.

"Does that mean we get to do this again?" he asked. His tone was playful, but a flurry of hope swirled in his grey-blue eyes.

Jazz arched her body, bringing them against each other inch by inch. "You said you'd make me come."

"And I plan to, many times if you'll let me."

Tipping her head, she nipped at his jaw, the groan that escaped him making her dizzy. "Let's start with one," she whispered. Then she kissed him.

At last, the frantic clash of their mouths seemed to spur Theo on. He rolled, taking Jazz with him so that she straddled him. Her hips flexed, and her body, instantly recognizing the advantage of the position, began to rock. Delicious friction sent stars ricocheting through her vision, and she arched back, gasping. It would only take a minute to gain the release her body was screaming for.

Beneath her, Theo panted, his face a mask of tension as he battled for control. His strong fingers dug into her hips, sending plumes of delicious pain through her. "Move up. I want to taste you," he commanded.

Words eluded Jazz, but she nodded, steadying herself against the headboard as she moved up his body. She tried to hold her weight, but Theo seized her, pulling her down. The first glide of his tongue made her forget her worry about suffocating him. "Fuck," she choked. She had always loved having his mouth on her. It was how he had first made her come. Jazz let the memories merge with the present and wash over her in a wave of desire. She was so close. Three flicks of his tongue, and she was nearly there. How did he maintain this spell over her?

Theo stared up at her with a look so close to reverence it would have made Jazz uncomfortable, were she in any mind to pay attention. "Holy shit," she panted, seizing a fistful of his hair to brace herself. If it hurt, he gave no indication. Then he sucked, hard, right at the pinpoint of her body, and Jazz came apart.

"You're so beautiful," Theo said, his voice muffled a barely contained shred. "So fucking strong and sharp and wonderful." He steadied her, fingers kneading her ass as she swayed, cherishing the aftershocks. "I love watching you."

"Take. Off. The. Boxers," Jazz managed, her thighs still shaking.

"Are you sure? We can wait a few minutes if you—"

Jazz reached back, taking him in her hand and giving him a firm pump.

Theo grunted, then obliged, shoving his underwear down over his hips.

"I have an IUD," Jazz said, catching his eyes. "Are you—?"

"My last test was clear, and I haven't been with anyone for... Let's say a long time and leave it at that."

"Good." With one motion, Jazz shifted her hips back, positioned Theo against her and eased down. She was so wet from his mouth and her arousal that there was no resistance, only an immediate filling of her body, her heart; he was the puzzle piece she had lost far too long ago.

Theo's entire body went ridged as she took him inch by inch. The tendons in his neck strained as his jaw clenched. "Fuck. Oh fuck, Jazz."

"I agree," Jazz hissed. She'd missed him. For fifteen years, she'd built a wall so high around herself that she couldn't acknowledge how much she missed him. No one had so perfectly fit her or kindled the same fire inside her. Jazz often heard it was impossible to truly love someone at a young age. Life was supposed to be lived, but now she wondered if Theo Bridger had been *it* all along.

Theo began to rock as if he were reading her mind, whispering to her as their bodies fell into an old, familiar rhythm. "I missed you, Jasmine. I missed you. I've felt whole these last few months here with you."

Jazz wanted to stop the flow of words. Wanted to tell him it was all too much for her. What he was doing to her body was already overwhelming. She didn't need the swelling ache rising in her chest as well. Tears burned the surface of her eyes, so Jazz squeezed them shut, glad for the brief reprieve from the sight of his face. He looked too much like the boy he'd been: vulnerable, pleasure-soaked, and completely besotted.

Theo's hips bucked, knocking away the scrambling in Jazz's mind and leaving only sensation. At her cry, he took the hint and repeated the motion, driving himself right into the core of her pleasure.

Jazz murmured a string of expletives, her movements becoming frantic. She was so close. Then, Theo took one hand off her hips, slipped it around her, and pressed his thumb directly where she needed it most.

"Fuck!" Jazz threw back her head, coming undone again, more violently than she could ever remember doing. The waves crashed through her again and again. It wasn't until she sank forward against Theo's chest, wholly spent, that he allowed himself to follow her over the cliff with a guttural cry.

What the hell was she supposed to do now?

Jazz's body was a pleasant thrum of pain and remembered pleasure. She lay still, not wanting to disturb Theo. They'd fallen back to sleep in each other's arms, and though she knew one or both of them needed to rise and tend to chores, she couldn't quite bear to leave the cocoon they'd woven yet.

Would he stay? Did she want him to stay? The answer to that question blazed to life in her chest. A resounding, all-encompassing *yes*! And what happens when he leaves again, Jazz asked her fickle heart. What then? At least this time, they'd get to say goodbye.

She had to get up. The animals needed tending, and she had to go to the bank with Valley. There wasn't time to fall in love. So, maybe enjoy each other for a while, her heart suggested, or perhaps that was her vagina talking. She sent them both a cease and desist before easing herself from the bed. One thing was sure: the man deserved a lie-in after his early morning performance.

By the time Jazz finished feeding the animals and showered in the downstairs bathroom so she wouldn't wake Theo, Valley was waiting for her outside.

"Coffee." Valley shoved the cup into Jazz's face before her ass even hit the seat.

"Thanks," Jazz said, grabbing the mug and throwing back a healthy swig.

"I know better than to take you anywhere without offering the necessary caffeine."

Jazz grinned at her friend. "I've trained you well."

Valley punched her arm, then threw her car into reverse.

"I thought you may be feeling worse for wear this morning," Jazz said, watching, as she always did, the roll of green fields as they wound down the driveway.

"I mean... does my head hurt? Yes. Am I going to let it slow me down? No. Well, maybe I can convince Joan to take the kids out this afternoon and let me nap."

"You know she will. She's too good to you," Jazz said, chuckling.

"She really is." The softening in Valley's voice at the mention of her wife sent an unexpected pang through Jazz's heart. It felt like jealousy, and she wasn't proud of that.

They drove in silence for a few minutes, but Jazz was aware of Valley's eyes travelling over her. Finally, she twisted in her seat. "Okay, why do you keep looking at me?"

"Something is different about you," Valley said, her voice ripe with suspicion.

Blood rushed up Jazz's neck. Surely Valley couldn't *tell*, could she? "Different, how?" She sipped her coffee in what she hoped was a nonchalant fashion.

"You're looser than normal, and your skin is glowing like you had a facial, but I know you didn't—Oh, my god! Did you and Theo have sex?"

Jazz gasped, inhaled hot liquid, and spat it all over Valley's dashboard. "How the fuck did you know that?" she rasped. Still coughing, she desperately searched for napkins or *anything* she could use to wipe the brown droplets racing down the car's interior. "What the shit! Don't you have kids? Where are the McDonald's napkins or baby wipes?"

"Those heathens aren't allowed in my car!" Valley yelled, aghast. "And now, neither are you." Valley's eyes darted between her dash and the road, growing wider as the liquid inched along the sleek curve of the glove compartment. "And they're six and ten, *Auntie* Jazz. I haven't had baby wipes in years."

With a growl, Jazz used the sleeve of her sweatshirt to mop up the coffee. She could practically hear Valley's eye start to twitch.

"Sooooo?" Valley needled once the mess was dealt with.

Jazz made an indistinct sound of exasperation and pushed both hands into her hair. "Yes, okay... we did. This morning."

"This morning!" Valley stomped the breaks in her excitement, making Jazz gasp and fumble her grip on the coffee cup, nearly spilling more liquid. "How was it?"

"Fucking transcendent," Jazz muttered, smacking her head back against the seat.

"I don't understand the problem." Valley guided the car into a parking spot on the main street and killed the engine before twisting in her seat to look at Jazz. "A kind, caring, sexy man wants to give you orgasms. What more do you want?"

"I don't know." To her dismay, Jazz's eyes prickled. "I haven't had time to think about what it means, and we sure haven't talked about it."

Some of the teasing light drained from Valley's face, and she reached over to squeeze Jazz's forearm. "Make sure you give him a chance, baby girl. Be open and honest with each other; you might be surprised by where it goes."

Jazz swallowed. Why did the idea of that scare her so much? "I'll try," she said.

Chapter Thirty-Two

JASMINE

VALLEY SLAPPED A BLANK cheque down on the counter at city hall, leaned across, snatched a pen out of the mug full sitting by the computer and glared at Ed Hamilton until he put down his ham sandwich and pushed himself to his feet.

"I'm paying the back taxes on Jasmine Joyce's property, and if I hear gossip about it, I'll know it was you, Ed Hamilton. Then you'll get a nice taste of the trouble I can cause... a veritable smorgasbord. Are we on the same page?"

"Uh," Ed stammered. A glob of mayo clung to his lower lip, wobbling as he spoke, and Jazz had to turn away, unsure if she would laugh or gage. "Yes, right away, ma'am." Ed trundled to the computer and began clicking.

Jazz leaned her shoulder against Valley's. "What kind of trouble can you cause him?" she asked in a hiss.

Valley shrugged and flashed her a wicked grin. "I've no idea, but if you say shit like that with enough confidence, you can usually get what you want."

"Wow," Jazz breathed, stepping back and giving her friend a once-over. Power Val is sexy."

Valley cast her a sideways look before tossing a sheet of blonde hair over her shoulder. "Bitch, I'm always sexy."

"I'm surprised to see you so soon," Ed commented as if suddenly snapping out of whatever spell Val had cast. He was squinting at the computer screen and seemingly, to Jazz's relief, oblivious to their conversation. "Here's the balance remaining as of today." He slipped a sheet of paper across the counter with one stubby finger.

"Wait... what?" Jazz looked down at the number at the bottom and shook her head, trying to grasp his comments. "What do you mean so soon?" Grabbing the paper, she slid it closer, blinking. "What the fuck?"

Ed *tsked*. "Ms Joyce, language please. This is the city hall."

"Cram it, Ed," Valley said, snatching the sheet from Jazz. "You're a grown man, and this is Jamieson Creek. And Jasmine, why didn't you come to me sooner? This isn't that bad. We could have worked something out and saved you months of stress."

Jazz shook her head. "It isn't right. I owe way more than this."

Ed's glossy brow furrowed, untrimmed eyebrows scuttling in to meet each other in the middle like reuniting caterpillars. "Your... guest—" he stumbled over the words as if it were dirty, "came and paid a large installment recently. He said you sent him in. You really should keep better track of your finances.

Valley pointed a finger at Ed. "I repeat, cram it." She filled out the cheque with a few flourishes of her pen and passed it over.

Only a few thousand left... that meant... fucking shit.

Theo put down at least twenty thousand dollars. Bile churned in Jazz's stomach, and she didn't know if she would vomit or spontaneously combust. She didn't speak, even when Valley took her by the elbow and steered her outside and into the passenger seat of her car.

"Okay, honey, you're scaring me," Valley said after getting in behind the wheel. She didn't start the vehicle, only twisted in her seat to look at Jazz.

"I'm going to kill him," Jazz whispered.

"I mean, with all that land, I'm sure you could find a nice secluded place to hide the body. However, I'm not condoning murder."

Jazz ignored her. "Who the hell does he think he is?"

Chewing her lip, Valley shrugged. "Someone who loves you and doesn't want to see you lose the place you love more than anything. I can attest to the feeling."

"You asked me, and I said I would pay you back," Jazz said, gripping her head in both hands as if that would keep it from exploding. "It's different."

"And do you remember what a fight I had to put up to get you to agree?" Valley threw her hands up, wincing when they smacked against the sunroof. "I'm guessing Theo knew you wouldn't accept his help, so he gave it the only way he thought he could."

The words were sandpaper on Jazz's skin. Valley was right. She would never have allowed Theo to put a cent toward helping her.

"He doesn't love me," she muttered instead. Her father used to say she was obstinate to a fault, and it was probably one of the few things he'd ever been right about.

Valley barked a laugh. "Yeah. Uh-huh. Whatever."

"He doesn't!" Jazz snapped.

Every pore on Valley's face oozed skepticism, at least they would, if the damn woman had any pores.

"We barely know each other," Jazz insisted, even though it was bullshit.

"You did the horizontal tango this morning. You screwed, fuuuckkked."

"Okay!" Jazz pressed her hands over her ears. "Please, no more."

"You cannot expect me to believe you feel you don't know him."

Jazz picked at a callous on her palm. "Fine. I do know him. All the important stuff, anyway."

Fine white scars.

Tears on his cheeks.

Her work rough fingers dancing over the ridges of his abdomen.

She swallowed heavily. "But now I owe him *money*. It changes our whole dynamic." Their dynamic wasn't even established yet. She had no idea where she and Theo stood, where she *wanted* them to stand.

Valley made a rude noise. "It isn't all about you, you know."

Jazz flinched in surprise. "Ouch. What the fuck?"

"I think he did it because he cares, not because of a male hero complex or ulterior motives. Theo is a good guy. He saw a chance to help someone he loves. It probably made him happy to do it, and he's allowed to seek happiness."

He deserves all the happiness he can get.

"Jazz, seriously. Him doing this does not mean you're weak or incapable. You're allowed a little help. We all need it sometimes. That sperm donor asshat of yours left you with a mountain of debt and an inner voice that keeps telling you you aren't worthy. Well, I'm here to tell you that voice is a fucking liar!" Valley flopped back against the seat, ranted out.

All Jazz could do was stare at her, the image of her ferocious, dear friend blurring before her.

Valley stared right back. "People are allowed to love you, Jasmine," she whispered.

To her horror, Jazz couldn't stop the tidal wave of emotion that seared up her sinuses and burst out her tear ducts.

Biting her bottom lip to stop it from quivering, she sniffed, blinked, and then shattered into messy sobs.

Chapter Thirty-Three

THEO

A FTER THE BEST MORNING of his life, followed by the deepest few hours of sleep he'd had in years, Theo woke up alone. His heart sank a fraction when he slid his hand across the sheets and found them cool, the bed empty. Jazz was gone. He wasn't sure what he'd expected. Her absence could mean anything, from the fact that she was out feeding the animals to the fact that she'd skipped town in order to never see his face again. If it wasn't for the fact he was in her room, Theo could almost believe the last twelve hours had been a wonderful dream. Sighing, he pushed back the sheets and groaned. He was weary but in a bone-deep, satisfied-to-his-core sort of way.

Gathering his clothes, Theo listened carefully at the door, ensuring Betty wasn't downstairs before slipping out in his boxers and going to his room. In the shower, he found at least three bite marks on his chest and couldn't stop the laugh that rolled out of him.

With his stomach furious at how long he'd ignored it, Theo went to the kitchen next. He was jamming a peanut butter sandwich into his mouth when the front door of the house slammed shut.

"Theo Bridger, where are you?" Jazz's voice cracked through the house sharp as a pistol retort.

Panic injected adrenaline into his blood at the anger in Jazz's voice. *Shit.* With an intuition that chilled him to his core, Theo knew she'd caught him. He thought he would have more time. Swallowing the lump of bread that had become concrete in his throat, he turned to face the door as she entered.

"What's wrong?" he said, though peanut butter had glued his tongue to the roof of his mouth. His nerves came alive at the sight of Jazz, each one buzzing with electricity. Theo was suddenly acutely aware of his hands and didn't know where the hell to put them.

The look Jazz gave him could have frozen over the river Styx. "Oh, I think you know," she growled.

Theo sucked at his lip, pretending to think. "You are mad that I didn't give you more orgasms?" he asked, attempting what he hoped was a seductive smile.

Please don't let there be peanut butter on his face.

Jazz snorted, advancing a few steps and brandishing a finger, with which she used to accentuate two words by poking him in the chest. "City. Hall."

Theo swallowed. "I see."

"What the fuck, Theo!" Jazz drove the flat of her palm into his chest, shoving him back. Her face was a mottled red, and her dark eyes burned dangerously.

"In my defence," Theo hedged. "I didn't think you'd find out so soon."

The dark wings of Jazz's brows dove lower, and Theo knew he'd made a mistake.

That is not an acceptable excuse... shit.

"How did you find out about the payments?"

"I saw the bills in your truck." He may as well be honest. It might be the only thing that would save him.

Jazz bristled. "Why the hell were you going through my truck?"

A bubble of irritation worked its way up Theo's esophagus. "You gave me your truck to take to town. A couple of months ago, when we got back from the fence lines... the night we... you—" He snapped his mouth shut. It wasn't going to do him any favours bringing *that* night up. "You said the credit card was in the glove compartment, but when it opened, it was like I was under a leaflet propaganda attack."

Ropes of glossy black hair swung around Jazz's face when she shook her head in confusion. "What?"

"In WW2, the Germans—no, never mind. The point is, I wasn't snooping through your truck. The papers launched all over the cab, and I had to pick them up." Theo took a cautious step forward, reaching out a hand. When Jazz didn't pull away, he laced his fingers with hers. "Jasmine, sweetheart. I promise I didn't do this because I expected anything or thought I could rescue or make up for the past. I wasn't trying to buy you or be your white knight. I only wanted your home, the place you love most in this world, to be safe."

"That's why Valley said you did it. She said you—" Her voice was thick with tears, and when she didn't finish, Theo didn't push.

When she looked up at him, her eyes glistened with tears. "She said I never let people help because, on some level, I don't believe I'm worthy of being loved."

Theo shut his eyes against the sudden burn of her words and the sight of her tears. "Therapists and their levels," he said. Cautiously, he tugged her forward. She came into his arms with a choked laugh.

"You may not believe you're worthy of love, but I *know* you are," he whispered against her hair. "Because I see the love that Valley, Betty, and the animals on this ranch have for you. And then there's me." He shrugged, brushing a kiss across her temple. "I'm disgustingly besotted with you, so the proof is in the pudding, darlin'."

Jazz went still. Even her breathing seemed to cease. Tears slipped off her chin when she looked up at him again. She moved to pull her hand free of his to wipe them away, but Theo stopped her. With the thumb of his free hand, he skimmed her jaw, catching the drops. He allowed his hand to slip up her cheek and through the wavy strands of her unbound hair. She was silk and iron beneath his hands. "I only thought you should know."

"I think maybe I'm a little lost," Jazz whispered. Her voice was tight, filled with a vulnerability that was unlike her.

"Would it be corny to say I was, too, until I found you again and realized I was finally home?"

Jazz squeezed her eyes shut, laughing, even as more tears rolled down her cheeks. "That would be the worst. I would kick you out if you said that shit."

Theo lowered his lips, brushing the shell of her ear as he spoke. "It's a good thing I didn't say it, then."

Her breathing hitched, and Jazz tipped her head to the side, displaying her neck. "That is a good thing."

The pulse point beneath his lips beat wildly. Theo rested his mouth there, breathing her, tasting her. Then, with a soft flick, he ran his tongue over the nearly translucent skin. Jazz gasped, body arching into his.

When she turned her head to meet his mouth, the truth of Theo's words flowed through him. He wasn't letting Jasmine go a second time.

Chapter Thirty-Four

JASMINE

*F*UCKING HELL, THEO BRIDGER *was destroying her.*

Jazz's back hit the fridge, and she hissed at the cold contact against her heated skin. Theo's dark head was bent before her as he rucked up her t-shirt with one hand and massaged her ass with the other. And his mouth... fucking hell, his mouth. It seared a path across her stomach, venturing downwards. When he slid an exploratory finger into the waistband of her jeans, Jazz's knees threatened to buckle.

"I want to taste you," he rasped, looking up at her from beneath his crescent of dark lashes, and *fuck*, she loved him. The knowledge hit her with a right hook to the gut. She loved him. How the hell was she going to deal with that?

The alarm must have registered on her face. Theo sat back on his heels, eyeing her warily. "What happened? Was that not sexy? It seemed sexy in my head."

"Oh god, no! It was sexy. I'm sorry." She pressed a hand to her forehead, forcing air through her nose. "It's just... today has been a lot. I think I need a moment."

Theo stood and, with both hands, brushed the hair from her face. "Tell me what I can do. Do you want me to leave you be for a while? Do you want to talk? Beer on the porch? Snack?"

The riot of emotions gripping Jazz's chest eased, and she laughed. "A snack and a beer sounds amazing. I'm sorry to cut things off that way." She waved a hand between them.

Theo shook his head before the words finished leaving her mouth. "Never apologize about asking for what you need," he said. "I will take nothing from you that you aren't one hundred percent ready to give."

"Okay," Jazz said, fighting another wave of tears. What the hell was wrong with her? She never cried, at least not before Theo Bridger reappeared in her life. "I feel bad; that looks painful." Biting her lip, she jerked her chin toward the bulge straining the front of Theo's jeans.

"He'll be fine, I assure you." Theo leaned in and brushed his mouth across hers in a whisper of a kiss. "I've been on this ranch, staring at that magnificent ass of yours, marvelling at that brain and that filthy, sarcastic mouth for months now... this is not the first unrequited boner I've had."

Jazz snorted. "Name of your band," she said, tears evaporating under the force of the grin spreading across her face.

"Don't tempt me, I'll do it." In a faux announcer's voice, he bellowed. "Please welcome to the stage, Grammy winners for album of the year, Unrequited Boner!"

"Well, you two seem to be getting along better." Betty's voice cut through their mirth, and Jazz yelped, hiding her face against Theo's chest. He jumped violently, then laughed harder when he glanced over his shoulder and saw the look on Betty's face.

"Just planning for my future," he said.

Jazz noticed he kept the front of his body carefully turned away from the older woman.

Leaning in, he whispered against her ear, "I'll meet you on the porch in five minutes. Poor Betty doesn't need a show."

Jazz shivered as his warm breath moved across her skin. "Okay," she said. "And I'm thinking you should probably stay with me tonight. Work on some more band names."

Biting her thumbnail, Jazz watched as Theo slipped out through the back door, then she slowly turned her gaze up to meet Betty's. She'd felt the woman's eyes on her for a good thirty seconds before she gathered the courage to turn to her.

"It is awfully nice to hear you laugh," Betty said. Her face had the sort of look that was usually a precursor to something sappy.

Jazz wrinkled her nose. "I laugh all the time."

"Mhmm," Betty said, turning to the fridge and pulling it open. "Can you do one thing for me?" she asked, peering into the chilly depths.

"What's that?" Jazz asked.

"Can you keep an open mind about that boy? Don't shut him out because you're scared."

"I'm not scared, and he isn't a boy," Jazz said, a huff to her voice she wasn't proud of.

"Whatever you say, dear."

It was ten pm before the tentative knock sounded on Jazz's door. Heart in her throat, she jumped off the bed and rushed to open it.

"I thought you'd changed your mind," she said the second it swung wide enough to reveal Theo on the other side.

"Holy shit." His eyes swept over her, one hand raising to grasp the door frame.

Jazz wore her only lingerie, a simple red lace bralette and French cut thong combo. She knew the crimson looked vibrant and sexy against her tanned skin. "Well, are you going to come in, or what?"

Theo surged forward, hands diving into her hair, guiding her mouth to his. "I'm so sorry." He growled against her mouth. "My mom called, and I haven't talked to her in ages. It was awkward. All I could think of was getting up here to you, and then I'd start getting hard. Not an ideal situation."

Jazz wrapped her arms around his neck, pulling him as close as she could manage. He was already hard, and she smiled against his mouth. "Well, you're here now. And laying on my bed, thinking about this morning and the things we're going to do to each other tonight, has had some advantages," she said. Taking his hand in hers, she slid it down her chest and torso and settled it between her legs where the thin fabric of her underwear was wet through.

"Fuck me," Theo ground out, his fingers slipping past the thin barrier to tease at the wet slick of her.

"Oh, I plan to," Jazz gasped, arching into his touch. "Thoroughly."

That statement seemed to dissolve Theo's ability to speak coherently. He pulled his hand free, then spanned both around Jazz's waist, and lifted her into his arms. Carrying her over to the bed, he dropped her onto it. She laughed as she landed, but he stole the sound from her mouth with a kiss that blasted heat through every inch of her nervous system. Theo sat back, pausing for a moment to stare down at her, one hand cupping the swell of his cock through his jeans

"I've not had a moment of peace from thinking about you today," Theo said, lips reuniting with her neck in a way that made her moan.

"It's only been a few hours since I saw you at dinner," Jazz said, laughing as he nipped at her jaw.

"Well, it feels like forever ago."

He moved down her body, following the trail he'd blazed before their earlier interruption. Jazz squirmed as his hair tickled across her lower belly. He hadn't had it cut while he'd been on the ranch, and it was growing shaggy, curling over his ears in a way that made him resemble the boy he'd been when Jazz first laid eyes on him. How could so much have changed, yet the visceral way she reacted to him, the way he broke through her shell to make her laugh, remained the same? Had she ever stopped loving him? Or had her heart gone dormant until he returned and brought it out of hiding? Fuck, listen to her. Corny enough to fill the concession at a movie theatre.

"Jasmine?"

"Hmm?" She didn't even mind her full name when he said it. It sounded like music instead of contempt when it came from his mouth.

"I wanted to make sure, after this afternoon, that you're alright with this?" He crouched between her thighs, ready to bring her mind-bending pleasure, but wanted to check with her—because he was *good*. Valley was right. She had to trust him with her feelings, with her heart. He deserved that.

"Yes, please," she breathed. Theo's dark stare was doing things to her core that only his mouth could relieve. The first languid stroke of his tongue brought her hips bucking up off the bed. Theo's broad palm spread across her belly, pressing, anchoring her, offering a delicious pressure.

He blew a hot breath across her, and she gasped. "Stop teasing me, damn it."

Theo chuckled, his mouth still on her. And *oh*, that was a new and curious sensation.

"So bossy," he admonished. "I fucking love it. Tell me what you want me to do all you like, Boss."

Jazz was an incoherent puddle of desire when Theo finally rose above her. She arched up, welcoming him into her body with a groan that resonated from his chest and reverberated through them both.

The urgency that thrummed between them that morning was gone. They sank into each other, determined to wring each second of enjoyment out of the hours ahead of them.

"I want to do this forever," Theo panted. One broad palm spread across her chest, and his eyes drank in the way her breasts threatened to spill out of the red lace she still wore.

"Okay. Forever," Jazz agreed. She wasn't entirely sure what she agreed to, but she didn't care if it meant Theo continued his deep, steady thrusting. She was a sunburst of need. "More," she begged, and Theo obliged, pressing in to the hilt then drawing back, teasing her with the silken tip. When she fell apart, he fell head first after her.

Chapter Thirty-Five

THEO

THE PROBLEM WITH FALLING in love with a farm girl was that relaxation was scarce. Theo groaned as Jazz shifted out from under his arm before the sky was light.

"Stay. The animals will be fine. Hunger builds character," he muttered, grabbing and successfully catching her by the waist to drag her back.

With a shockingly feminine giggle, Jazz tumbled back into the warm embrace of the blankets, and Theo bundled her up against his chest.

"You know perfectly well I can't stay here. And if I recall correctly, you also work on this ranch."

"Talk bossy to me. I love it when you do that." Theo nudged his nose into the sweet-smelling skin beneath her jaw, making her squeal.

"Stop, the horses are hungry." She wiggled away, the action sliding her pert ass right across his lap. "Besides, you promised to help me at the market today."

Theo groaned and buried his face in his pillow. "Unrequited boner," he grumbled, making Jazz laugh harder.

"I'll requite it later," she said, patting his head. "Now get up and help me, lazy asshole."

"Yes, ma'am."

"There's a goat in my truck." Theo came from the kitchen, arms laden with cartons of eggs, and stopped. Gruff was peering at him through the windshield of his truck. Seriously? He'd left the door open for thirty seconds.

"There's a snake in my boot," Jazz said from behind him in an oddly flat, robotic voice. Theo turned to her, unable to keep from laughing despite his confusion.

"Um, pardon me?"

"You know... Woody? When you pull the cord?"

Theo stared at her blankly.

"Woody and Buzz?"

"Woman, sometimes I wonder if it's just me or if you make no sense at all."

She gave him a sunny smile, throwing out a sideways kick that landed squarely on his ass as she went by. "It's just you; now get that sweet ass in gear before the goat shits in on your truck seats."

Theo was sweating by the time he had the pop-up tent and tables set up for the market. Jazz was shuttling boxes from his truck and set the last one down with a groan.

"I remember why I only do this a couple of times a year now," she said, rubbing her forearm over her brow.

"Farmers markets... not for the faint of heart," Theo said. Seizing his bottle of water, he drained half in four long pulls. When he recapped it, he found Jazz watching him. There was a look in her eye that made his blood heat.

"Can I help you, Miss Joyce?" he asked.

"I was just... recalling some things," she said, eyes twinkling. Fuck he liked her like this. This was his Jazz. The knowledge that *this* person, funny and bright, was still under the protective layers she had built made his heart feel too big for his chest.

Theo extended a hand, joy flooding his blood when she reached out and threaded her fingers through his. With a tug, he brought her against his chest. "Did any of those recollections have to do with my mouth on your pussy?" He breathed the words hot and light against the curve of her ear. Low enough that only she could hear. Jazz shivered violently against him.

"Maybe." Tipping her head back, she perused his face for a moment before her eyes rested on his lips. "The memories are fading, though. I think you may have to reenact it when we get home. Remind me what it was like."

"I'll remind you right now," Theo growled. "This place must have a bathroom."

"You're not doing anything to me in the Jamieson Creek Recreation Center bathroom, Theo Bridger."

"Fine," he grumbled. Dropping his head, he let it rest against the fragrant curve of her neck. He could live here, sustain himself on the taste and smell of her skin. The heat of her body against his.

Jazz released a throaty laugh, and the sound seemed to have a direct connection to his cock. Fuck. Did he really have a hard-on at a *farmer's market*?

"You have to stay in front of me for a minute," Theo said. "This is a family place. And I am now in an... unseemly state."

Jazz rocked back on her heels, and Theo seized her by a belt loop, afraid she would step away. "Now you're worried that it is a family place?" she asked, her voice soaked in laughter. "You propositioned me like thirty seconds ago."

"Yeah, yeah, I got a bit out of hand. If you want me to calm down, stop being so unbelievably sexy."

Jazz snorted. "I'll work on it."

"Theo Bridger? Is that you, man?"

The unfamiliar voice chucked a bucket of ice water over Theo's raging libido. He glanced past Jazz and stared at the man leaning over their still-empty tables, grinning. Recognition niggled at him, but it took the other man stepping forward with his hand outstretched for the past and present to merge and provide Theo with a name.

"Scott, hey, how are you?" With no avenue of escape, he leaned around Jazz and shook the outstretched hand. God, the last thing he needed was for the originator of Boner Bridger to see him now... with a fucking boner.

What the hell had he done in a past life to deserve this?

"I'm good, really good. Hey Jazz. I didn't know you were in the market scene."

Jazz flashed a warm smile at the big man. "Well, sometimes, if I have an abundance of eggs and have made enough other things to sell."

Theo frowned. He hadn't even asked Jazz what she had in the boxes. She was very accomplished at distracting him. He caught her eye, not missing the jerk of her chin toward his... regions. He gave her a slight nod, indicating the situation had been resolved.

"So, catch me up," Scott said, spinning his ball cap around so the brim lay over the back of his thick neck. "What are you up to these days?"

Ah, there was a question he loved.

Theo cleared his throat. "I was in the military for a while. Done now, I'm trying to... well, I'm thinking of doing music full time." Holy shit, that was the first time he'd said it out loud. A little geyser of excitement spouted in his gut.

Scott smacked him none-too-gently on the shoulder with the back of his meaty hand. "That's right, you've been playing at Dad's place quite a bit! I really need to make it in there and have a listen." He shrugged, a giddy grin crossing his bearded face. "Chrystal and I have a new baby, so I don't get out much these days."

"That's wonderful, congratulations. Boy or girl?"

"Little boy, Max." Scott's grin could have blinded pilots flying over. "Best thing that's ever happened to me. You got any kids?"

Behind Scott, Theo saw the line of Jazz's back go ridged. He swallowed hard, a sudden choking sensation tightening his vocal cords. Finally, steeling himself, he nodded. "One," he managed. "He would have been a teenager, probably taller and more handsome than his old man. Maybe again, one day, I'll get lucky."

Scott blinked, clearly speechless. "I'm, I'm sorry, man."

"We appreciate that," Theo said. Jazz stared at him from behind Scott, her eyes wide, wet. *Thank you* she mouthed.

The truth was he'd never considered kids as more than an abstract idea until Jazz had told him about their baby. Now, he couldn't seem to escape the idea of her holding his son in her arms.

What if he was as terrible a father as his own?

Fuck, Scott was looking at him expectantly, obviously waiting for the answer to a question he'd asked. "Sorry, man. What was that?"

"I asked if you were living here now?"

Again with the hard questions. Did this guy know what he was doing to Theo?

"I... I'm here temporarily, but—" Theo paused, catching Jazz's eyes over Scott's shoulder. She stared at him, frozen, waiting. "I'm seriously thinking about a permanent relocation."

He wished he could read that expression and understand the look that flashed through her eyes, but she turned away before he could decipher what it meant. Did Jazz want him to stay? Because he realized with lightning-strike certainty he never wanted to say goodbye to her or Jamieson Creek again.

The two men chatted for a bit longer, and then Scott left, promising to bring the baby back to their booth when he found his family. Theo turned back to the table and found that Jazz had them laden with goods.

"Eggcellent selection you have here," he said, straightening a pile of egg cartons.

"Oh, don't start that again." Jazz grinned at him, and his gut did the geyser again.

Theo longed to ask her what she thought about him staying. How she felt about them continuing what they had started, but he kept his mouth shut. Now wasn't the time. People were beginning to mill around, buying goods and chatting.

"Jasmine?" Theo asked tentatively.

"Hmm?"

"What the fuck are these?" Theo held up the little garment he'd grabbed off the table. They looked like tiny pyjama tops. Delight filled him at the blush that flooded Jazz's cheeks.

"They are—" She wrinkled her nose and bumped her finger against her thigh. "Goatie coaties."

Theo had to bite his bottom lip for a moment before he could reply. "So, let me confirm here... coats for... goats?"

"Baby goats, yes." She shrugged, refusing to meet his eyes. "Or... for lambs. They get cold easily, and... well, it is fucking adorable, okay? Have you ever seen a lamb in pyjamas?"

"Jammies for lammies?" Theo couldn't help it; he doubled over, laughing so hard that he snorted. "Oh my god, Jasmine Joyce. You make tiny clothes for baby animals!"

"Shut up! I'm still tough." She tried to sound petulant, but her face shone, and she lost the battle with her own laughter. It took a few minutes for them to regain control, and when they did, Theo pulled her back into his arms.

"I am in awe of you, Jasmine," he said, kissing the top of her head. "Don't ever change."

Theo couldn't stop watching her. It was an incurable condition, a compulsion. Jasmine drew his eyes with the faith of the north, drawing a compass needle. He never wanted to stop looking at her. He knew convincing Jazz to let him stay would be the hard part. Her bruises were fading, but they still hid beneath her skin, tender spots inflicted by the people who were supposed to love her, including him. Guilt and regret were bile in Theo's throat. If only he hadn't been under his father's spell all those years ago. If only he'd seen he could fight instead of falling into the pit of pain, hiding in his soul and nearly drowning.

"I can feel your eyes boring into me, Bridger," Jazz threw over a shoulder as she passed with a sack of feed over the other. "That tells me you're not working hard enough."

Shaking his head, Theo dropped his gaze. He was mucking stalls. That job did not require his full attention, but he knew better than to tell her that.

He hummed as he worked, allowing melodies to bubble up and flow through him. The music hadn't felt purposeful for a long time, but today, words pinged through his mind as wild as the balls in a Bingo machine.

You're everything I want to look at
The only one I see
Turn around, I need to know
That you notice me

The words rattled around in his brain. They *felt* like they could become something but had a long way to go before they actually were. Still, the restlessness signalling the urge to create took up residence in his fingers. He longed to grab a pen, scribble the words, and manipulate them until the itch eased and the song took shape.

Theo was so lost in his mind he didn't hear Jazz come back into the barn. When she laid a hand against his sweating back, he jumped.

"What were you singing?" she asked. "It sounded nice."

"I was... it was nothing. Yet."

"Yet?"

He studied her, trying to put words to the feelings music stirred inside him. Jazz's skin glowed with exertion, damp hair curling into ringlets at her temples. *Fuck*, he loved her. He'd never stopped. No one had ever lived up to the woman who stood before him. He'd given no one a fighting chance because he hadn't wanted to. Theo had always only wanted Jazz.

Forgetting to answer her question, he reached out and tugged her against him, hugging her close. Her scent was that first whiff of home after a long time away. That singular smell that wrapped itself around your bones and brought boundless comfort.

Jazz was still in his arms for a second, then hers rose, wrapping around his waist. They stood that way for a long time, in a bubble, a haven, while the world kept turning around them. Theo never wanted it to pop.

"Jazz?" he finally whispered against her hair.

"Yes?" Her voice emerged from against his chest, strangely soft. Vulnerable. It was clear she knew what he was going to say.

"I don't want to leave."

The arms anchoring him tightened. "I don't want you to, either. But I'm also terrified, Theo. If there is one thing I know for certain, it's that you have the power to destroy me."

Hearing the words was a balm over the anxious flaring of Theo's heart, but he hated that she was fearful of this, of *them*. He hated being the reason for it. "Can we talk about what that means?"

"We can, but... not yet?" she asked against his chest. "I want to enjoy feeling this free for a while."

"Tell me when you're ready." He left unsaid that he would wait, possibly holding his breath until she was. Theo dipped his head, searching her mouth and brushing his lightly against hers. Jazz fell into the kiss hungrily. Breathless in seconds, Theo began backing her against the wall. All day, working at her side behind the market table, watching her interact with her friends and neighbours, he'd fallen further and further. It was a tangible sensation, falling back in love with Jasmine. And god, he wanted her. All day, he'd waited for the moment he could get his hands on her.

"Do you care that I was just shovelling shit?" he asked against her lips, making her snort.

"No, you were wearing gloves. I trust you weren't rolling around in it?"

"Nah, I leave that for Titus to do."

"Perfect, then kiss me. I've never been fucked from behind over a straw bale before."

Theo growled against her lips before slipping his tongue inside to battle hers.

Boom!

A shot echoed through the barn. Jazz froze in his arms.

"What the fuck?" she asked.

Theo's heart went wild, an instantaneous wave of nausea threatening to take him to his knees. Blood rushed in his ears, and he pressed his palms against them as another shot rang out.

"Fucking hell!" Jazz yelled. "They're hunting on my land."

Hunting.

Theo repeatedly ran the word through his mind, trying to attach meaning to it.

Hunting. Hunting.

He was in Jamieson Creek. He was at home with Jazz. They were both safe.

Jazz was pulling gear off the pegs on the wall when she noticed his distress.

"Theo?" she dropped the saddlebags and came to him, digging her fingers into his hair and lifting his head so his eyes met hers. "What is it?"

Theo shook his head, breathing out in a sharp exhale. "I'm... I'm fine. The shot. Loud noises, it happens sometimes."

It was all he needed to say. Understanding flooded her face, and she came over, pulling him close. Her fingers found the hair and his nape and combed through. "Breathe," she said, her voice calm and steady. "You are safe. I'm so sorry, I didn't even—"

"No. No, it's fine." Even as he said the words, a fine tremble clutched at his muscles. He locked them, trying to will away the shaking.

"I've got you, okay? I've got you, Theo."

Theo nodded against her shoulder, hating himself for the weakness but loving how her arms tethered him, held him to this time and place where, for once, things felt right. He allowed himself another moment of comfort, then pulled back.

"I'm alright," he managed to say after a moment. The sudden burst of panic was subsiding, but he still hated to relinquish his hold on her. "What do we do?"

"I'm going to go chase those fuckers off my land," Jazz said, turning back to her task. "Will you grab Ghost from the small pasture for me?" Without looking, she held out a halter in his direction. "Actually... Goliath is faster."

"Jazz, do you think that is a good idea? You said he spooks easily."

"He'll be alright. I can cover more ground on him." Her jaw was set with determination, and Theo knew arguing would be pointless.

"Give me David's too, then." There was no way he was sending her out there alone. He had to get his head on straight and go with her, keep her safe. Thank god she couldn't hear his thoughts, or she'd kick his ass for thinking she needed his protection.

Jazz paused, rotating slowly to look at him. "Why?"

"Because I'm coming with you." Theo left no room for argument in his tone, stating it as a matter of fact, but he saw in her eyes that she still longed to do so.

"Theo," she said, straightening. "You—"

Anger spiked through Theo's chest. "Don't. You will not use that to keep me here. I don't do well with loud noises or gunshots, no. But that will not have me cowering in the barn when there's a chance of you being hurt trying to protect our home."

Our home.

The words plunged through the air around them, as heavy as stones through the water. Jazz's dark eyes searched his face, but finally, she nodded. "Of course not. I'm sorry."

"You wanted to protect me," he said, forcing a weak smile. "That is a feeling I understand."

Chapter Thirty-Six

JASMINE

T HE STORM ROLLED IN from nowhere. Jazz found quad tracks, and she and Theo followed them along the river for a few miles before the slate grey clouds rolled in and the sky opened up.

"Fuck!" Jazz slammed a closed fist against her thigh. "This is pointless. They're long gone with those quads."

"Can we report it?" Theo asked, wiping at the steady stream of rain coursing over his brow.

"Yeah, it will get me nowhere, though." Anger burned a hole in Jazz's gut, and she fought to keep her voice steady. "The ranch backs onto Crown land. They're allowed to hunt there if they have proper tags. Conservation may come and check, but there is no way to prove they were on my land. Not this close to the boundaries."

A crack of thunder split the sky without warning. Goliath shrieked, pitching his body up and sideways. Jazz, unprepared for the horse's antics, found herself suddenly weightless before her ass connected with the muddy ground. The air left her in a sharp gasp, and her eyes flooded with tears as pain echoed through every bone in her body.

Theo kicked David forward, nearly losing his seat as he grabbed for Goliath's reins, but the horse, sensing his revolt was in danger of being quelled, reared back and spun away. The horse whinnied again before violently kicking his heels and taking off through the field alongside the river.

"Shit!" Theo yelled. For a moment, he looked unsure if he should pursue the horse or check on her, but concern for Jazz won out, and he faltered. Jazz held up a hand to stop him when he swung a leg over David's saddle to dismount.

"No! Please, can you go after him?" she gasped. "I'm fine. Only winded from the fall." She was embarrassed as hell, but she left that out. She hadn't been thrown from a horse since... the thought brought a rush of anguish surging up her throat, and she squeezed her eyes shut, blocking it before it could grow to consume her.

Theo cast her one more look, concern sharpening his features, then whirled his horse. "Come on, old man, let's get that asshole." David's hoofbeats had died off by the time Jazz finally forced herself to her feet, attempting to wipe the mud from her butt but only smearing it around.

"Fuck!" Jazz's voice broke, and she allowed herself an indulgent few moments of tears before swiping them away, worried that Theo would come back and see her.

Another boom of thunder made her jump. The rain, which had been unpleasant before, changed tact and crashed from the sky with torrential force.

The urge to sit under a tree and cry nearly overwhelmed Jazz, but she pulled the hood of her jacket up and put her head down, heading in the direction Goliath, David, and Theo had gone.

♪ ♩ ♫ ♪ ❀ ♪ ♫ ♩ ♫ ♪ ♪

Lightning split the sky. Through the fog, Jazz saw a flash of brown, and then the squeal of a terrified horse ripped through the wind. A cry rang out, and then silence.

349

He'd gone down. Jazz knew it without having to see what had happened. The river was too full, tearing away chunks of the river bed under the bank so the ground looked stable, but it wasn't.

"Theo!"

A shape became visible, and Jazz broke into a run, slipping and falling into the mud again. With a growl, she shoved herself up. David stood on the bank in a lone shape, head hanging, water and mud dripping from his mane and tail. She didn't see Theo anywhere.

Jazz's heart rioted, attempting to outdo the storm for noise. Her trembling hands were so numb she could barely grip David's hanging reins.

"Fuck!" she screamed the word, raw and piercing into the wind. She forgot about Goliath and what it would mean to her and the ranch if she lost him. Theo was a pulse point in her brain. *Help him.* She had to help him. It was her fault Theo was in that river. Her fucking fault. Acid pushed at her throat, threatening to gag her.

Jazz scraped the rain from her eyes with frozen hands and looped the reins on the saddle horn.

"It's alright, sweetheart." Jazz ran her hands over the horse's trembling form. She couldn't see an injury, but he was so wet and muddy it was impossible to tell. With a jerk of his head, the horse cantered away toward the trees. Jazz couldn't spare the time to catch and safely tie him. She would have to hope he didn't go far.

Jazz cupped her hands across her brow, trying to see through the rain, the dim light. "Theo!"

The river was swelling, pushing the boundaries of its banks. Then, a flash of colour caught her eye.

A few hundred meters down from where she stood, Theo was half submerged, clinging to a system of roots hanging from the eroding bank. As she got closer, Jazz saw he wasn't holding on. His head lolled, and the water smashed his body against the steep, rocky bank.

Swallowing a sob, Jazz paused, forcing herself to assess before she moved forward. She would be no good to Theo if she ended up swept away in the riotous water.

The gnarled roots that kept Theo from heading downriver looked strong. He wasn't holding on, but one of the branches had snagged on his belt. Jazz had no idea how she'd get him up from the bank. She needed David. There would be a rope on his saddle. Dropping one hand, she ensured her knife was still at her hip. Fumbling with her frozen fingers, she raised two to her lips and whistled sharply.

Please, she prayed. Please listen.

The horse was well trained, but with the storm and the rain, he may not come. The drum of hoof beats brought tears to her eyes, and she blinked furiously. The last thing she needed was more obstruction to her vision.

David nickered, stopping in front of her and pressing his wet head against her chest.

"You're a good boy," she rasped. "Beautiful, brave boy."

The leather ties were impossible to unknot. They were swollen tight with the wet. Growling, Jazz pulled her knife free and cut the straps. Uncoiling the rope, she fastened it to the saddle horn and looped it around her waist before gathering the excess.

"Stand," she told David before moving to the bank. Jazz struggled to keep from slipping into the river twice before she managed to slither far enough down the bank to reach Theo.

"Hold on," she whispered over and over as she worked the rope over his shoulders and around his chest. It would have to do. Praying she didn't drop it with her shaking hands, Jazz pulled her knife from its sheath and cut through the leather of his belt. Theo's body jerked back, carried by the water before the rope cinched tight. She couldn't stop the cry that shredded her throat. Or the reflex to dive forward and grab him.

The water bit the skin of her face and neck with sharp teeth. Jazz spluttered, pushing into the clay as she fought to keep from sliding forward into the roiling depths.

"David! Back!" she yelled. "Back!" An eternity passed, and Jazz's throat squeezed shut in terror. Theo's body was bobbing in front of her, his face thankfully above water. She had no idea if he was breathing. If he was alive. But she would not let the river have him.

"Back, David!"

Then, the rope around her waist went taut, and she slid backward up the back. Pain screamed through her ribs as rough bark ate through her clothes. The rope was so tight it threatened to cut her in half, but then, her feet were on the ground. Stumbling upright, Jazz swallowed back the urge to vomit. "Back!" She yelled again, gathering the rope and lending her weight to the horse's efforts. Theo's dark head emerged, and she flung herself forward, grabbed his armpits and yanked him up and onto solid ground.

"Theo," she choked out, pressing her fingers to his neck. His pulse beat under her fingertips. A huge welt marred the skin across his brow and temple.

Ignoring her trembling, Jazz yanked off her sodden jacket and draped it over Theo. It was wet but warm from her body heat and somewhat waterproof. What the fuck was she going to do? Then, a memory smashed into her.

The satellite tracker. Stumbling to her feet, Jazz ran back over to David. Again, she used her knife on her tack, slicing the ties that held her saddlebags in place. Pulling them down, she slipped her way back to Theo.

When she pulled the little black box out of her saddle bag, praying it had charge, she nearly dropped it in the mud. Blair had insisted she carry it, and when she said they were too expensive, he'd shown up with one anyway. Jazz had been mad at the time, but now she swore she would kiss Blair when she saw him again.

A tiny red light flashed when Jazz powered the device on, and she sobbed in relief. She stabbed the button that would send an emergency message—Blair had preset that as well, bless him—and then slipped it into her pocket.

Please. Please let it work.

Jazz pulled Theo to the edge of the trees as carefully as she could. She knew they couldn't go far. The tracker would send out a location, not a live signal. But if she wanted him to be alive when help arrived, she had to get him warm and dry.

Dropping the saddle bags, Jazz unfurled the thin emergency blanket she always kept inside. Why hadn't she been more prepared? Cocky asshole, she scolded herself. So sure nothing would happen to her here, on her property. Now, Theo's life was at risk because of her.

Body heat. Pulling wet clothes off Theo's unmoving body would be nearly impossible. Unzipping the vest he wore, she used her knife to cut his henley up the middle, exposing his chest. Then she pulled off her shirt and pressed her body against his core. It was an effort, but Jazz managed to get the blanket over them both and then fling the vest and jacket over the top, creating as close to a waterproof cover as possible. Then, there was nothing else but to will her heat into Theo's body and pray to whoever would listen that his heart would keep beating.

It was the longest night of Jazz's life. She wasn't sure when the rain stopped, but as warmth seeped into Theo's body, she began to tremble. The aftereffects of adrenaline and cold threatened to swamp her. She clutched Theo to her. *Please.*

Please, someone, come. His breathing remained shallow, but even and with warmth, a bit of colour returned to his pale face.

She must have slept because when she closed her eyes, the rain still pelted the ground, and when she opened them again, it was quiet, aside from the roar of the river and the chores of night bugs returning to their songs. Jazz poked her head from under the blanket, only to be greeted by inky darkness. She listened, praying she'd hear something to indicate help was coming, but nothing was out of the ordinary. Off to her left, she could make out David's dark outline. She'd unsaddled him and given him his head, not wanting to tie him with the thunder and lighting. Seeing him there, waiting when he could have gone home, made her want to cry.

"Jazz?"

The croak of Theo's voice made her jerk violently. "Theo?" pulling the blanket down so she could see him in the faint moonlight, Jazz ran her hands over his cheeks. "Can you hear me?"

"Yeah. Where are we?"

"We're by the river at the base of the cliffs."

"Shit." His voice was weak, and the few words seemed to exhaust him. Theo closed his eyes, head lolling.

"Theo?" Jazz ran her hands through his hair. He didn't answer.

Chapter Thirty-Seven

JASMINE

D AWN STAINED THE SKY coral when Jazz gave up on trying to sleep. Her stomach repeatedly growled so loudly that she was no longer worried about predators. The sounds of her furious belly would scare them away. Then, there was her full-to-bursting bladder. She would have to leave Theo alone and hated doing it.

She squeezed her eyes shut, stoically ignoring both angry organs, when she heard a rumbling. Jazz's eyes shot open.

Was that... quads?

Someone was coming. Her system dumped a load of adrenaline into her blood that made her thankful for her strong pelvic floor.

Poking her head out from the pile of clothes, Jazz blinked at the fresh light. She must look like a groundhog poking out of its hole. The day glowed with a post-storm, washed-clean quality. David was contentedly grazing a few feet away, the terror of yesterday forgotten. He lifted his head, nickering when he saw her. Jazz grinned.

Rolling from the pile of clothes, she carefully tucked them around Theo. The early morning air hit her bare skin, raising an army of gooseflesh across her top half. Jazz didn't care about the cold or the fact she was only wearing a bra and muddy jeans or that her stomach was eating itself. She stood stock still, listening, trying to pinpoint a direction. South. South! Hallefuckinglujah.

Striding into the trees a few steps, Jazz peed, buckled her jeans back up, and checked on Theo.

"Help is coming," she whispered, brushing the matted hair off his brow. "Only a bit longer, and help will be here."

She removed her shirt from the pile and pulled it on, leaving Theo with the coats. Then, she began to pace at the edge of the trees while the rumbling of engines slowly grew louder.

Blair was astride the first quad that came through at the trailhead. Jazz's throat instantly closed at the sight of his familiar face. Fighting the tears, she waved both hands over her head, pointing to where Theo lay. Two more vehicles arrived bearing the Search and Rescue emblem on their hoods. They formed a half circle around Jazz and killed the engine.

"Thank god," Blair said, barely swinging his leg off the machine in time to catch Jazz as she threw herself into his arms.

"You came. You came. Oh, Blair, thank you." Her voice broke, and she settled on squeezing until Blair made a choked sound. "Theo is over here," she said, hurriedly wiping at her cheeks. "He's hurt. Hurry, please. David slipped at the edge of the bank, and Theo went down. He hit his head and fell into the water. He was in the water for about fifteen minutes before I was able to get him out."

"Is he still bleeding?" The first SAR member, a bearded man in his thirties, grabbed a pack off his quad and approached the clothing pile that was Theo.

"No, I got it stopped fairly quickly," Jazz said, hustling to keep up to the man's long strides.

"Good. And his temperature?"

"I was able to bring it up to what seemed fairly normal." It had been far too long since Jazz had taken first aid. She added it to her mental to-do list.

"Any vomiting?"

"No."

"Has he regained consciousness at all?"

"Once, very briefly," Jazz answered.

An older man with silver threaded through his blond hair caught up to them, carrying a foldable backboard. "I radioed the location for the helicopter. We're lucky; there should be enough space for them to land here."

Jazz stayed out of the way while the older man examined Theo. Blair and the younger man, who introduced himself as Anthony, came to stand beside her.

"He used to be a paramedic in Vancouver," Anthony said. "He'll make sure your friend is safe to transport, and the helicopter should be here any moment."

"Thank you," Jazz said, her voice rasping with emotion and thirst.

Blair wrapped an arm around her, tucking her against his chest. "Are you doing alright?" he asked. His hand started rubbing circles between her shoulder blades, and Jazz leaned into the familiar touch.

"I'm fine."

Anthony eyed her skeptically. "I'm getting you some water and a protein bar. You are going to sit down and ingest them while we wait. No arguing."

Jazz opened her mouth again to protest that she was alright, but Blair pinched her side, shutting her up.

When she was settled with her back against a pine tree, using sips of water to turn the protein bar into a cement-like substance and forcing it down her throat, Blair came to sit with her.

He settled down, crossing his long legs at the ankles as if they were having a casual picnic. "What the hell were you doing out here so late in the day?"

Jazz looked at him sideways, working to swallow the bite she had in her mouth. "It's my fault," she finally managed. "We heard gunshots. I wanted to try to catch whoever was hunting on the property. Goliath freaked out when the storm rolled in. He threw me and took off. Theo followed him on David. I was so worried about something happening to the horse... It didn't occur to me how dangerous it was for us to be out here. I was so mad they were trespassing, hunting. Fuck—" She scrubbed a hand over her face. "That horse is my money maker."

"Plus, you love Theo," Blair supplied. "And you are worried about him. It is okay to admit that, Jazzy. I'm not going to crumple into a mess of snot and heartbreak."

Jazz dropped her chin to hide the tears that blurred her vision. She was so fucking tired. So tired that her soul felt crumbled, like a discarded ball of paper. "Yeah. I do. I love him. Though it is pretty weird you were the first person I told and not him."

He shrugged, but didn't meet her eyes. "It's sort of how we roll though, isn't it? Best friends and all that."

"I'm sorry, Blair. For everything. You deserved better than what I gave you."

Blair nodded, seeming to digest her words for a moment. Then, he took her hand, squeezed it, patted it twice, and put it back against her thigh. "You haven't seen Goliath since he took off?"

Jazz shook her head, her scrambled brain trying to keep up to the conversation twist. "I have no idea where he is or if he's okay. Once I found Theo... well, he was all that mattered."

"Once we get him out safely, I can come back and look for Goliath."

"You don't have to do that."

Blair gave her a look that said *shut the fuck up* as clearly as any words.

"Alright," Jazz whispered. "Thank you."

A heavy thrum began to pulse in the air, growing steadily closer. David, lingering not far away, whinnied, his eyes rolling in fear before he spun and darted into the trees when the helicopter floated into view. Jazz shot to her feet, teetered and would have fallen back to the ground if Blair's arm hadn't snaked around her waist.

"Steady," he murmured. "You've had an ordeal, too. Don't forget that."

"I'm f—"

"Yeah, yeah. You're fine," Blair muttered. "I know. You're always fine; don't need anyone."

Nevertheless, he kept his arm firmly around Jazz, bolstering her as they watched the helicopter hover and finally land beside the river.

Time passed in a blur as Theo was checked over again and loaded onto the aircraft.

"Are you riding with us?" One of the paramedics called to Jazz.

Her attention swivelled from the helicopter to where David had disappeared to Blair.

"Go," he said, and his tone left no space for argument. "I've got the rest. I'll call Valley and get her to grab you a change of clothes and meet you at the hospital. Take care of Theo, the dude is a class act. I like him."

Jazz ran to seize him in a quick, fierce hug before jogging back and climbing into the aircraft.

It was a couple of hours, and a bit of grumbling about next of kin, before the nurses allowed Jazz into the room to see Theo. He had a severe concussion, mild exposure, and three bruised ribs. But, the words that glowed bright as a brand in her mind were, "he will be alright."

She'd wasted so much time with him. Blown past his confessions of how he was feeling for her because she was too fucking scared to tell him the truth. *Her* truth. She loved him and would not make the mistake of not telling him again. The moment Theo opened his eyes—and he would open them—she was going to pour her heart out to that man.

A harried-looking nurse showed Jazz to the room, then ducked out again without so much as a word. Swallowing hard, Jazz sank into the chair beside the bed.

"Oh, Theo," she breathed. "Look at you."

His face was sallow, and inky bruises bloomed from his temple and trickled down his jaw. An I.V. tethered his hand to a bag of clear liquid. Some machine or another was quietly beeping out a rhythm, but the most prevalent sound in Jazz's ears was the hushed song of his steady breathing.

Reaching out a trembling finger, Jazz stroked the smooth expanse of his forearm. The pristine spot where the inky black hair didn't reach. It always flexed so deliciously when he moved his fingers along the guitar strings. Jazz thought it may be her favourite sight in the world. She could get lost in watching it.

"I'm so sorry. You told me not to take Goliath. I was foolish. You might even say hot-headed, and I'm so sorry."

A shoe squeaked in the hallway, and a different nurse entered. Her grey hair was pulled back in a stylish, messy bun that Jazz suspected wasn't purposeful. The dimpled smile she flashed at Jazz put her instantly at ease.

"Hello sweetie, how's our handsome guy doing?" the nurse asked as she set a chart down on the little table and went to the I.V. bag, checking the levels.

"He's alright, I think," Jazz said, her voice wavering. "I was only allowed in to see him a few minutes ago."

"I hear you saved his life," the older lady said, flashing Jazz another smile. "Well done."

"It was my fault he was out there at all." To her horror, tears brimmed and spilled over her cheeks before she could stop them. "I wasn't thinking, and then the storm came in so fast." The words spilled out of her, a confession like she thought this dimpled, sweet woman could absolve her.

The woman leaned an ample hip against the counter. "What's your name, honey?"

"Jazz."

"My name is Tracey. I'm glad to meet you."

"The same." Jazz sniffed wetly, then winced. "Sorry."

"Darling, in my line of work, I've heard much, much worse."

Jazz couldn't help but smile at that. The woman was so unapologetically kind.

"Now, Jazz, I don't think this boy would agree that what happened was your fault," Tracey said, taking up her bustling once more. "I'm guessing he may blame the weather, sure... perhaps the horse he fell from, but I have a feeling it won't be you."

Jazz shook her head. "He'd never blame David."

One thin, pale eyebrow rose. "I can only assume that's the horse?"

Heat prickled Jazz's cheeks, and she nodded.

"Well, if he's a smart boy, which I'm sure he is, he will know that blame never got anyone anywhere. It doesn't change the past; all it does is foster anger. I never saw the point in it myself."

"If more people thought the way you do, the world would be more peaceful," Jazz said. She turned her gaze back to Theo. "He's really going to be okay?"

"He will be. He will certainly have some healing to do. Concussions are no small matter. Headaches will plague him; he may have trouble with his eyesight. But he will be alright in the grand scheme of things."

"Good." Jazz blinked hard. "When will he come to?" She longed to hear his voice. She wasn't sure she could fully trust that he was okay until she did.

Tracey reached out a hand and squeezed Jazz's shoulder. Jazz had to resist the urge to lean into her and sob.

"They should have told you when they brought you in. He's only sleeping now. It's different. He's had a healthy dose of painkillers and is probably exhausted. His body will need lots of rest for the next while."

Jazz nodded, unable to take her eyes off Theo's face. He looked peaceful, and she said a silent thank you to whatever powers may be for ensuring that he wasn't suffering from pain.

Tracey gave Jazz's shoulder another squeeze as she left the room. Laying her head on the bed, inches from Theo's hand, Jazz plunged into sleep.

Chapter Thirty-Eight

JASMINE

A HAND ON HER hair pulled Jazz out of sleep. She bolted upright into a sitting position, ignoring the clench of pain in her neck. "Theo?"

But his face was still slack with sleep on the pillow in front of her.

"No, honey, it's me." Valley's voice cut through the fog of sleep, still clinging to Jazz.

Jazz turned, her foggy brain piecing together where she was. Valley was crouched beside Theo's hospital bed, one hand on Jazz's back. "Oh. I thought—" Jazz shook her head. She felt mushy-brained, as if it wasn't computing things as it should.

Valley's blonde brows drew together, concern etching lines between them. "I know. I'm sorry. I was trying to not startle you."

"It's okay." Jazz rubbed a hand over her face and yawned so hard her jaw cracked. "What time is it?" she mumbled.

"Just after three o'clock."

"In the afternoon?"

Valley chuckled. "Yeah, man. I love you, but if it's three a.m., I'm in bed."

No wonder her neck hurt. She'd been asleep, bent over the bed for several hours.

Valley's teasing expression dimmed, and she studied Theo briefly before straightening. "I had to finish up with a couple of clients before I could come. But I brought you a few things." Valley hoisted a bag to show Jazz. "A change of clothes, toothbrush, deodorant." At the last, she wrinkled her nose. "Thank goodness I thought to throw that in."

"Shut up," Jazz said, but the words held no real fire. She stood from the chair, feeling as though her body had moulded itself to the thing. Taking the bag, she set it on the bed by Theo's feet before wrapping her arms around Valley. "I'm so glad you're here."

The words hiccuped a bit, and Valley squeezed her tight. "I'm glad he's alright," she said. "That you're *both* alright. I would have killed you if you died."

As Jazz released Valley, she caught a whiff of herself and winced. "Holy shit, I do stink," she muttered.

Valley laughed and pushed her away. "Go clean up and change. I'll sit with him until you get back."

Jazz hesitated, her eyes darting back to the bed. How did such a big man look so small? "You won't leave?"

Valley shook her head. "I wouldn't dream of it."

"Thank you."

"Unless I get bored or hungry," Valley added as Jazz took the bag of clothes and went to slip out of the room. Smiling for the first time in what may have been years, Jazz ignored her friend and went in search of a washroom.

Theo didn't wake up until ten-thirty that night. Jazz was in the chair, her head propped in her hand, watching Theo's video from the fair. When the rasp of his voice made Jazz drop her phone in surprise.

"Who's the goof singing?"

"Theo!" She jumped to her feet, leaning over the bed to run gentle hands over his cheeks. "You're awake."

Theo squinted at her, brows creased in pain. "It would appear so."

"Are you okay?" Jazz asked, lowering her voice. "What do you need?"

"Water, please."

Carefully, Jazz helped him sit up enough that she could lift the glass of water to his lips. "Don't drink too much," she cautioned.

He took a few swallows, then sighed in relief. When he spoke again, his voice was smoother. "Thank you."

For the first time, Theo seemed to register his surroundings. His grey eyes tracked around the room and then down his body. With a small intake of breath, his gaze flew to her. "Are you hurt? Did you find Goliath? Is David alright?"

At the flood of questions, Jazz shushed him. "I'm not hurt; David is alright; Blair took him back to the ranch after they airlifted you out..." she paused, chewing at her lip and trying to smother the rush of anxiety. "I don't know about Goliath. Blair was going to go out on Ghost and look for him." That had been this afternoon. Jazz hadn't heard from him since.

Theo's hand searched for hers, and she wrapped both hers around it, relishing the vital warmth of his touch. "You scared the shit out of me," she whispered. She was aching to say so many things to him, but they could wait. For now, he needed to rest and heal. "I should have left you in the river for all the trouble you've caused me."

"Witch," Theo said, grinning, then wincing as it stretched his bruised face. "Kiss me, please... carefully."

***

Theo slept on and off for the better part of two days. Jazz only went home once. As she pulled up to the house, driving at a snail's pace to avoid all the dogs bombarding the truck, her heart began to pound.

Goliath.

The horse stood in the yard, pressed as close to the fence separating him from David and Ghost as he could, his head hanging. He'd slipped free of his brida, which hung by the reins around his neck. It had been dragging; sticks and clumps of grass hung from it like a forgotten fishing line. Clumps of burdock matted his once glossy mane and tail.

Jazz climbed out of the truck and strode toward him. "You fucker!" she growled. "You absolute fucker." The horse snorted, jerking his head as she approached, but decided his relief at seeing her was more significant than his need for dramatics. Jazz wrapped her arms around his sweaty neck, pressing her cheek to the hot velvet softness there while she soaked his coat with tears. "You fucker," she whispered again, hugging him until he huffed in displeasure.

Leading Goliath slowly to the barn, Jazz stripped off his tack. He had a few minor saddle sores from rubbing after the prolonged wear, and there was a cut on his right front leg an inch above the hoof. It didn't seem to bother him and didn't look deep. After debating whether she should call in a vet, Jazz cleaned each thoroughly, rubbing a protective ointment over each wound. Then, she portioned out a healthy measure of oats. She'd never seen the stallion so overjoyed to be inside his stall. He trotted over to his water trough, taking a few long gulps before moving to the feeder, snuffling contentedly.

Swiping at her cheeks, Jazz turned away. Her boys had come out of their ordeal, not unscathed, but alive and well. It made her knees wobble with relief.

"Goliath is back!" Jazz announced as she shoved open the door to Theo's hospital room.

She stumbled to a stop when she took in the scene. Theo was sitting on the edge of the bed. A nurse bent over him. The woman straightened, giving Jazz a sharp look, and Jazz realized she had been about to pull the I.V. needle from Theo's hand. Jazz winced and slipped to the side, remaining quiet until the nurse finished. He looked pale, whiskers cutting across his cheeks in dark slashes, but his eyes sparkled when he smiled at her.

"Alright," the nurse said as she tidied up. "You're free to go, Mr. Bridger. No more adventures. I don't want to see you back here."

"Yes, ma'am," Theo said, holding Jazz's eye until the woman left. Then he beckoned her over. "He's back?"

Jazz rushed across the room, careful not to jostle him when she sat on the foot of the bed. "Yes. I pulled in, and he was standing all sad in the yard."

"Is he hurt?"

Shaking her head, Jazz reached over and picked up one of Theo's hands. "No, a few minor things, but he's no worse for wear. Came out of this better than you," she said. She strove to make her tone playful, but the memories of that day still made her heart pound like it was attempting to escape from her chest.

Theo was watching her with a look that made Jazz want to squirm.

"Stop it. What's that face?" she said, pulling her hand free of his and crossing her arms over her chest.

"I don't know—" Theo said slowly. "Gratitude, maybe? You saved my life, Jazz."

When she shook her head, he shrugged. "Don't worry about it. It's my face, and it can look at you however it wants to."

"Touché," she said, fighting back a manic urge to simultaneously cry and laugh.

Theo's face fell soft, and he leaned over to kiss her, apparently forgetting he had broken ribs. With a sharp hiss, he nearly toppled onto her lap. Sweat popped up on his brow, and he wrapped his arms tightly around his chest.

Jazz helped him straighten, then wrapped her arms over his, hugging him gently. "Let's get you the hell out of here, hey?"

"Fuck yes," Theo muttered against her neck. "Please take me home."

Chapter Thirty-Nine

JASMINE

FOUR DAYS AFTER BEING airlifted off her property, a grumpy, unshaven Theo went home with Jazz to the ranch. Despite Theo's sour mood, Jazz couldn't contain her joy when they pulled into the driveway. They were *home*. At last.

Titus threw back his head at the sight of Theo, and Jazz reached out, seizing the dog's collar as he was about to jump.

"Thanks," Theo said, ruffling Titus' ears, then moving down the line to greet the other canines. Loki studied him with a strong side eye before consenting to a pat. "Getting bowled over by that dude would not have felt good."

"Let's get you inside. The risk of further injury is too great out here."

Hovering near his elbow, Jazz followed Theo into the house. He still suffered bouts of dizziness the doctor said could last for a while, and his ribs made it difficult for him to move.

In the hall, he headed to his room, stopping when Jazz made a slight sound in her throat.

"I was thinking you may be more comfortable in my bed," she said. Blood rose to blanch her cheeks, and she quickly added, "It's bigger."

"It *is* a mighty fine bed," Theo agreed, one side of his mouth tipping up. It was the closest thing to a smile she'd got out of him in days. "I have very fond memories of it."

"Listen to you." Jazz brushed back an errant strand of hair off his brow. "You sound like a real cowpoke."

Theo snorted. Shaking his head, he caught her hand as it dropped. The stubble of his unshaven jaw tickled across her palm as he pressed a kiss to the sensitive skin.

"Thank you for bringing me home, Jasmine."

The word *home* imbued her with a warmth that made her stomach fizz. It was a conversation they needed to have, but it could wait. She knew without a doubt that she wanted Theo to stay. For the rest of their lives if that was what he wanted.

All the confessions, the raging emotions, jammed up in her throat, trying to spill out of her, but the weariness oozing off Theo had her swallowing them back. "How about a shower?" she said.

Theo closed his eyes for a second as if battling back tears. "God, yes," he whispered.

"Come on. I'll help you."

"I don't need—" Theo began to say, but then a slow, wicked smile carved through the tired lines on his face. "Actually, I'm scared I might fall while I'm in there. Please, Jazz, can you join me, keep me safe?"

Jazz bit back a smile, shaking her head at the bubble of joy threatening to crack her ribs open. "I will join you, but there will be no funny business."

"Oh, no, ma'am. I wouldn't dream of executing any *funny* business." Theo's voice dipped into a raspy growl on the last words. Goosebumps erupt across her body in response. The man's voice was magic, and he knew how to use it. Tugging her closer, Theo pressed his lips to the silky skin below her jaw.

Jazz shuddered violently. "Theodore Bridger, I am serious. You just got out of the hospital"

"I love it when you're stern." Slipping his hands from her waist, he gripped her ass, pressing himself into the cradle of her hips. "Makes me want to be a bad boy, so you'll punish me."

"Theo." His name, meant to be a reprimand, came out as a quivering whisper. "We can't. You're injured."

"I'm fine." He ran his nose along the column of her neck as he spoke, his words soft as mist on her skin. "Unless you count a bad case of blue balls as a medical issue. If so, we're in luck because you're qualified to help me with that."

What the fuck was this man doing to her.

"I missed you so much," he murmured when she chose to ignore his remarks.

"I was there with you every day," Jazz laughed, trying, without much enthusiasm, to free herself from his embrace.

"Yeah, but I couldn't hold you," Theo said against her hair. "I couldn't take you in my arms and fuck you whenever I wanted."

Jazz's body became a single pulse point, and his touch was the lifeblood that kept it beating. "God, Theo." She rolled her head back, allowing him better access to her neck, before she remembered. "Wait, no. We can't. You had a head injury. The doctor said no strenuous activities until you stop having dizzy spells."

"Well, how the hell am I supposed to know if it's the injury making me dizzy or you," Theo said, his voice taking on a tone of exasperation.

"Come into the shower," she said. Seizing his face between her palms and kissing him, obviously too chastely for his liking. He plunged his fingers into her hair, trying to deepen it. "Theo!"

"Fuck! Fine." Some of the fight went out of him, and he slumped against her. "What if we do something that isn't strenuous?"

Dragging him into her bathroom, Jazz tugged the hem of his shirt over his head. A huge black bruise spread dark as an ink stain over his left side, and she winced at the sight of it. "Oh," she whispered.

"I'm fine, Boss," Theo said. "I promise."

Jazz held his gaze, searching the depths of his beautiful grey eyes. He was fine. She could see the truth reflecting back at her. He was exhausted and in pain, whether he would admit it or not—but there were no storm clouds.

Without looking away, Jazz stepped closer, her fingers moving to unbuckle his belt. His eyelids drooped, and a rumble sounded in his chest. As she worked the jeans over his hips, it was evident he'd not lost hope in some "activity."

"How can you be this excitable after all you've been through?" She waved a hand at the bulge straining his black boxer briefs before she moved to turn on the shower.

"Well, you see, this beautiful fucking woman who happens to be the love of my life just took off my pants, and since I'm only slightly broken and not in any way that really matters, here we are."

Jazz froze, her back to Theo, the cold water rushing over her hand. Pulling in a shuddery breath, she adjusted the knob and turned back to him. "What?"

"I said you're fucking beautiful?"

"No..."

Theo held his hand out, and Jazz laced her fingers with his, letting him pull her back into his arms. "I said, you're the love of my life, Jasmine."

"Oh," she managed to croak. "See, that's what I thought you said." The crooked smile that toyed with his mouth brought tears rushing to her eyes.

"I haven't stopped loving you since the day I walked into the convenience store and saw you yelling at that kid. I thought he was going to piss himself."

"He... he was stealing, and Mr. Boland was already losing so much money, he couldn't afford—"

Theo shut her up with a swift press of his lips. His heat and taste branded her mouth, and she closed her eyes, relishing it. "I... I love you, too," she whispered. Fear and excitement thrummed through her. She'd spent the last fifteen years pushing Theo Bridger from her thoughts, memories, and fantasies. It was a rush of relief to let go... lift the walls around her heart, and allow him in.

The small bathroom steadily filled with steam as they stared at each other, their admissions dancing around them along with the plumes of mist.

Cupping her cheek in a rough palm, he brushed his mouth against hers once. Twice. When Jazz leaned in, seeking more, Theo pulled back, pressing a kiss to the centre of her forehead. "Let's get in before the water runs out." His hands dropped to her shirt, popping each button free until he could slide it from her shoulders.

They finished undressing in silence. Theo took Jazz's hand, never relinquishing it as he drew her into the shower stall with him. Pulling her close so her back rested against his chest, the water slicking their skin, Theo used one hand to bundle her hair and pull it over her shoulder. Fingers achingly gentle, he smoothed all the errant strands, then slipped both arms around her waist. Pushing his face into the dip where her shoulder met her neck, he held her. They stood for a long time in the rush of hot water, shrouded in steam and content to breathe each other.

"I love you," Theo whispered against her skin, coaxing a shiver from her by lapping up the drops of water running down the column of her throat.

"I love you," Jazz answered, her breath hitching when one of Theo's hands trailed down her stomach to the juncture of her thighs. She didn't protest. Her body had done a fair job convincing her brain that it would be alright. The insistent press of his hard-on against her ass had done its job in making up her mind and dispelling any hope she had for him staying relaxed.

When his fingers delved between her folds and found her slick, Theo groaned, dragging his teeth over her naked shoulder. "I need you, Jasmine." His voice was taut with an emotion she couldn't name. He sounded... raw. Naked, in more ways than the physical sense. "Please, I need to be inside you."

"Okay. Yes," she managed. His fingers had begun a steady sweeping rhythm over her swollen flesh, making *her* dizzy. "But be careful, or else."

"Promise," Theo rasped. Placing one broad palm between her shoulder blades, he pushed, bending her forward to brace against the shower wall. Jazz sent a silent thank you to whatever gene was responsible for her height. Theo's fingers never relinquished her clit, even as he seized himself in his free hand and brushed his hard length forward and back over her. A whimper escaped Jazz, and she bit her lip, attempting to quell it.

"Don't," Theo said. "I want to hear you. I want to go to sleep every night and dream of the sounds you make while you're coming all over my cock."

"Fuck." It was all Jazz could manage to whimper. She pressed back, desperate for him to fill her.

Theo pushed inside her with one long, rough thrust. Jazz cried out, stars pinwheeling across her vision. The angle and the dance of his wicked fingers threatened to plunge her into oblivion before they even started.

"You. Are. Mine. Jasmine." Theo punctuated each word by nearly withdrawing from her body's grip and slamming back home again.

Jazz's head hit the shower's tile wall, and her legs shook, but she didn't care. A guttural sound tore out of her.

"Say it," Theo gasped, his breathing ragged and hitching. "Say that you're mine."

"I'm yours!" Jazz sobbed. "Fuck Theo. I've always been yours." She barely managed to get the words out before she was coming, her body clenching his, squeezing the thick weight of him like it would never let go. Embracing him so tightly, she felt the moment he followed her over the edge.

Chapter Forty

THEO

"I'VE BEEN THINKING."

"Three words that strike fear in any man's heart," Theo muttered, laughter erupting out of him when Jazz reached up and pinched his bare nipple. Catching her hand, he pressed a kiss on her palm. "Go ahead, Boss; what were you thinking?"

"I was *thinking*—" she enunciated the word hard, tipping her head enough to cast him a side-eyed glare, "that, though I will still be paying you back the money you gave to City Hall, we should become... partners." Her voice was hesitant, touched with shyness, and the tone made a little swell of love expand and burst in Theo's chest. He would do anything for her and spend his life ensuring she never doubted it.

"I will be your partner in any way, shape or form you will have me, Jasmine."

"Shh—" she reached up, pressing a palm firmly over his mouth to quiet him. "Stop being so ridiculous." Theo promptly nipped at her palm, loving how his laughter made her head bounce against his chest. He didn't know if he'd laughed as much in his entire life as he had in the last few weeks with Jazz.

"What if you did some sort of music therapy here," she continued after it was clear he wouldn't interrupt her again. "I've always dreamed of expanding what I started here at Sunrise with the recovery ranch. Maybe we could put in some cabins. The plans have always been this foggy sort of dream, but I think they're finally coming together. You could have music classes, and maybe we could teach riding and give people some animal therapy experience?" The words came out slightly breathy as if she'd been storing them up and they'd escaped in a rush. Theo didn't miss the word *we* and those two little letters filled him with blinding joy.

"I think that is brilliant." Theo tangled his fingers into the riot of her hair, pulling it back from her cheeks. Some of the strands were damp from the exertion of their activities a few moments before. "But, sweetheart, are you sure you want to share this place with that many people?"

"I'm only thinking of a few at a time; I think the most benefits would come with keeping it small. I want to bring Valley in as well to do onsite counselling. This way, we could also keep people out of the house, which ensures we have our own space."

Our own space.

The words made Theo's heart so buoyant it could have floated into the sky, free as a helium balloon slipping from a child's grasp.

"So many people are struggling, Theo. I want to help as many as possible. I've been given this amazing place, and I think it's my calling to do this."

Theo lay quiet so long that Jazz sat up to look at him. He didn't hide his emotions from her. He belonged to Jasmine Joyce and wouldn't do her the injustice of not trusting her with his whole self. Jazz's compassion and her dreams for the ranch did not surprise him, but how her words had taken his throat in their teeth did. Tears burned his eyes, and he swallowed hard before he could speak.

"You're amazing," he said, cupping her face between her palms. "I am in awe of your soul, your heart, Jasmine. I'm in awe of who you are." He brushed his lips against hers and lay back, pulling her body down and cradling it with his. "And I agree. My journey with mental health has led me all over the map, and if I can be a guide for others and help them stay on a straighter path to healing, then I will do whatever I can."

Jazz's breathing hitched as she nodded against his chest. "So, you're in?" she whispered.

"I am in one hundred percent."

"Where were you all day?" Jazz asked when Theo entered the kitchen. She was leaning against the counter, brandishing a carrot she was supposed to be chopping at him.

"Hello to you too, Boss," Theo said. Crossing the room, he took the carrot from her hand, set it on the cutting board, and looped her arms around his neck. "I missed you," he murmured, brushing his mouth over hers. She tasted of home. The fading weeks of summer were passing quickly in a flurry of farm chores, garden harvests, and as much sex as Theo's concussed brain would allow him.

"I missed you, too. While I was doing all the work by myself," Jazz quipped, pulling back to give him a narrow-eyed look. Betty saved him by bustling in from the garden, her arms full of fresh greens.

"Those carrots won't chop themselves," Betty scolded, throwing Theo a wink over Jazz's shoulder.

"Yes, chop chop." Theo ducked in time to avoid the orange missile Jazz launched at him. They both broke out in laughter at Betty's squawk of outrage.

When they calmed, and it was clear Jazz was once more absorbed in her task, Betty caught Theo's gaze, her own growing wide as she tried to convey a silent question to him. Theo knew what she was asking. Fighting back the massive grin that attempted to take control of his face, he gave her a single nod. Betty clutched her hands under her round chin, looking like she was about to emit a loud-pitched shriek. Instead, she squeezed her eyes shut briefly, took one deep breath, and clapped her hands together.

"I have to head home early tonight, and I've had a wonderful idea," she announced.

Jazz looked up from her task, jaw working as she hurriedly chewed a pilfered chunk of carrot. "What?" she asked around the food, making Theo shake his head. He'd tease her about being raised in a barn later.

"I'm going to pack this supper up for you, and you can go on a little picnic," Betty announced. Her tone was no-nonsense, but Jazz opened her mouth as if she might argue. That had been Theo's primary concern. He loved the woman with all his heart, but she did not do well with being told what to do. Luckily, he'd planned for her bullheadedness.

"I would love that," he said, slipping an arm around Jazz's waist. Pressing his face into the curve of her neck, he whispered. "I haven't fucked you under the stars yet. I want to see your skin painted with moonlight."

He'd played his cards right. A full-body shiver trembled through Jazz. She twisted to check that Betty was looking the other way before she arched her back, pressing her ass squarely into his groin. Theo hissed. He had to let her go before the plan ended up in him being known as "Boner Bridger" again.

"Go put on something comfy, and I'll meet you out back in ten minutes," he said, kissing her cheek before stepping back.

When Jazz stepped off the deck wearing a loose yellow sundress that floated around her long, tanned legs, with her curtain of black waves hanging around her shoulders nearly to her waist, Theo thought his heart might stop. He watched her cross the yard, a lump forming in his throat. He was incredibly nervous but calm simultaneously, as though each moment of his life had led to this one. He'd always been meant to stand here on this rolling green lawn, outside a little ranch house, watching the love of his life, the most stubborn, generous, sarcastic, glorious woman he'd ever met, walk toward him.

If tonight's plan worked in his favour, they would do this again in a few months, surrounded by their families and friends. But Theo knew this was the moment he would remember until the last breath left his body. Jasmine, streaked with coral light from the setting sun, dressed in the colours of a sunflower, walked toward him with the mischievous tip to her lips that he loved more than words could describe. She was his. She held his heart between her hands, and even if she threw it away, he would never give it to another. He didn't care that it had only been a few weeks since they'd exchanged *I love yous* and made plans for their combined future on the ranch; this life had always been it for him.

Chapter Forty-One

JASMINE

THEO'S EYES NEVER LEFT Jazz as she crossed the lawn toward him. The late summer sun was sinking past the mountains, staining the land in bright streaks of orange and coral. She was glad she chose the yellow dress. Valley had forced it on her during a recent thrifting trip, and at first, Jazz had sworn she'd never wear it. Now, seeing how Theo's eyes drank her in, she vowed to send Valley a thank you card.

He waited for her with the picnic basket clutched in one hand and a blanket draped over his arm. Beside him, Titus and Loki were playing a raucous game of tug-of-war with a tree limb swinging dangerously close to the backs of Theo's legs, but he seemed oblivious. The way he watched her brought each nerve ending in Jazz's body crackling to life. Emotions danced in his grey eyes as they tracked over her, and whether he was aware of it or not, he'd pulled one corner of his full bottom lip between his teeth. He took her breath away.

When she came to a stop in front of him, neither spoke, as if they were both scared to break the spell that engulfed them. Finally, with a shaky inhale, Theo set the basket down and snaked an arm around her waist, pulling her tight against his body. He was already hard. Jazz couldn't help the smile that escaped to play across her mouth just before Theo's crashed into it. Both his big hands tangled in her hair. She knew he loved it when she wore it down and had run back to her mirror to unlace her braid before coming outside. He wrapped ropes of it around his fists, using it to tip her head back to the perfect angle as he deepened the kiss. The sounds of the dogs playing, the cattle lowing in the far field, and the insistent grumble of chickens melted away. They were in their own universe of touch and breath and battling tongues.

Finally, Theo pulled his mouth away with a groan. "We need to go, or I'm going to take you right here on the lawn," he rasped against her heated cheek. Jazz released a shaky, pent-up breath.

"Let's go to bed," she said, arching her hips to press against the bulge straining at his jeans. "I'll make sure that isn't unrequited. We can eat later."

Theo pressed his mouth against hers in a closed-mouth peck, much more chaste than the last, and hummed deep in his throat. "Patience. With the plans I have for you tonight, you'll need the fuel."

"Hmmm, the only reason I'm not trying to convince you to change your mind is because I'm very intrigued," Jazz said. Slipping her hand into his, she jerked her chin at the picnic basket. "Where are we off to, then?"

"The clearing," Theo said, tugging her along.

Crossing through the field, which led to the little clearing with the creek, took only a few minutes. It had always been her grandmother's favourite place on the ranch, and Jazz often visited when she wanted to feel close to her. As they reached the break in the trees, Theo pulled her to a stop. "I love you," he murmured. "Jazz? You know that I love you, right?" His voice had so much emotion that Jazz's eyes flew to his. They were glossy as if he were fighting tears. Her heart skipped in alarm.

"What is it?" she whispered, pressing a palm to his cheek. "What's wrong?"

Theo shook his head. "Nothing. Everything is more right than it has ever been in my life. Come with me."

Leading her by the hand, Theo took Jazz through the trees. He angled her toward the creek's bank where the little wooden bench sat. With a frown, Jazz noticed his guitar case propped against the arm. Past it, she saw something else odd. The rocks along the bank had been moved, forming some pattern. Pulling her hand free from Theo's, she took a step closer. They were words. And then, like one of those pictures where you unfocus your eyes to see the 3D image, her brain made sense of it.

Marry Me?

Jazz inhaled so sharply that she nearly choked. Spinning on her heels, her eyes flew to where Theo had stood, but he wasn't there. He was closer behind her, on one knee, clutching a ring box in a violently shaking hand.

"Jasmine," he said, then stopped, swallowing thickly. "I hope you'll say yes because that took a ridiculous amount of time. Who would have thought spelling two words would take me so long?" He wrinkled his long nose, and for a moment, he seemed to teeter on the edge between laughter and tears. "But, more than that, I hope you'll say yes because I love you. I love you and want to spend the rest of my days doing the best I can by you. I want to laugh with you, cry with you, fight with you. I want to do all of it, the mediocre and the amazing moments that go into creating a life together. Jasmine Elizabeth Joyce, will you marry me?"

Words and emotions formed a dam in Jasmine's throat, clogging it. She pressed both hands over her mouth and sank to her knees on the soft earth in front of Theo. She wasn't sure when the tears began rolling down her cheeks, but when the warm breeze blew over the water, she realized her face was wet.

"I—" It was all she could manage. Alarm flashed across Theo's face, and she rushed to reassure him. What the hell was wrong with her? She had to say something.

"Jazz?" he whispered. "You're starting to scare me; I don't think I've ever seen you speechless for this long." He held the box extended to her and shook it the way he would if he were trying to lure Goliath into his stall with a bit of grain. "I still have that dare, you know. I'll use it if I have to."

That broke Jazz from the trance. A laugh burst out of her. Then a sob. She launched forward and threw her arms around Theo, taking them both to the ground as she kissed him. The ring box fell to the side, forgotten as he wrapped her in his embrace.

"Yes!" The word finally exploded out of her as if her brain had finally caught up and remembered its duty was to animate the rest of her, including her vocal cords. "Yes, I'll marry you, Theo. Of course, I'll fucking marry you!"

Tears escaped Theo then, too, even as he laughed. "There she is," he murmured, laughing as he rained kisses on her cheeks. "There's my girl." He framed her face between his palms, staring down at her, unabashed by the tears that spiked his lashes. "My Jasmine."

Suddenly, he dropped his hands and bolted upright, keeping one arm around her in an impressive show of core strength. "Wait, where did the ring go? I want to see if it fits."

Jazz twisted around, spotting the little black box lying a few feet away. Without dismounting from Theo, she reached out and grabbed it. She placed it back in his hand and looked up at him, her heart beating up a storm in her chest. It was happening. She was going to spend the rest of her life with Theo Bridger.

Theo wet his lips, his eyes holding hers for a long moment before dropping to the box. It seemed so small in his big hands, such a minuscule thing to hold such a world of meaning. Carefully, Theo pulled back the lid. Jazz had never been a jewellery girl. She had a delicate gold necklace with a tiny rose charm that belonged to her grandmother and the engagement ring her father had given her mother. She never wore either of them. She feared them being broken or lost in the rough farm work. When she married Blair, he gave her a simple gold band that had belonged to his mother. She'd returned it when they split up.

This ring was different. Though it would still have to be protected, Jazzknew the moment she saw it that Theo had considered her lifestyle when he chose it. The ring was little more than a wide band, with no large protruding diamonds that would catch on things; only three small emeralds smoothly sunk into the silver. Tiny etchings decorated the circlet, vines, and flowers writhed around the little gems. Jazz had never seen such a unique ring; she loved it instantly.

"Oh, Theo. It's so beautiful," she breathed.

"It reminded me of you," he said. "Unique and beautiful without being obvious. I also got you a silver chain so you could wear it around your neck while working." He lifted the little cushion that held the ring to reveal the necklace coiled below. His thoughtfulness stole her breath. Had anyone ever *known* her the way he had? Bothered to see her for all that she was without shying away?

"It is beyond perfect. Put it on for me?"

The slight tremble in his fingers when he lifted the ring and slipped it onto her finger only made Jazz love him more. She leaned back in his lap to look at him, using both hands to brush the hair off his brow before tracing her fingertips along his temples, down the white line of scar tissue beside his eye, and then the ridges of his jaw, the ring glinting on her finger in the rising moonlight.

"It fits," she whispered. And she meant the ring, but also so much more.

Epilogue

TWO YEARS LATER

J<u>ASMINE</u>

Bathe you in moonlight,

with stardust in your hair

Spin you up in sunshine,

You're everywhere

Everything I love

The only one I see

Turn around, I need to know

That you notice me

The notes of Theo's song still fluttered in Jazz's ears. Their vows finished, she clutched his hand and they wove their way down the path leading past the tidy row of new guest cabins. They'd both agreed the clearing by the creek was where they would take their photos.

The last thirty minutes played on a loop in her mind, cementing themselves into treasured memories. Theo had looked up at her from his guitar, eyes like storm-clouded oceans, and sang as if she were the only person in the world.

Jazz would hold that moment in her heart for the rest of her life.

"I want your music to welcome me home after a long day," she'd told him, standing beside Valley and Betty, staring at him over their joined hands.

It had been over in a rush and lasted an eternity. Time slowed to a warm, syrupy pour as they vowed to love each other until the end. Jazz was still discombobulated a couple of hours later, but pleasantly so, as if she'd drunk just enough to coax a pleasant heat in her veins and fizz in her head. Which was entirely possible. Her glass of crisp white didn't seem to have a bottom. She wasn't entirely sure who was refilling it.

"How are you doing, baby girl?" Valley appeared beside Jazz, where she stood, surveying the scene unfolding around her.

Her wedding—her and Theo's—at last. The two years since Theo proposed had passed in a blink. But *this* day, the moment they officially stitched their lives together, couldn't come soon enough, in Jazz's opinion.

Their picnic at the creek had been eaten cold after the blanket was utilized for non-picnic activities, and they'd joked about heading straight to City Hall and making Ed Hamilton marry them. But the more they talked and planned, the more one dream shone above the rest. They wanted to set their plans for the ranch into motion before anything else. The sooner they could build the cabins and launch the other initiatives they wished for, the sooner they could begin helping people.

Now, it was done. They built six cabins tucked off in the nearest field, with a cookhouse and communal space. They no longer had anyone stay in the house. That was for Jazz and Theo only—well, and Betty and whichever dog managed to sneak inside. There was already a waiting list of people who wanted to book time on their rescue ranch—people looking for their second chances.

Jazz pulled a deep breath in through her nose and gazed around her, full of contentment and a little in awe. Friends and family spread over the back lawn, taking shelter from the last rays of the summer sun, sipping drinks, and laughing. Children ran wild, fuelled by excitement and sugar, courtesy of the candy bar Theo insisted they set up. Valley's two were playing with the daughter of Theo's oldest brother, and they seemed to be contriving to ride one of the goats.

"I am... completely, utterly, wonderfully happy," Jazz said, smiling over at her friend. "Except... I have to pee." With a defeated sigh, she smoothed down the thick skirts of her wedding dress.

Valley laughed, tipping her glass to drain the last drops of wine before she reached back to set it on the table. "Come on, princess. I'll give you a hand."

Jazz never thought she'd be the type of girl who would purchase a dress that would require assistance for her to go to the bathroom, but life was full of surprises. The lace gown with its long, sheer sleeves and plunging v-neckline had called to her the moment she saw it in the store's window display. The skirts were just voluminous enough, made up of ragged edge layers of alternating lengths, that it was too dangerous to pee alone. Thank goodness for wonderful girlfriends.

While washing their hands, Valley caught Jazz's eyes in the mirror. "I hope you know what you have accomplished these last couple years, how you've... well, how you've come into yourself. It is stunningly beautiful. I'm really fucking proud of you."

"I—" Jazz was momentarily taken aback by the emotion in her best friend's voice. "I know." And she did, she realized. In the past year, she had worked hard with her therapist on allowing herself to be vulnerable, and loved.

"Like, really proud Jasmine. Of the steps you've taken with your mental health, relationship, and the ranch." Valley's voice broke, and tears shone in her eyes. With a squeak of alarm, Jazz rushed to wrap her arms around her friend. Seconds after she'd done it, she knew even that small gesture wasn't something that would have come so easily a year ago.

"You alright?" she whispered against Valley's golden hair. Her friend sniffled but nodded.

"Fucking weddings," she mumbled against Jazz's shoulder. "They get me every time." After another moment, Valley leaned back, bracing her hands on Jazz's shoulders, her crystal eyes searching Jazz's. "I've wanted this for you, and seeing you marry the man you gave your heart to all those years ago makes me a bit mushy. I love you so much."

Jazz's eyes blurred at that, and she blinked rapidly. "I love you too, but I don't want to wreck this makeup!"

"Of course not. You need to sweat that off later!" Valley rolled her eyes up to the ceiling, waving a hand before her face. "And I don't mean on the dance floor!"

"Tears of laughter will make just as much of a mess," Jazz said, laughing.

"Okay, okay." Turning to Jazz, she grinned. "Let's get out there. You've got a gorgeous husband waiting for you, and I want to go tell my wife I love her and her ass."

At that, Jazz let out an unladylike cackle and threaded her arm through Valley's.

Theo was standing on the porch when Jazz left the house. He held a hand out, and she took it. Pausing for a moment, she stood anchored simultaneously to two of the people she loved most in the world. Then Valley slipped away, pressing a quick kiss to Jazz's cheek before skipping down the stairs.

With a gentle tug, Theo brought her close. "I've dreamt of marrying you since I was nineteen years old," he said, grinning down at her, his grey eyes bright with excitement and love. "But I can honestly say I didn't see the canine ring bearer coming."

Jazz stared into her husband's face—that would take some time to get used to—and smiled. "Loki's feelings would have been hurt if he wasn't included." Theo pursed his lips, nodding. "I get it, but what about Titus? I think he's sad he didn't get a chance at the job." Theo pointed to where the massive white mound lay snoring by the buffet table. He may have some of the guests tricked, but Jazz knew he'd be up the second a single pea hit the ground. Jazz turned in Theo's arms, settling her back against his chest and relishing the warm heat of his cheek when he brought it to rest on top of her head.

They stood for a moment, staring out at the small gathering, content to share a moment of peace. On the lawn under the big white pavilion tent, Theo's mom, Abby, danced a two-step with Joe. Jazz could hear the bright chime of her laughter over the music. Valley and her wife Joan were sharing a moment away from the inquiring eyes of their children. Jazz smiled when Valley reached up and swept a strand of dark hair off Joan's brow. Was there anything better than a wedding to remind people of their own love stories?

"I'm happy your mom and brothers could make it," she said. Blair and Theo's second eldest brother, Oliver, seemed to have hit it off and were engaged in an animated discussion over something.

"Me too. I have a long way to go in repairing our relationships, but for the first time, I think we're all in a place where we want to try."

"They really never saw the damage he did?" Jazz asked. It was a continuation of a conversation that often sprang up between them. Like weeds, they always tried to address the thoughts, pulling them from the earth and throwing them away.

"No, but I think they're starting to. I believe they are beginning to recognize their own scars for what they are."

"Well, husband, if you taught me one thing, it's that even old scars can be healed with time and patience."

Theo

Husband.

The word rang through him, clear and sharp, reverberating through his body like the toll of a bell. The grip of the happiness squeezed his chest so tight it bordered on pain.

"Turn around," Theo breathed against the shell of Jazz's ear. She obeyed, twisting in his arms to kiss him, but something tucked in the low bodice of her dress caught his eye. Theo frowned. "What is that?"

Remembrance dawned across Jazz's face, and she shoved a hand down between her boobs, fishing around. With a noise of triumph, she pulled out a check. "It's the last installment of the money I owed you."

Theo closed his eyes, letting his head fall back as he prayed for patience. "Jazz. You literally vowed an hour ago that what's mine is yours, and what's yours is mine."

That haughty, stubborn chin rose, and Theo ached to take it in his hand and kiss her senseless. Their bedroom was only one flight of stairs away; guests be damned.

"I don't care," she said. "This money was from before we were married. I said I would pay you back, and this is the last payment." Her eyes shone with steely resolve, and her jaw had the firm set that he both loved and feared. Theo took a beat. He knew this woman and her moods, emotions, and stubborn pride as well as he did the face that looked back at him from the mirror. "Alright." He plucked the check from her fingers and shoved it into his pocket. "Have it your way, then."

"If we're going to open up the guest cabins, you'll need every dime you can get," she said, triumph shining on her face. Fucking hell, she was beautiful. Beautiful and his, at last, for the rest of their lives. Theo had longed for this day since he was nineteen years old. Before he understood life and the blows it would land. Before he comprehended the damages that marriage could cause. Not theirs, though. He'd make sure of that. Theo would do whatever it took to make Jazz happy. He knew she would do the same for him even if she hissed and spit along the way.

So, he didn't argue with her logic. Because, really, they'd been sharing bank accounts for at least a year. It hadn't taken them long to twist their lives into a rope of committed contentment. Nodding, Theo grinned and tugged her forward into his arms. "Kiss me, wife," he commanded. And, for once, Jasmine Bridger did what she was told.

Bonus Epilogue

SIX MONTHS LATER

THEO

Something was wrong with his wife.

Theo watched Jazz as she slept, curled up against his side, her head resting in the cradle of his shoulder. It was a chilly spring evening, and they'd done something they rarely did: curled up on the couch and turned on a movie. Theo thought he could count the times he'd sat on the sofa in the ranch's living room on one hand, and he'd been there nearly three years.

They had a total of three DVDs in the house: *Toy Story*, *Trolls*, and *The Princess Bride*. Jazz had deliberated for five minutes before she'd finally slipped *Toy Story* into the player.

419

"Then maybe you'll get my super cool references," she said, sticking her tongue out at him. She'd been asleep before the opening credits finished.

It wasn't unlike her to be tired. She worked her ass off every day from dawn until dusk, but there was a quality to that exhaustion Theo had never seen. As if it had gotten into her bones and taken over her body. It controlled her. And Jasmine Bridger did not let anything but her own mind tell her what to do.

Theo stared down at her sleeping face. His love for her was so ferocious sometimes it resembled physical pain. If she was sick... the thought snatched the air from his lungs. His eyes scoured her face, searching for other clues. Blue crescents pillowed her eyes, and he was sure her face was thinner. Her already sharp cheekbones seemed to press taut against her skin.

With a little moan in her sleep, Jazz tucked tighter into him, and then she did something, a small gesture, but one that sent pieces sliding into place like the jackpot on a slot machine. Her hand slipped between their bodies to press protectively against her abdomen.

Oh.

Could that be it? Theo tried to think when the last time she'd mentioned having cramps or asked him to make her chocolate chip pancakes in the middle of the night. His wife wasn't one to ask for help, but she was getting better at admitting when she was suffering. Theo did his best to make sure she felt safe enough to be vulnerable with him. It was something he was always conscious of, showing up for her. It was odd he couldn't remember. They'd been so busy with all the changes they were making to Sunrise and the popularity of the new cabins that, many nights, they both fell into bed too worn out to even talk.

Stretching an arm out, Theo managed to snag the remote and shut off the television. Then he hooked an arm under his wife's legs, keeping her head pressed to him with one palm curved around her skull. She was a tall woman, but, thankfully, Theo was taller, and the years of physical labour had done him favours in the strength department. He managed to stand without jostling her too much.

There was no way to know at the moment if his suspicions were correct or not, but Theo was going to pamper the shit out of his wife either way. She'd spent plenty of time caring for him in her unique, sometimes prickly ways, and she deserved her turn.

She barely stirred when Theo tucked her into their bed. Pulling the quilt around her, he stepped back, staring at her. He could watch her for hours, but if she woke up and found him, she'd probably scream and punch him in the nuts. Smiling to himself, Theo tugged off his jeans, brushed his teeth in their ensuite bathroom, and then burrowed his way into the bed. Jazz mumbled something as he pulled her against his chest.

"Shhh," he crooned, running a hand over her hair. "Shh. You're okay, Boss. Just rest."

Jasmine

Something was wrong with her husband.

Jazz studied Theo as he ate. Betty had left early that evening, citing a need to go home and tend to her garden. Jazz wasn't fooled, though. Word spread around town that she'd been seen with Patty, the pub proprietor, on more than one occasion. However, she'd left them alone, and Jazz realized with a stomach-hollowing sensation that she and Theo hadn't touched all day.

It was a little thing to worry about, but her emotions were out of control lately. What if he was unhappy?

Ask him, you idiot.

And what if he said he'd made a mistake? She was being unreasonable; she could see it, but her brain was taking the thoughts and running wild with them, entirely without her permission. She'd been working hard in therapy to overcome this sort of thing, but it was far too easy to fall back into old habits.

She shovelled another bit of pasta into her mouth. It was probably hormones. When was her period due?

Jazz stopped chewing, stillness settling over her as she plunged into cold realization, sobering and all too familiar. The last time she remembered having a period, it had been... January? Holy shit, was that right? She remembered Theo bringing her a hot water bottle for the cramps and how nice the heat felt in the drafty living room of the ranch house. She'd taken the rare indulgence of a day on the couch. Had they been so busy that she didn't notice her period had been absent for two months?

Holy shit. Holy fuck.

A wave of hot nausea washed over Jazz. She clamped her lips shut, worried her dinner would reappear right then and there. Knowing she was late, other signs began to click into place. How tight her bra had become... she'd chalked that one up to marriage—Theo had a habit of making chocolate chip pancakes in the middle of the night—and the fact she'd been famished lately... so, that was another one.

How was she this slow-witted?

"Will you come down to the creek with me after dinner?" Theo's voice cut through the fog swirling through Jazz's brain and made her jump.

She looked at him. "I... yes. I guess so."

He was watching her, a fathomless look in his stormy eyes. She wondered what their depths held. A sharp need to have his touch on her rose in Jazz, and she battled back the urge to go to him and curl up in his lap like a lost kitten.

Once they'd cleared the dinner dishes and wrapped up in warm jackets, Theo threaded his fingers through hers. "I love you," he said, bringing their joined hands to his lips and brushing a kiss across them.

Abrupt tears flooded Jazz's eyes, and she blinked hard. "I love you, too."

Theo held her gaze for a long moment, then opened the door. Titus jumped up, tail sweeping a potted plant off the little outside table in his excitement. Jazz sighed.

"I'll clean it up when we get back," Theo said, patient humour in his voice.

They went into the field, following the thin trail worn through the grass by their many trips across. To Jazz's surprise, low flickering lights shone from between the trees.

"What is this?" she asked when they drew closer. This spot had become their private oasis, their sacred space on the ranch. They'd even asked guests to respect that boundary and leave it for them.

Around the bench was a half circle of small solar lights flickering like golden flames, illuminating the shallow, running water so it sparkled like diamond shards. A tinkling sound filled the clearing, and Jazz glanced around for a moment before she discovered the source of the sound.

Frowning, she stepped closer. From one of the trees hung a gorgeous wind chime. It was constructed of raw cut chrystals and thin metal tubes. When the stones swayed against the tubes, they resonated with various clear notes.

"Did you put this here?" she asked Theo, though she already knew he had.

His warmth suffused her back, and then she was against his chest, his strong arms cinched around her, holding her close, steady, safe. The clamouring anxiety inside Jazz instantly calmed. "Yes."

"It's beautiful," she whispered. Leaning back, she rolled her head to look at him.

Theo smiled and brushed a kiss over her cheekbone. "Thank you. I want to talk to you, Jasmine."

A stone plunged through her belly. "About what?"

"About our baby."

She couldn't help it; she jerked in his arms. "What?"

Theo raised his free hand, cupping her chin, holding her steady with firm but gentle pressure, ensuring she continued to look into his eyes. "We've talked about it some, but I worry I've never adequately expressed how I felt."

He was talking about the baby they'd lost.

"Alright." She drew the word out, hesitant. With the work she'd done with her therapist and the weight of finally having told Theo, she struggled less to talk about the baby. However, it still wasn't something that came easily.

"I want you to know, just because I wasn't there doesn't mean I care any less or don't love the child we made." The sound of his thick swallow was loud in her ear. "My greatest regret will always be not being there for you. Not being able to hold you through the grief, not being able to walk that path at your side. It kills me—" his voice broke, and he swallowed again. "It kills me you made the journey alone."

"It's in the past, Theo," Jazz whispered, though her sinuses burned with a storm of emotions. "We don't need to go back."

"Remembering him and honouring his existence isn't going back, Jazz. It's acknowledging we lost a part of ourselves, and a small piece of us will always be missing. And that's alright. That's what loss is. It's an empty space, love that has nowhere to go. It isn't something we get over, but move forward carrying."

Tears were openly streaming over her cheeks now, but Jazz made no move to wipe them away. She just listened as her husband told her what was in his heart.

"I put this here so you would have a spot to come remember, to cry, and celebrate who he could have been—" his voice thickened again, and he stopped, clearing his throat. "And if you'll let me, I'll come too, and if the wind wills it, he and I can make music together."

"Theo," Jazz hiccuped, the one word suffused with all the awe and love filling her.

"It's a rainbow, Jazz. Do you know why?" he whispered.

She shook her head, and he turned to her, pressing his forehead to her temple, their tears mingling on each other's skin. "Because, Boss," he said, pulling his hand from her grasp and pressing it to her abdomen. "You have our rainbow inside you. We made it through the storm."

Content Advisement

SCSR deals with some themes that some people may find difficult. These themes are **discussed on the page**, but all happen **prior to** the story's timeline. Please put your mental health first.

Off-Page Themes:
*Loss of parent

*Loss of pregnancy/late-term loss

*Self-harm/Cutting

On-Page Themes:
*Light drinking, mentions of being drunk, but no descriptive scenes

*Descriptive sexual scenes

*Profanity

*PTSD military flashbacks

*Physical injury resulting in a hospital stay (full recovery)

Acknowledgements

As always, there are plenty of people to thank for their help and guidance throughout the journey of writing this book. But the two who are foremost are my wonderful author friends, Shea West and Becky Tzag. Thank you both for your insights and ideas, reading multiple drafts of SCSR, even though I failed both of you as beta for your books. Your support means so much!

Thank you, husband, for your never-wavering support of me!

Thank you to LPP for cheerleading, sharing, and generally helping me not crumble to imposter syndrome.

Bethany, at Brightly Editing, thank you for BRIGHTENING up this work!

And Kim at KBG Designs for the lovely cover, thank you!

About the author

L.E. Wagensveld is the mother of four human children, four furry ones, and wife to her best friend and biggest supporter. Despite being outnumbered, L.E. holds her own thanks to caffeine and good old-fashioned stubbornness.

For as long as L.E. can remember, she's been a passionate wordsmith. From crafting poems about her pets as a child to the various piles of unfinished manuscripts sitting in her magic cloud, she has always found writing a necessity for her life. L.E. loves helping others discover the words they are looking for to express themselves, and at work, they have dubbed her The Blurb Queen. In July of 2024, L.E was announced the grand prize winner of the Dragon Blade Publishing Write Track Contest for her historical fiction novella, The Courtesan's Touch.

L.E.'s Stevenson Family novels focus on friendship, family, and love in a small town. L.E. is an unashamed romance lover, a passion she attributes to her late maternal grandmother, who was rarely without a Harlequin novel close at hand. In her novels, L.E. seeks to create an escape for her readers, a place to go when they need a smile or some warm and fuzzy feelings. L.E. looks forward to a life full of words and sharing each story by story.

Follow her on Instagram @L.E.Wagensveld

Check on the SCSR Spotify Playlist

https://open.spotify.com/playlist/3FoVONrP9GVszfZxG3
b43i?si=4cbd0c9263114341

Scan Me to Listen!

Also by L.E. Wagensveld

When a rom-com, Scooby-Doo, and Ghost Adventures collide...

Branson Hobbs, aka Sonny, chases ghosts for a living. But what his fans don't know is that he also talks to them. When Sonny created his paranormal investigation show, Haunted, it was the perfect cover for his abilities. Still, he and the friends who made the show a reality didn't expect fame. Sonny is sick of it all after five seasons, but stepping away isn't easy. Determined to ensure the fifth season is the best yet, the producers straddle the Haunted crew with a social media star, whatever the hell that is.

When she meets the hulking ghost hunter Sonny—a name so incongruous with his demeanour that it's almost laughable—Isadora Hernandez wonders if she's made a terrible mistake. As if chasing the paranormal wasn't scary enough, Sonny Hobbs makes her sweat for more reasons than she cares to admit. But as the crew travels into the British Columbia interior, Isa finds herself swept up in the adventure and captivated by Sonny's unexpected kind-hearted charm.

Nature gets fierce, and after digging up more mysteries than they bargained for, the Haunted crew must ask themselves if they're pursuing the supernatural or if something else is going on at the Hideaway Hotel. They'll do everything they can to figure it out, but the most challenging part for Sonny will be not falling for the Influencer...

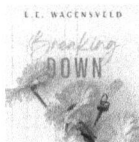

Get your engine revving with this funny and heartwarming story of one woman's happily ever after with a grease-stained knight.

Carmen Maclean is unmoored from her home and city when a long-term relationship turns violent. Determined to protect herself, Carmen heads to the small mountain town where her little brother lives, but her plans take a turn for the worse when car trouble leaves her stranded on the side of a lonely mountain highway.

Sawyer Stevenson is a divorced small-town mechanic, scared to let himself fall in love again. Lately, he's taken to burying his emotions in ways that border on scandalous. When he is tasked with fixing a Beetle better left to the junkyard, Sawyer is willing to accept the challenge. He didn't count on meeting Carmen or the feelings she would stir in him.

Carmen and Sawyer can't get enough of each other despite knowing it won't be long before they have to say goodbye. Nothing matters to Sawyer but keeping Carmen safe when danger follows her to Willow Brook. For the first time in as long as either can remember, they are looking forward instead of back, but what exactly does the future hold?

When one kiss forever changes their friendship, Sam and Charlotte must make a choice. Will they take a chance on love? Or will they remain in the friend zone, where they've always been?

Charlotte Baker never thought of herself as obtuse. But when fireworks ignite between her and one of her oldest friends, her feelings are a complete surprise. Now, Charlotte can't stop thinking of that night or how it felt to be in Sam Stevenson's arms. One thing is certain: She'll never think of Sam as a brother again.

Sam Stevenson has loved Charlotte Baker for most of his life. He's shut the feelings away and never told anyone how he feels, especially not Charlotte. But, during his brother's wedding, with drinks flowing and love in the air, Sam's feelings get the best of him. Kissing Charlotte changes everything. Sam doesn't know how he'll ever see her and not touch her, talk to her, and not taste her.

Now, with their friendship on rocky ground, an emergency pushes them together once more. The question is, where do they go from here?

L.E. Wagensveld draws listeners in with compelling characters and weaves stories you love. Breaking Through is her latest, following up her debut BREAKING DOWN with another Stevenson sibling who doesn't want to upset the friend zone.

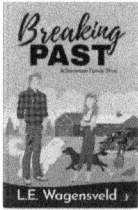

River James tried to leave Cascade Creek more than once. Now, she's resigned herself to a life in the town where she grew up, and she's happy, even if, sometimes, it feels as though something is missing.

When she meets Jake Maclean, it's clear the man has his burdens, yet she can't stop thinking about him. His shyness, talent, and kind heart endure Jake to River faster than she would have liked. She's open to a future with Cascade Creek's handsome interloper, but Jake is much more resistant. The question is, can she make him see that he and his future are worth fighting for? Or will Jake successfully drown their chances of love in his past pain?

Jake Maclean loves his family. So, he knows they're better off without him. When Jake moves to Cascade Creek to escape his past and the pain he's caused, he isn't looking for a new beginning. Living in the tiny town is supposed to be his penance, not a second chance.

It takes a feisty woman with eyes that look into his soul,

a three-legged dog, and the unflagging support of his sister Carmen to help Jake shed the pain of his past. Will he be able to embrace his new life and a chance at love? Or will the struggles of his past get the better of him again?

For more, check out:

http://www.lewagensveld.com

Milton Keynes UK
Ingram Content Group UK Ltd.
UKHW030147051224
452010UK00001B/74